Threads That Weave Us

A Novel by
Manjula Pothuri

Cover design by:
Manjula Pothuri

ISBN: 979-8-9990340-3-8

First Edition Published by:
Ramadia Publishing
E-mail: greenjute.manjula@gmail.com

For more information, visit: www.manjulapothuri.com.

For Nana and Maa—
Mr. N. J. Prabhakar and Mrs. Indira Prabhakar,

whose strength, grace, and love continue to guide me.
And for all who keep showing up for love,
even when it's hardest to do so.

Acknowledgments

This book began in heartbreak but grew into a testament of love, resilience, and hope.

To my dad, the late Mr. N. J. Prabhakar—your presence continues to guide me, even in your absence. You were my greatest hero, and this story is a tribute to your spirit.

To my Maa, Mrs. Indira Prabhakar—you sacrificed so much for us, and even through memory loss, you continue to love me fiercely. The way you remembered the day I was born is a gift I will carry forever.

To my daughters, Ramya Pothuri and Divya Pothuri—you remind me every day why stories matter. Your laughter carried me through my grief and filled this journey with joy.

To my husband, Raghu Pothuri—you are my anchor and my safe place.

To my father-in-law, Mr. Gopal Rao—your blessing and belief in me give me strength and remind me to continue telling stories that matter.

To my friends—you offered listening ears, encouragement, and laughter when I needed them most. You are my greatest gift.

And finally, to every reader who finds this book—thank you for letting these characters into your heart. May they offer you solace, hope, and the courage to keep going, even on the hardest days.

Chapter 1

Weight of my tears

Gravel fractured beneath his truck's tires—crack, grind—splintering through her.

Red taillights flared like wounds in the dusk. They pulsed, then drifted away. Away.

She ran—bare feet shredding on stone, lungs burning, the taste of metal blooming on her tongue.

"Dad!" The word tore loose, jagged, then dissolved into smoke before it reached him.

The lights pulled farther away—until the road opened like a mouth and swallowed them whole.

Anna jolted upright in bed, her breath ragged, her nightshirt clinging with sweat. The echo of red taillights still burned behind her eyes. A dream—but not just a dream. The same night. The same leaving, the wound that never closed.

The faint aroma of Grandma's roasting coffee beans drifted up from the kitchen—her morning ritual, steady as the sunrise.

She rubbed her eyes and glanced toward the doorway. Sam, her little brother, stood outside his room, rubbing his eyes, his pajama top askew. "You look like a goofball," he mumbled, blinking at her.

Anna scrunched her face at him as she brushed her hand over his hair. He ducked away with a sleepy scowl, though the corner of his mouth twitched into the smallest smile.

It was the same every morning—his half-hearted resistance, her unspoken win. And maybe, deep down, he liked that she never stopped trying.

The shower roared to life. Hot water pounded her skin—scalding. Steam curled in heavy ribbons, clinging to her throat. Some mornings were like this—when the water thundered, but the past thundered louder.

No matter how many years passed, the low growl of her father's truck still followed her into sleep. She was thirteen again, sitting at the kitchen table with a smudged pencil while Sam stacked blocks.

He passed close enough that she caught the faint trace of his aftershave, but he didn't look at her. Didn't even slow down.

Keys yanked from the hook. Boots striking the floor. The slam of the screen door.

And red taillights bleeding into dusk—her birthday collapsing into silence.

She pressed her palms to the tile. Tears salted her lips, softened by the trace of strawberry shampoo.

Her thirteenth birthday should have been cake and candles. Instead, she heard her mother crying behind closed doors, then the rattle of Grandma's old Corolla pulling into the drive.

The hiss of the shower pulled her back, the spray drumming her shoulders, heat wrapping around her like a heavy cloak, damp strands of hair sticking to her cheeks.

Four years later, she still woke to the echo of that night—daughter abandoned.

Now at seventeen, she was the one wiping her mother's sweat, calming Sam's fears, pretending everything was fine.

Piece by piece, she had learned how to keep the walls standing— almost enough to forget she was still just a child herself. *Almost.*

On their way down the hall, Anna paused at her mother's door and eased it open with two fingers. Sarah slept on her side, breath shallow, the sheet rising and falling like a small, careful tide.

Her wrists looked too thin, her collarbones sharp as folded wings. A lock of hair clung to her damp temple, the faint scent of lavender lotion still lingering.

Anna closed the door gently, the sound of her breath loud in her ears. "Come on, sweetheart, breakfast's ready," Grandma Sophia called.

The kitchen light spilled across the worn wood floor. Bacon sizzled in the pan, spitting gently while the coffeepot burbled in the background.

Sophia reached for the comb she kept by the breadbox and tugged Sam toward her. "You get in a wrestling match with your sheets again?" she teased, running the comb through his stubborn cowlick. Sam wriggled free with a scowl, but his grin gave him away.

Watching them, Anna felt the tug of something steady, a thread of normalcy she clung to even as the edges of her world kept unraveling.

The space their father had left. The space their mother was leaving, piece by fragile piece. And Anna, anchored by love yet splintered by loss, pressed back against the wind, carrying whispers of colder days to come.

Chapter 2

Borrowed light

Even as the chill crept in, the town held its glow. October sunlight spilled across CreeksVille, red-gold trees and sharp autumn air sweetening the streets.

As Anna stepped off the bus, Mrs. Thompson leaned from the window, her familiar smile waiting for her.

"Tell your mom we're all praying for her. We're rooting for her."

"I will. Thanks, Mrs. Thompson."

Shop bells chimed; leaves chased each other along the curb. Out here, the world felt lighter.

Fall was her favorite—clear skies, red-gold trees. She paused at the bakery window, where cakes stood like tiny cathedrals. Someday, she thought—France, Le Cordon Bleu, her own café. Warm bread on the counter. Sunlight in the windows.

Her sneakers crunched over the sidewalk, treetops blazing against a crisp blue sky. For now, it helped.

Mrs. Cole waved from the café, the scent of cinnamon drifting into the street.

"Hey, sweetheart! Can you drop this off for your mom?" she asked, handing over a warm paper bag.

"Of course. She'll appreciate it."

Her phone buzzed—time to head home.

The creaky front door gave way just as rain began to patter on the porch roof. Warmth met her—firelight chasing back the dark.

Grandma's worry lines, lavender mingling with the fire's crackle.

"How was your day, sweet pea?"

"Math got canceled. Best news." Anna kissed her cheek and set the bag on the counter.

She dropped her backpack, kicked off her shoes, and carried two mugs down the hall. Cookie tucked between her lips; she nudged her mother's door open. Anna smiled, though a hollow ache whispered the truth she wasn't ready to face: her mother was fading. "Hey, Mom," she said, setting the mugs down.

Sarah's arms opened, and Anna folded into them. Even in frailty, her mother radiated quiet strength.

"Super-duper! How was your day?" Sarah grinned. Her face alight despite the shadows under her eyes.

Anna sat on the bed, sipping chamomile. The silence between them held more than words ever could.

Then came running feet. Sam burst in, laughter spilling ahead of him as he leaped onto the bed. Sarah wrapped both children close, laughter bubbling as they tickled each other. Later, Grandma joined, settling into the armchair with a sigh, her shoulders easing. "How about a family game night?" she asked, eyes twinkling.

Excitement rippled through the room. Banter and teasing filled the space, each roll of the dice pushing the worries a little farther away. For a while, they clung to this—

to the firelight,

to laughter,

to love.

But when the laughter faded and the fire dimmed, the shadows in the house grew heavier.

That night, long after the house stilled, Sam padded toward the kitchen for water. Passing their mother's door, he slowed. A thin strip of light spilled from the half-open bathroom.

Then—gagging. A muffled cough.

He peeked in. Mom bent over the commode, thin shoulders trembling. Anna knelt beside her, one hand firm on her back, the other pressing a damp cloth to her neck.

The sharp tang of antiseptic clung to the heavy air. Sam's fingers curled against the doorframe. His mother's fragility. His sister's steady hands. The picture burned into him.

He backed away, retreating without a sound. Under his blanket, silent tears soaked his pillow.

Now he knew—it wasn't just tiredness. Something inside his mom was breaking.

And in the middle of it all, Anna—calm, unwavering, a light refusing to go out. He clenched his fists beneath the covers. I'll be strong, too, just like Anna.

The wind carried the sharp bite of autumn. Change was coming—quiet, unyielding, unstoppable.

Later that week, Anna knelt beside Sam's bed, noticing the worry clouding his eyes.

"What if she doesn't get better?" he whispered. "What if she leaves us, too?"

Anna's chest pinched. "She's fighting hard. And we're with her."

"Is she scared?"

"Maybe, but she's brave. Like you."

"Will you stay till I fall asleep?"

"Always."

She settled beside him, blanket drawn close—a small protection against questions neither dared to ask. As Sam drifted to sleep, the rhythm of his breathing brought her quiet peace. Stars still shone beyond the clouds—a quiet reminder to hold on.

Her phone buzzed: Appointment confirmed—Oncology, 9:30 a.m. She turned it face down, switched off the light, and stared at the ceiling.

"The rain had stopped. The clouds hadn't. Tomorrow would bring more questions. She would meet them. That was all she could do."

Chapter 3

A child's prayer

The next day, while walking home from school, Sam and his best friend Jacob ambled side by side, backpacks bouncing on their shoulders.

"My mom says we pray when we need help or want to say thank you," Jacob said, skipping over a crack in the sidewalk.

Sam nodded slowly. "Yeah? Do you pray a lot?"

"Sometimes," Jacob said. "And sometimes… we light a candle, too."

Sam slowed, eyes wide as he turned to Jacob. "Wait—you light a candle? Does that really make God hear you better?"

Jacob shrugged. "Maybe. My mom says it helps us feel close to Him."

They walked for a moment before Sam blurted out, "Can I… can I come with you next time? To light one?"

Jacob looked surprised, then grinned. "Sure! I'll ask my mom. She won't mind."

"Okay." Sam stared at the ground as they walked, kicking a pebble ahead of him. "I just… I think maybe it'll help."

That night, as the house settled into quiet, Sam sat on the edge of his bed, his small hands fidgeting nervously with the hem of his pajama shirt.

The lamp cast shadows along the walls, shapes that seemed to wait and listen. At the window, the moon sagged low, its pale light seeping through thin curtains.

Sam hesitated. He'd never prayed before—not like this. Jacob's words echoed in his mind: *"Just talk to God like you're talking to anyone else."*

Taking a deep breath, he slid off the bed and knelt on the rug. The fibers tickled his knees, grounding him in the moment.

He folded his hands awkwardly; his fingers squeezed together like he was holding on for dear life.

"Um. Hi, God." His voice was barely above a breath. He cleared his throat and tried again, a little louder this time.

"I don't know if you know me. I'm Sam. I'm seven. I'm Jacob's friend."

He paused, his gaze darting to the shadows that seemed to inch closer in the room's corners.

"So, um, my mom... she's really sick. I heard the doctors say it's cancer, and I don't know what to do.

Could you...Could you please help her? Stop the coughing and the throwing up? She's always tired now, and I just want her to feel better."

Sam felt a lump rise in his throat. He blinked rapidly, determined not to cry.

"And thank you for Anna. She lets me play games on her laptop even when I don't ask. She makes the best cupcakes. And... I think she cries in the shower."

He hesitated again, unsure how to finish.

His hands unclasped, falling to his lap. "Please, God, just make her better. I'll do anything—I'll be good, I'll get good grades," he whispered.

He wished he had a candle too—just in case it made God listen harder.

Sleep found him with the words still echoing in his head.

While Sam prayed for a miracle, Anna prayed only to be strong enough. And between their two prayers, the house held its breath.

The next morning, Sam awoke to the smell of pancakes wafting through the house. His mom was feeling a bit better and had decided to make breakfast.

He, Anna, and Grandma Sophia gathered around the kitchen table, their plates piled high with fluffy pancakes drizzled with syrup. It was a rare treat, and they savored every bite.

It was the best Friday ever.

As they ate, laughter and chatter filled the room—a reminder that joy could still find its way into their lives despite the challenges they faced.

Sam stole a glance at his mom. Her smile looked real today—not the tired kind she wore when she was forcing it. He didn't say anything. But something in him believed his prayers from last night had been heard.

Sam didn't say it out loud, but he felt it—grateful for his family, for pancakes, for one good morning.
When he left for school, Sam hugged his mom tightly, whispering a silent prayer of thanks—and hoping God was still listening

Chapter 4

The night whispers

The nights were quieter now—too quiet. No arguments. No footsteps pacing. No promises unkept.

Sarah had learned to live inside the silence.

For the first year after Jake left, she clung to hope, believing he would return—if not for her, then at least for their children.

But time had stripped that illusion bare. What remained was a man lost in his own fog, resentment festering over sacrifices he believed he'd made.

Four years had passed since his departure, leaving a void Sarah had long stopped trying to fill. She never saw Jake as a villain—just a man adrift, blurred in the flickering hospital lights of her long shifts.

Whenever she asked him to be there for Sam, his replies were sharp, his words cutting like the scent of burnt coffee—bitter, lingering. But for their children, the real sacrifice was his absence.

In the long stretch of months that followed, Sarah fought to keep their family afloat.

She called Jake after the diagnosis—too weak to hold the phone to her ear. She set it on speaker, hands trembling as she leaned against the counter for support.

"I thought you should know," she said, her voice barely steady. "It's cancer. Stage Two."

There was a pause—long enough to let hope crawl in before his words crushed it.

"So now you need me?"

Not "What are the doctors saying?"

Not even "How are the kids?"

Just that.

As if her illness excused his absence. Sarah blinked back the sting in her eyes and ended the call quietly.

"No. I don't."

She hadn't realized Anna was in the doorway until she felt her arms wrap tightly around her.

Anna pressed her cheek to her mother's shoulder and said with quiet fire,

"We don't need him, Mom. Never will."

And somehow, Sarah knew they'd be okay.

Sarah's gaze drifted toward the mantel, where her father's photograph stood—a reminder of a very different kind of man.

Unlike Anna, who knew only absence, Sarah remembered the warmth of laughter and hugs with her dad.

After her father's funeral, Sarah sought solace in the loud beats of club music, the air thick with smoke and neon. The bass pounded through her ribs until she could almost forget the hollow ache inside her.

That's where she hung out with Jake most evenings—a mirage of escape, a crooked smile, a drink in hand, a promise of escape she mistook for hope.

Later, when her mother begged her to come home, Sarah chose defiance instead. She married Jake, believing she was escaping grief. She never guessed she was walking into another kind of absence.

Looking back, she tried to untangle the anger she carried toward her mother in those turbulent years.

In contrast, Sarah's admiration for her mother ran deep. When she apologized for her youthful defiance, Sophia only smiled, dismissing it as teenage angst and choosing instead to be grateful for the grandchildren who filled her days with joy.

Observing her mother's strength in the face of grief and hardship profoundly influenced Sarah's understanding of resilience and motherhood. Those memories resurfaced often, guiding her through moments of despair.

One evening, as she tucked Anna into bed, she whispered, "We're going to be okay, sweetheart. I promise."

The words stayed with Anna for years.

Watching Sophia become the pillar of their home grounded Sarah. She saw how her mother nurtured Sam and managed the house with grace.

Sarah often woke to the soft murmur of Sophia's prayers drifting from the kitchen, the kettle's whistle rising like an anthem of endurance.

That unwavering presence gave Anna a sense of security amid the chaos—something Sarah could never thank her mother enough for.

Sophia often reminded her, "We can't control what others do, but we can control how we respond."

Over the years, Anna absorbed those words, her quiet resolve filling the gaps Jake left behind.

Amber and violet streaks lit the winter sky. Sarah sat in the living room, shawl pulled tight against the cold, divorce papers in hand. Their sharp edges cut against the blur of recent days, the decision heavy as a quilt—fear and liberation stitched into every fold.

As Sam lay cocooned in his comforter, his faint snores rising and falling like waves. Sarah curled into the corner of the small living room. The old shawl brushed her skin—familiar, scratchy, warm.

Outside, the wind rustled dry leaves along the porch, a scraping sound that came and went like an old song she couldn't quite place.

The paper crinkled under her grip, brittle as if it might shatter. Her name—Sarah Bennett—stood beside Jake Buchman's, unyielding.

Her hands, though pale and thinner than she remembered, didn't shake.

Not this time.

She looked out the window, where the stars blinked faintly through a veil of clouds. A breath caught in her throat. She hadn't cried yet. Not for this. She wasn't sure why.

Then, quietly, as if testing the stillness, she said, "Can we talk?"

Anna glanced up from the hallway, sensing something different in her mother's tone. She padded over, the scuff of her socks on the wooden floor the only sound.

The couch let out a sigh as she sat beside her mother, and the throw between them rustled as Sarah pulled it around both their shoulders.

Sarah spoke gently, her words carrying quiet resolve. "I filed for divorce from your dad."

Anna's lips parted, but no words came at first. Her gaze dropped to the papers, then back to her mother's face. The warmth from the fireplace cast flickering shadows across Sarah's cheekbones—lines deeper now, etched with both pain and peace.

"It'll be in the newspaper," Sarah added. "Everyone will know."

Anna drew in a breath, the scent of burning wood hitting the back of her throat. "Grandma knows, right?"

Sarah nodded slowly. "Yes."

A long pause hung between them, heavy and unspoken.

"Why now?" Anna asked, the words low and tight around the edges.

"The doctors don't think I'll survive this cancer."

A log cracked in the fireplace, startling them both slightly—a reminder that time kept moving, even in the hardest moments.

"Mom, stop!" The words tore out of her as her fingers curled into the blanket, knuckles pale. She blinked fast, the sting of tears sharp and sudden.

Sarah's eyes, glazed yet steady, locked on her daughter's. Her thumb traced soft circles over Anna's skin. "Shhhh...my baby girl. Everyone must leave eventually," she murmured.

"But I don't want to die as his wife.

I want to die as my mother's daughter."

For a moment, neither of them breathed.

Anna's shoulders trembled as she leaned in. "I'll be okay, Mom," she said fiercely. "I promise. I'll take care of Sam."

Pride bloomed in Sarah's chest, warm and quiet and full. She tucked a strand of hair behind Anna's ear, her hand cool against her daughter's warm cheek. "I know you will. You're stronger than you know."

A gust of wind rattled the windowpane, but inside, the air stood still—thick with truth, pain, and love.

Sarah looked down once more at the divorce papers. This wasn't just about Jake. It was about reclaiming herself. She no longer wanted a name bound to abandonment.

Instead, she chose the one her mother had given her.

She folded the papers, smoothed them flat on the coffee table, and felt it—not relief alone, but something more profound, heavier, more final.

Pride—quiet, unshakable, and hers alone.

But warmth can't stop the days from moving forward.

The next day came, as all days do—whether you're ready or not.

Chapter 5

When the clouds wept

Winter had settled in, cloaking the world in stillness. The wind rattled softly against the glass, but inside, warmth lingered in the quiet corners.

The hospice nurse moved with practiced care, adjusting Sarah's IV line, checking the oxygen levels, and noting vitals with gentle efficiency.

Sarah's lips parted. Her words came as a rasp, barely louder than breath. "Can we have the room, please?"

The nurse paused, then offered a reassuring nod. "Of course," she said with a kind smile. "I'll be right outside. Just press the bell if you need anything."

As the door clicked shut behind her, the stillness deepened—closer now, almost intimate.

A single bedside lamplight pooled in the corner, illuminating the frail figure beneath the thick comforter. The air was thick with the sterile scent of medicine, mingled with the soothing aroma of lavender.

Sarah breathed in shallow whispers, every inhale a labor. The monitor's beep cut through the room, steady as an hourglass marking the seconds she had left.

Anna sat beside her, her fingers laced with her mother's, feeling the warmth that was slowly fading. The moment pressed into her chest like a stone.

"Mom." The words broke in the still air. "I don't know if I can do this without you."

Sarah's eyelids fluttered open, her gaze locking onto her daughter's. Despite the frailty in her body, there was a flicker of strength in her eyes—a quiet, enduring love that seemed to transcend time and space.

"Yes, you can." Her tone was faint. "You're not alone. And you'll have Grandma and Sam. You'll be okay."

The words offered her a fragile sense of comfort amid heartbreak. A tear slipped down her cheek, warm against the chill of the moment, but she nodded, drawing strength from her mother's unwavering gaze.

She stayed there, holding her mother's hand, feeling the warmth ebb until the room grew still, hushed like the calm after snowfall.

Snow swirled into the night, white flakes drifting like lost memories.

Anna sat beside the bed, her fingers still curled around her mother's limp hand.

What once comforted her was gone, replaced by an unbearable absence.

No beep. No breath.

Sam was asleep in the next room. He didn't know yet.

Anna swallowed hard, her throat tight, her chest aching. She had told herself a thousand times this day would come, but nothing could have braced her for the moment itself.

The lamp's dim light traced the bed sheets where her mother lay, once rising and falling, now still.

Anna squeezed her mother's hand one last time, pressing it to her forehead, willing the moment to freeze, to reverse, to be anything but what it was.

A quiet knock at the door broke through the stillness. Sophia stood there, wrapped in her thick cardigan, her eyes knowing and heavy with unspoken grief. No words were spoken—none were needed.

Anna slowly shook her head, the grief that had been held at bay for so long breaking through, a quiet, breathless sob escaping her lips like a fragile bird taking flight.

Sophia crossed the room, and in an instant, Anna was in her grandmother's arms, shaking, crying—mourning the loss that felt like a living thing, clawing at her heart.

A floorboard creaked from the hallway. Sam.

He stood there, small and vulnerable in his pajama shirt, clutching the sleeve of his shirt. His hazel eyes darted from Anna's tear-streaked face to the still figure in the bed.

He didn't ask. He didn't have to.

Anna wiped her face and opened her arms. Sam ran into them, burying his face against her shoulder, seeking the warmth only she could give.

The three of them—Anna, Sam, and Sophia—held each other in the quiet of a room once filled with Sarah's laughter.

The world kept turning. The wind battered the windowpane, a dirge for what was gone. Below, the town moved on, oblivious to the hollow ache in their home.

Tomorrow, there would be phone calls to make, arrangements to handle, and a funeral to plan. But tonight—just for tonight—they allowed themselves to grieve, enveloped in the cocoon of shared sorrow.

The night stretched long, sorrow wrapping them in its cold embrace.

A light knock broke the silence. The nurse entered quietly, her eyes carrying the calm empathy of someone who'd stood in rooms like this before. She offered only a respectful nod toward Sarah's still form.

"I'll need to take some notes and begin the process." Her voice carried care, as if unwilling to disturb the peace that had settled over the room.

Sophia guided Sam out, her arm around his shoulders, whispering soothing words he likely wouldn't remember.

The nurse moved with reverence, confirming the time, making quiet notations.

"She went peacefully." The words were a small kindness offered back to the grief in the room.

Anna wiped her cheeks and nodded again. "Thank you." Her voice came out rough, scraped from somewhere deep inside her.

The nurse stepped back, giving her space. "Take your time. I'll call the team. They'll come when you're ready."

She slipped out, leaving the door slightly ajar. Anna stayed where she was, her hand clasping her mother's, unwilling to let go. Down the hall, the echo of a phone call drifted faintly, a reminder that while her own world had stopped, beyond the snow-dusted windows, morning was still coming.

Chapter 6

Goodbye mommy

The night unraveled slowly, each hour longer than the one before. Icicles clinked faintly against the window; a fragile rhythm Anna longed to stop.

When the doorbell finally rang, it felt as though the world had come to claim what was theirs. Anna stood in the doorway, a hollow ache stirring as she clung to her grandma's hand.

Sam bent down to kiss their mother goodbye, whispering, "Goodbye, Mommy. I love you."

Memories crashed over her—nights curled on the couch, laughter thick in the air, stories lit like warm sunlight.

Now, those moments seemed like fragile echoes, fading into the cold, unforgiving winter air.

She shut her eyes tightly, yearning to return to that sunlit kitchen, where the world was a tapestry of safety and her mother was an unwavering force, invincible against all odds.

In the depths of her heart, she could almost hear Sarah's voice—a melodic blend of love and encouragement—whispering that Anna was never truly alone.

"Remember, Anna," her mother had said, her eyes sparkling with wisdom, "love never really leaves us. It becomes a part of who we are." Those words were now a promise that defied the cruel reality of loss.

As the paramedics prepared to carry Sarah away, Sophia leaned down, kissing her daughter's forehead with a tenderness that belied the pain in her heart.

Her body trembled, as fragile as the threads of their shared memories. "Until we meet again, my baby girl," she whispered.

Anna buried her face in her mother's shoulder one last time, sobbing like a child, her grief raw and unfiltered. Sam gently held her hand—a quiet gesture of comfort in the storm.

Together, they stood on the edge of goodbye, bound by love even as the world pulled Sarah away.

Anna inhaled deeply, the scent of lavender still faintly lingering in the air, a reminder of her mother's presence, both comforting and heartbreaking.

With resolve building in her chest, she stepped forward, ready to embrace the pain of loss but also the love that remained.

As she turned away from the door, the nurse assured Anna that her mother's love, a guiding light in the dark, would always be with her.

And in that moment, Anna knew she would find the strength to carry on, even when the world felt impossibly heavy.

When dawn broke, golden light filtered through the curtains, too bright and indifferent to the room's heaviness. Sarah's room was empty, the crumpled bed a stark reminder of a life that had once breathed vitality into this home, now shadowed by loss.

The world does not wait. The ambulance was already at the door, papers waiting to be signed. The world had come knocking. It was time to say goodbye.

Though her heart ached, Anna felt something stir within her—a flicker of resolve igniting in the depths of her grief.

She would honor her mother's strength and love by carrying on.

For Sam.

For Grandma.

And for herself.

As news of Sarah's passing spread, neighbors and friends gathered to offer support, reflecting a mix of sympathy and shared sorrow. While Mr. Cole and Grandma made funeral arrangements, Sarah's friend Jane, who owned the local floral shop, stepped forward.

"I'll take care of the flowers," she said gently, offering more comfort than words alone could give.

Sam and Anna exchanged polite greetings with everyone who entered their home. After a few minutes, Sam slipped away from the crowd. He padded into the kitchen, opened the refrigerator, and poured himself a glass of milk with careful concentration.

Reaching into the old cookie jar, he pulled out two of the oatmeal cookies his mother had baked just days ago. He sat quietly at the table, crumbs clinging to his fingers, milk cooling in his hand.

Yet even with the sweetness of her cookies on his tongue, the emptiness pressed in, turning the once-familiar space hollow and strange.

The knitted shawl lay untouched on the sofa, a poignant reminder of her warmth. Its once-vibrant colors seemed muted under the dim light, as if grief had drained them of their life.

Sam hesitated before stepping forward, his fingers grazing the fabric. With quiet reverence, he lifted the shawl to his face, breathing in deeply, searching for the familiar scent of her—of comfort, of home.

The faintest trace remained, wrapping around him like a whisper of a memory, fragile but still present.

Slowly, he turned and went to his room, the shawl clutched tightly in his hands. Once inside, he carefully tucked it beneath his pillow, a quiet promise to himself.

When the hours stretched endless and the stillness grew too heavy, this part of his mother would remain—a thread of love, faint but unbroken, glimmering in the dark.

Chapter 7

No tears left

A gray mist clung to the streets, ice pellets striking the hearse's black roof in a measured rhythm, as though the sky itself was mourning.

The sharp bite of winter air mingled with the lilies outside the funeral home, their sweetness settling over the mourners like an offering of condolence.

Inside, the air was thick with unspoken sorrow. Dim lighting cast long shadows across the room, candlelight flickering against the polished mahogany casket.

Low murmurs wove through the space, broken by muffled sobs and the shuffle of shoes against the worn wooden floor.

Nothing could have truly prepared Anna for this day. She had known it was coming—her mother's health had steadily declined.

But the stillness of her body resting in the open casket shattered her fragile composure.

A light drizzle beaded against the windowpanes, mirroring the quiet grief of Anna, Sam, and Sophia. Anna's gaze flickered to Sam, her little brother.

He sat stiffly on the hard pew, legs dangling just above the floor, the wooden edge pressing into him as though the seat itself demanded a grown man's posture he did not yet have.

The dark suit swallowed his slight frame, fabric too grown-up for a child who should've been chasing games in the yard. Since their mother's passing, his round eyes carried a weight beyond his years.

He fidgeted, tugging at the stiff collar. "It's itchy," he muttered. Then, spotting Jacob across the aisle, he lifted his small hand in a quick wave. Jacob waved back shyly, clutching a crumpled program.

For a heartbeat, Sam's face softened, the child in him breaking through the stiffness of the suit.

A wobbly smile tugged at Anna's lips. She wrapped an arm around him, the warmth of his small body anchoring her. "We'll go home soon, okay?"

Beside them, Sophia sat rigid in the front pew, her gaze fixed on the children even as the casket loomed before her. Their small bodies leaning into each other made her grief both heavier and more bearable.

The lilies in the air carried her back to another funeral, long ago. The day she buried her husband had been the most excruciating of her life—or so she had thought.

Now, standing before the casket of her only child, she understood that losing a child was a pain without equal. Sarah, once the brightest in any room, now lay in stillness.

Sophia tightened her hands, the small ritual giving her a fragile sense of control. But control gave way to memory. She saw Sarah again—laughing so hard her whole body shook, joy spilling into every corner of the house.

On other days, when sorrow pressed too close, Sarah would sing at the top of her lungs, off-key and without rhythm, until everyone was laughing with her.

And when Sam needed a doctor's shot, she'd squeeze her eyes shut before he did, wincing louder than he ever did, then wrapping him close in her arms.

The lilies' perfume pulled her back. The hush of the chapel pressed in once more, grief folding over her like a heavy shroud. She gripped the pew tighter, as if holding onto both memory and moment at once.

Sam leaned close and whispered, "Will Dad come?"

Sophia's heart faltered.

That was the very question she had been grappling with: would Jake come? Her stomach twisted at the thought. Would their dad show up after all these years, after being little more than a ghost in their lives?

A part of her wished he would—for Anna, for Sam. They deserved the comfort of having a father present, especially on a day like today.

But another part of her dreaded his return. Jake had been nothing but heartache—the burden Sarah had carried too long. His presence, if it came, would only stir more chaos.

All through the service, Sophia's gaze kept drifting to the door, half-dreading, half-hoping. But when the final prayer ended, the doorway remained empty.

Jake had not come, and Sophia wasn't sure whether it brought her relief or disappointment—but she knew one thing: Anna and Sam deserved better.

As the service ended, the hushed shuffle of feet echoed through the room, a quiet symphony of sorrow. Sophia rose with the others, her body moving as if through a nightmare, each step unbearably heavy.

Standing with Sam and Anna, their warmth reminded her that love could withstand even the deepest heartache.

Neighbors lingered near the pews, sorrow in their eyes as they looked toward Anna and Sam. Mrs. Jones, their elderly neighbor, pressed a handkerchief to her lips, her eyes red-rimmed. She had known Sarah since Anna was a baby and had watched her grow into a strong mother.

Around them rose a chorus of condolences. A woman leaned in, thick with emotion, her hand resting gently on Anna's shoulder, while another reached out to squeeze Sam's small hand. "We are here for you and Sam."

The outpouring of love wrapped around them like a heavy quilt—comforting, with the care once shown to Sarah now extended to her children.

Sam looked up at Anna, his small fingers tightening around hers. He said nothing, but his grip told her what he couldn't say.

Sarah's love lingered—in every glance, every touch, every quiet promise left behind.

The ache of it all anchored Sophia as she reached for Anna and Sam, their small grips grounding her. Anna laid a gentle hand on Sam's narrow shoulders, pulling him closer. They stood—three hearts stitched by loss yet held together by love.

Anna thought she could almost hear it—her mother's laughter, bright and untamed, reminding her that love does not vanish.

The storm had passed, leaving a hush that felt tender, worn yet enduring. Anna felt it echo inside her—not absence, but a shift. The ache stayed, but so did the thread—fragile, unbroken—guiding her forward.

Chapter 8

Tulips always bloom

The scent of lilies still lingered in the hallway—faint, wilting—long after the last condolence guest had gone.

The days following the funeral blurred together. The house had grown quieter, emptier, missing Sarah's warmth, her laughter, her presence that once filled the spaces between.

Every corner held a memory, each one a comfort that ached as much as it comforted.

Anna had expected grief to erupt like a volcano—violent, shattering. But it wasn't. Grief was quiet. Lingering. A shadow that never receded.

Graduation loomed on the horizon, a moment she once looked forward to with excitement. Now, it felt hollow. What was supposed to be a celebration of freedom now felt like another step away from everything she had known.

Graduating with honors would have been her mother's proudest moment—a milestone Sarah had dreamed of witnessing.

Anna found herself taking on roles she had never imagined—balancing her grief while trying to be a constant source of strength for Sam.

Neighbors dropped by often. Their arms were full of casseroles and warm breads, bundled in tea towels or foil. Some offered to walk Sam home from school or drive him to soccer practice. It wasn't pity that brought them to the doorstep—but genuine love.

The kind that remembered birthdays, showed up unasked, and lingered in the quiet after everyone else had gone. Their kindness didn't erase the ache—but it blunted the sharpest edges of it.

When the dishes were put away and the door shut, reality waited at the kitchen table.

The week after the funeral, Anna and Sophia sifted through papers, Anna's fingers tightening around a bank statement that revealed her mother's careful savings. Three thousand dollars. The house was paid off. The car, too.

A breath of relief passed through her. At least they had a roof over their heads. It wasn't much, but it was home.

The weeks turned into months. They found solace in the little things—preparing meals together, tending to the small garden Sarah had loved, sharing quiet stories of her. Sophia became their rock, constantly reminding them that they were not alone.

Stability gave them room to breathe, but grief had its own clock. It showed itself in different ways—most clearly in Sam.

Sam's sorrow was loud in its silence. Anna felt it too, in her own way.

Despite the love surrounding them, Sam struggled. The school grief counselor tried to help, but nothing could erase the emptiness he felt when he walked through the front door and realized she was no longer there.

One evening, his chest felt tight as he trudged home, kicking at loose stones along the pavement.

"I should have prayed harder and lit the candles," he thought. "I should have asked God to make her better and keep her here."

The guilt weighed on him, a child's innocent belief that maybe, just maybe, he could have changed fate.

But then Anna would ruffle his hair, or his grandmother would hold him close, and for a little while, the pain would ease.

In the still moments, Anna would sit by the window, staring out at the world beyond, wondering how everything could keep moving forward when their world had stopped.

"This too shall pass," she murmured to herself.

She had read about the Buddhist concept of impermanence once in her world religions class.

Nothing is permanent.

Not joy.

Not suffering.

Not even grief.

She clung to that thought, whispering it like a prayer, hoping—believing—that the ache would be lighter one day.

That one day, they would find their way forward.

Life, in its stubborn way, kept offering new chapters—even when she wasn't ready.

Prom night slipped in quietly.

Early spring had begun to unfurl itself—a gentle breeze carried the scent of thawing earth, and the trees wore a light fuzz of green.

In the front yard, beneath the window where her mother once sat, a small cluster of tulips pushed through the soil—bold, certain.

Sarah had planted them years ago, saying tulips were stubborn things, always blooming even when the world hadn't quite thawed.

Anna knelt that morning, her fingers brushing the petals. Grief pricked at her, but beneath it stirred something fragile. It felt wrong to celebrate when everything still hurt—but she knew her mom would have been disappointed if she didn't go.

Her mother would have made a fuss—draping fabric swatches across the couch, comparing hairstyles from magazines, insisting on curling every strand herself. Sarah would've cried. She always did, even during middle school dances.

Instead, it was Sophia who helped fasten the dress, her hands gentle but trembling slightly as she zipped up the back. "You look lovely, my Anna," she said, pride shining in her eyes.

Anna turned toward the mirror, catching her own reflection—and then her mother's necklace. The delicate silver chain lay against her collarbone, the tiny sapphire stone catching the light. Sarah's favorite. She had always said it brought calm.

Sam stood in the hallway, wide-eyed. "You look like a movie star," he declared, and Anna laughed through the lump in her throat.

Mrs. Cole arrived at the door just before her date, holding her camera like a professional. "Come on, let's get some pictures before it's dark." She guided Anna onto the porch, arranging her with gentle hands. "Tilt your chin up just a little. That's it. Beautiful."

Laughter bubbled up—real and unexpected—between the flashes, while her date lingered at the curb, shifting nervously with his hands in his pockets.

For a moment, the sadness eased. The grief was still there, woven into the edges of everything. But so was love. So was the strength of those still standing beside her.

That night, as Anna stepped into the car and waved goodbye, the sapphire glinting at her throat, she felt her mother with her—not in body, but in every detail, every memory.

And that was enough.

She didn't look back as the car pulled away. She didn't need to. Her mother was everywhere—in the garden, in her steady grace, in the sapphire at her throat. In her. Always.

Chapter 9

The heart of CreeksVille

The afternoon sunbathed CreeksVille in a honeyed haze. Banners and balloons read, "Congratulations, Graduates!" as families hugged and laughed across the high school lot.

Anna stood on the steps of the high school, watching the scene unfold.

Around her, classmates hugged their parents, posed for pictures, and made plans.

She swallowed hard. Mom would have been here today.

Anna didn't have to wonder—she knew exactly where her mom would have been standing, right in the front row of the bleachers, camera in hand, beaming with pride, tears in her eyes, calling out her name the loudest.

"That's my girl!"

She could almost hear her mother, almost feel the warmth of her hug.

But she wasn't there. No matter how hard Anna tried to focus on the celebration, the ache of her absence weighed on her chest.

A touch on her arm pulled her from her thoughts.

"Anna, you did it!"

She turned to see her grandmother, Sophia, and Sam grinning with pride.

Sam, dressed in a too-big button-up shirt and slacks, jumped up and down, holding a tiny bouquet he had picked himself. Anna blinked rapidly, willing away the tears.

She smiled, pulling him into a tight hug.

"Thanks, buddy," she said, a grin tugging at her lips.

Sophia stepped forward, cupping Anna's face gently. "Your mom is here, sweetheart. She would never miss today."

Anna let out a shaky breath, nodding. She wasn't alone.

Even though Mom wasn't physically there, she lived in the love surrounding Anna today.

With her grandmother's steady hand in hers and Sam's unwavering support beside her, she let herself breathe in the joy of the moment—even if it was bittersweet.

After the ceremony, the town square buzzed with excitement.

Her classmates scattered toward bonfires and backyard feasts, but Anna turned down the familiar street toward the bakery. Work meant responsibility, bills, and keeping life stitched together—and right now, that mattered more than parties.

Her friend Stacy had invited her to join her family for a graduation party, but Anna didn't want to let Mrs. Lewis, the bakery owner, down. Besides, the extra money would help with bills, including property taxes, home insurance, and utilities.

Mrs. Lewis had to leave town urgently to welcome her grandbaby, who arrived two weeks early, and Anna agreed to cover her shifts.

Romance felt like a faraway idea—right now, the only boy she spent any real time with was Sam, her wide-eyed little brother.

Responsibility had aged Anna beyond her years, yet she carried it with quiet grace.

As she stepped into CreeksVille's cozy French bakery, a drift of coffee and warm, buttery cookies greeted her. She tied her apron neatly and smiled warmly at customers savoring flaky Danish pastries.

This time of year, the town came alive—sunlight dancing on the lake, families out on the trails, kayaks dotting the lake, and the scent of lilacs drifting on the breeze.

Mrs. Lewis had run the bakery for as long as Anna could remember, her pastries woven into CreeksVille like church bells and summer fairs. People came for the food but stayed for her warmth— an extra cookie here, a kind word there.

A lifelong friend of Sophia's, she took Anna under her wing after Sarah's passing, treating her like family and quietly admiring her strength.

Anna gathered used plates and empty coffee mugs, her thoughts interrupted by Lizzy's cheerful exclamation.

With a grin, Lizzy thrust a balloon marked *Congrats!* Into Anna's arms, while balancing a small homemade cake in her other hand, its single candle flickering brightly.

"Make a wish," she teased with a wink.

Anna laughed, light and unguarded, as Lizzy pushed the cake closer.

Before she could answer, the back door creaked open. Her eyes lit with joy. "I couldn't stay away. A new grandbaby or not—I wasn't about to miss this."

Behind her, the rest of the bakery staff trickled in—Carlos from the kitchen, Mira, the college student who helped on weekends, and even old Mr. Hartley, who delivered the morning bread.

They gathered around the counter, a makeshift little family.

"Go on, sweetheart," Mrs. Lewis said. "Let's mark the moment."

Anna took a breath, made a silent wish—one she didn't try to put into words—and blew out the candle.

Joyful applause filled the bakery. As the cake was cut and slivers of frosting-smeared celebration were passed around, Anna looked at the faces smiling back at her.

She still missed her mom—that ache would never fade. Yet as laughter filled the bakery and vanilla lingered in the air, she felt it—the quiet truth her mother had always promised: she wasn't alone.

Chapter 10

It takes a village

The scent of warm bread clung to the air as Anna brushed flour from her hands, the ovens' purr settling something deep inside her. With every shift, the bakery's rhythm stitched itself into her, familiar and kind, as if it had always been hers to keep.

Later that day, as the bakery wound down, Lizzy nudged Anna playfully.

"You've got quite the fan club," she teased. "Everyone here adores you."

Anna smiled, cheeks warming. "I'm just lucky to have such amazing people in my life."

Amid the clatter and chatter of the bakery, Anna found something more than routine. It was a place where friendships blossomed, laughter lingered, and hope quietly thrived.

In flour-dusted mornings and trays of cookies, she discovered a strength that didn't need to shout.

She was held—not just by her own resolve, but by a community that saw her and stayed.

CreeksVille still moved with comforting familiarity—leaves crisping gold, school buses rumbling past tidy porches.

The town felt smaller now, as if it could no longer hold all that was growing inside her.

As she and Lizzy wiped down the bakery counter, Lizzy bumped her shoulder.

"So, Miss Honor Student, what's next? College, big city, fancy new life?"

"College can wait," Anna said. "But maybe I'm needed more here—at least for now."

Lizzy raised a brow. "You sure? Or just scared to leave?"

Anna paused for half a second before rolling her eyes. "I'm sure. Someone's gotta keep this town running, right?"

"Good thing you've got me," Lizzy grinned. "Otherwise, this place would fall apart."

As days bled into weeks, the question of college returned again and again—unspoken in conversations, loud in quiet moments.

"Are you still thinking about college?" Grandma asked from the rocking chair beside her.

Anna swallowed. She had been. Once. But now?

"I'm thinking about it." Her words came out quiet, uncertain. But part of her wondered if this was where she was meant to be right now.

Sam was still adjusting. The house still felt like it had missing pieces. Then there was the bakery—her part-time job that, lately, felt like the only place where things made sense.

Mrs. Lewis had been kind, patient, and willing to teach her everything she needed to know. She felt calm in those quiet moments, kneading dough or frosting cakes.

"*I think Mom would have wanted you to follow your dream*," Grandma once said.

Her fingertips lingered on the sketches of croissants and éclairs, the scent of butter and coffee rising in memory as if Paris might still open its arms.

But she thought of Grandma, of all the sacrifices that had built this small, quiet life. With a trembling breath, Anna closed the book, setting it aside like a letter she would never send.

Paris would wait, but Sam could not. Dreams, she told herself, could be given away when love asked her to stay.

The low autumn sun slanted through the bakery's windows, casting amber light on the polished counters.

Lizzy had a way of lighting up every room. Her playful energy was a welcome contrast to Anna's quiet steadiness. In the warm light of the bakery, their hands stayed busy, and their minds found ease in the gentle rhythm of work.

When Anna started working at the bakery, Lizzy sensed a kindred spirit. Both women carried heavy responsibilities, though their challenges were different.

Their early conversations were lighthearted and playful, but deeper topics soon emerged, strengthening their bond.

One afternoon, Lizzy sauntered into the kitchen, her trademark grin firmly in place. She fanned herself dramatically with a pancake spatula, blowing a loose strand of hair from her face.

"Anna, are you trying to knead your way into some baking hall of fame? Because at this rate, you'll have arms like Mike Tyson!" she flexed dramatically.

Anna, elbow-deep in dough, rolled her eyes but couldn't hide her smile. The sticky warmth of the dough clung to her fingers, the scent of yeast and vanilla filling the air.

"Lizzy, if you spent half as much time baking as you do cracking jokes, we'd have twice as many pastries."

"Oh, please," Lizzy retorted, grabbing a rolling pin and tapping it against the counter for emphasis.

"You're the one who needs a distraction. When was the last time you even took a day off?"

Anna wiped the back of her hand across her forehead, feeling the slight sheen of sweat from a hot summer afternoon. The bakery's fans whirred overhead, circulating the warm, sugar-laced air.

"And when was the last time you didn't meddle in my life?"

Lizzy smirked, unbothered. "Meddling is my love language, darling. Besides, someone must ensure you don't turn into a dough-obsessed recluse."

Lizzy's playful banter often masked her genuine concern for Anna, but Anna knew better. Beneath the jokes and exaggerated theatrics, Lizzy's loyalty was unshakable.

Over time, Anna and Lizzy became inseparable.

They bonded during early morning shifts when the sun streamed through the front windows, and during slow afternoons filled with the scent of lemonade and sugar cookies.

Lizzy admired Anna's resilience, while Anna appreciated Lizzy's ability to find humor in even the bleakest situations. Their friendship grew naturally, with each supporting the other quietly and meaningfully.

Lizzy's husband, Bob, was the epitome of a gentleman. He served as a captain at the local precinct, earning the town's respect and admiration.

Though Lizzy and Bob didn't have children, they found fulfillment in each other and their tight-knit community. Lizzy's eyes softened as she pressed the peach iced tea into Anna's hands. "Paris will wait," she said quietly. "Sam can't."

Her words landed gently, like truth Anna had been trying not to name.

"You're doing an incredible job," Lizzy added, her tone firmer now.

"Taking care of Sam, showing up here every day, holding everything together. That's not nothing, Anna. Let others be your strength, too. It's okay to lean."

Anna's eyes misted. She blinked hard, then whispered, "Thanks, Lizzy. I don't know what I'd do without you."

Lizzy grinned and nudged her. "Good thing you won't have to find out."

She sipped the peach iced tea, let its sweetness linger, and whispered into the hum of the ovens, "Mom, I chose him. I hope you'd be proud."

Chapter 11

Let me be your shelter

The morning rush had just ended, leaving the bakery calm and filled with the lingering scent of buttery pastries and fresh espresso.

As Anna reached for a tray of scones, she suddenly heard a loud crash behind her. Spinning around, she saw Lizzy standing over a toppled tray of Berry tarts, her apron splattered with sticky jam.

"Well, that's one way to make a statement," Lizzy said, trying to stifle a laugh as she grabbed a towel.

Anna covered her mouth, eyes wide before bursting into laughter, even as they scrambled to clean up the mess before Mrs. Lewis walked in.

The smell of warm strawberries and caramelized sugar filled the air, making the whole thing seem even more ridiculous.

Later that afternoon, the oven betrayed them—overheating and charring a whole batch of bread. Smoke curled through the kitchen while Anna and Lizzy flailed at it with towels, laughing even as their eyes watered.

"If this keeps up, we might need to offer 'charcoal loaves' as a new special," Lizzy joked, coughing through the smoky haze.

Despite the chaos, Anna felt a deep camaraderie as they worked together to salvage the day.

Just as they managed to air out the kitchen, the small bell above the entrance chimed.

Mrs. Lewis entered and set down her purse near the register.

Her eyes swept over Lizzy's berry-stained apron, the tray of cooling, misshapen pastries, and the open kitchen window still letting out the last remnants of smoke.

She arched an eyebrow. "Should I even ask?"

Lizzy wiped her forehead dramatically. "Just another thrilling day in the bakery business."

Anna let out a small laugh, rubbing the back of her neck. "We might have had a few mishaps."

Mrs. Lewis simply shook her head, but her expression had no frustration—only fondness. She walked to the counter, tapping her fingers lightly against the worn wooden surface as if weighing something in her mind.

Then, with an exaggerated sigh, she said, "I leave you two unsupervised for a few hours, and you nearly burn down a piece of CreeksVille history."

Lizzy gasped dramatically, clutching her chest. "How dare you doubt our professionalism?"

Mrs. Lewis snorted. "Oh, I don't doubt you two—just your ability to keep the place standing."

Anna laughed, shaking her head. "We only smoked up the kitchen a little. Nothing a fresh coat of paint won't fix."

Mrs. Lewis rolled her eyes. "All I ask is that you don't make me the talk of the town by accidentally turning this bakery into a bonfire."

Lizzy grinned, wiping her hands on her apron. "No promises, boss."

Mrs. Lewis sighed, smiled, and shook her head. She walked to the counter and glanced around.

"You two do make quite the team."

Anna and Lizzy exchanged a knowing look, assuming she was still teasing them.

Lizzy smirked. "If you mean 'team of professional chaos creators,' then yes, we do."

Anna chuckled. "I promise, we haven't burned anything important."

But Mrs. Lewis simply smiled, shaking her head.

"No, I mean it."

Something in the way she spoke made Anna pause. Lizzy straightened, her playful expression softening as she realized Mrs. Lewis wasn't just talking about their morning mishaps.

Mrs. Lewis glanced around again, taking in the bakery she had poured her life into. Then, after a quiet pause, she said,

"I'm thinking of stepping back a bit—letting you two handle more of the day-to-day."

Anna's eyes widened, caught completely off guard. "Are you sure?"

Mrs. Lewis nodded. "Absolutely. You've got the skills and the heart for it. And Lizzy will keep you in line."

Lizzy grinned, throwing a playful wink at Anna. "You bet I will."

What began as a job soon became comfort. The rhythm of kneading, the laughter in the kitchen, the ring of the doorbell as regulars asked after Sam.

It wasn't Paris or college, but it was something she was building—day by day, with her own hands. And for now, it was enough.

And then there were the people: Mrs. Lewis, with her gentle wisdom and unwavering faith in her, and Lizzy, whose lightness could make even the hardest days bearable.

The customers came in every morning, laughing, gossiping, and asking about Sam, Grandma, and life. It felt like belonging.

The bell above the door jingled as Mrs. Grady picked up her usual coffee and scone. "Did you hear? Emily Riley's thinking of retiring. Word is, her nephew might take over Pine Valley."

Lizzy arched a brow, leaning on the counter. "Oh, great. Another big-city type who thinks he can run CreeksVille better than we do."

Anna smiled faintly, wiping flour from her hands. "It's probably just a rumor."

"Mm-hmm," Lizzy said, wagging a finger. "And rumors have a way of showing up on our doorstep with fancy shoes and too much confidence."

Anna laughed, shaking her head, but she thought no more of it.

As the days unfolded, Anna no longer measured success by where she was going, but by the steadiness of each morning.

The laughter in the kitchen. The patient rhythm of flour-dusted hands. The way the doorbell chimed when regulars walked in, asking how Sam was doing.

That night, as Anna locked up, her reflection in the bakery window looked tired but content, flour still dusting her sleeves.

For a flicker, she thought she saw her mother's smile there too—faint but certain, baked into the very walls.

She didn't know what came next—but for now, she had her hands in dough, friends in the kitchen, and Sam's laughter waiting at home. And that felt like enough.

Chapter 12

Lean on me

As Christmas neared, CreeksVille shimmered under frost, the air sharp with the promise of snow. Inside, Grandma Sophia sat by the hearth, firelight flickering against her frailty.

Lavender and tea scented the room—a fragile comfort against the grief that lingered. Her gaze fell on Anna—proud, helpless, quietly disappointed.

"Anna, have you thought this through?" she asked gently, a flicker of hesitation in her eyes.

Anna shifted in her chair, staring into the flames. The question settled heavily in the air.

The flicker of firelight tugged Sophia backward in time. She had grown up in CreeksVille, built a life as a librarian, and married an elementary school teacher. The echoes of laughter and chatter from the nearby park floated through the open window now, reminding her of the vibrant life she once shared with her husband.

But grief was an unwelcome companion. She had lost him to colon cancer, a heart-wrenching journey that tested her resilience. For years, she cared for him, balancing full-time work while tending to an ailing spouse and raising her teenage daughter, Sarah.

There had been days when time felt like an endless stretch of love and laughter—and nights when exhaustion pressed her to the edge.

The scent of pine from the holiday decorations wafted through the air, pulling Sophia deeper into memory.

After her husband's death, she juggled two jobs to keep the family afloat, her heart heavy yet resolute. In those years of absence, Sarah had fallen for Jake—a choice Sophia often blamed herself for. If she had been home more, could she have changed it?

Sophia's gaze returned to Anna; echoes of memory entwined with new worry. Her granddaughter was the same age as Sarah when her father passed, yet the burden she carried was not the same.

From the kitchen drifted the smell of freshly baked apple pie, sweet and familiar, like a hug from the past. For all her fears, Sophia found hope in this new generation—resilient in its own right, the flickering lights on the tree twinkling like stars in a dark sky.

Sophia knew how much potential Anna had—so bright and full of promise. But the reality was hard to ignore.

She reached out, resting a hand on Anna's. "Keeping Sam at home isn't just about love," she murmured. "The social worker was clear—without a steady income, custody could slip away."

The thought of Sam ending up in the foster system sent a chill through her, a dread sharpened by the warmth of the fire. She couldn't bear it, and she knew Anna couldn't either.

In the hallway, Sophia paused by Sam's room, her eyes misted with memory. For all her fears, this—this bond between them—felt like hope.

When Mrs. Lewis announced she was stepping back, she offered Anna the full-time role—a lifeline, but not without cost.

Accepting it meant dropping out of community college, a sacrifice she felt she had to make to support her brother.

Meanwhile, Sam sat at his study table, oblivious to the weight of the decision hanging over Anna. The scratching of his pencil against the paper filled the quiet room, a rhythmic reminder of his determination. He was focused on his homework, struggling but determined. The teachers at his school were understanding and aware of his challenges.

With his sister and grandmother as his primary guardians, he felt a sense of stability, unaware of how much they did to keep life steady for him.

Anna woke early each morning to make breakfast for Sam and herself, the smell of eggs and toast filling the air—a comforting routine that grounded them. Her spare time went to helping Sam with homework and attending PTA meetings. All the while, she pursued part-time classes at community college while Grandma stepped in to watch over Sam.

Despite these challenges, Anna believed they managed well until the social worker's unexpected visit. Anna had applied for legal guardianship of her eight-year-old brother.

Her attorney and the social worker advised her that securing a full-time job could significantly enhance her chances of gaining custody.

As she reassured her grandma and insisted this was a temporary situation—a bridge to a brighter future, she promised to continue her education once things settled down, her heart filled with hope against the backdrop of uncertainty.

Anna's heart swelled with love as she tucked Sam into bed, lamplight soft across his face. She pulled him close, breathing in the faint scent of his shampoo, clinging to the fleeting peace of the moment.

She knew she needed Sam as much as he needed her. But at his bedside, the questions pressed in—the judge, the job, the fear of failing him. Families are supposed to hold together, especially at Christmas, when everything shines with joy.

Anna sat on the porch with Lizzy, the evening sun sinking low, the first stars blinking awake like distant dreams.

"I just don't know how to have both Sam and my dream," Anna whispered. "Every decision feels like it pulls me further from one or the other."

Lizzy leaned closer, her gaze firm. "You don't have to choose Anna. You can hold on to Sam and still reach for your dream. Start small. Keep moving forward without letting go of him."

Anna looked down at her hands, doubt pressing cold into her chest. "It feels impossible. I don't want to let him down. He's already lost so much."

Lizzy's smile was warm but certain. "You won't lose him. That bond is too strong. Remember—pursuing your dreams doesn't mean abandoning him."

Anna's throat tightened. "I just want to be the sister he deserves."

"And you are," Lizzy assured, resting a hand on her shoulder. "One step at a time."

As the horizon burned in orange and violet, Anna felt a flicker of hope take root. "Thank you, Lizzy. I needed this."

"Always," Lizzy replied. "You're not alone."

Later that night, Anna tucked Sam into bed, pressing a kiss to his forehead. His breathing slowed, gentle as the heartbeat of home. She lingered, whispering, "I love you, little buddy. Always."

Beyond the windows, Christmas lights twinkled against the dark. Anna felt a quiet certainty—not only in her dreams, but in the family she was building with her own hands.

Chapter 13

The wind beneath my wings

CreeksVille's streets shimmered with holiday lights, storefronts dressed in garlands, and the faint sound of carolers drifting between houses.

After work, Anna sat at the table, papers spread before her—custody applications, financial statements, letters of support from the bakery and school. Each page, smudged by her anxious fingers, was a mosaic of hope and fear.

Nearby, Sophia rinsed a tea mug, steam curling toward her face, her eyes clouded with worry. "You've got everything in order, sweetheart. The judge will see where Sam belongs.

If it comes to a crucial point, I can request custody. However, heaven forbid, if anything were to happen, you would have to navigate the entire process all over again.

Anna nodded, but the knot in her stomach twisted tighter, a heavy stone weighing her down. Only three days remained until the hearing, and doubt gnawed at her resolve.

"What if it's not enough? What if they think I'm too young?" Sophia crossed the room, resting her hands on Anna's shoulders. 'You've done everything for that boy. No judge could overlook that.

The next day, even beneath makeup, Anna wore exhaustion like a second skin.

"Late night again?" Lizzy teased at the bakery, concern lacing her words.

Anna forced a smile. "Just preparing for the hearing. I keep worrying I'm missing something."

Lizzy squeezed her hand. "It's going to be fine. You've got us. We're all in this together."

Gratitude swelled in Anna. "Thank you. I don't know what I'd do without you."

"Now go home and rest," Lizzy urged.

Sophia and Mrs. Lewis stood beside Anna and Sam as they entered the family court, the air thick with tension and anticipation, much like the early holiday season that enveloped the town.

The faint scent of pine lingered in the hallways, a reminder that warmth and togetherness were just around the corner, even amidst the uncertainty.

Lizzy and Bob joined them, their presence a reassuring embrace against the looming challenges.

Inside the courtroom, the air felt charged—echoes of quiet hope mingling with the distant chime of church bells. Heart pounding, Anna took her seat.

Her breath caught as the judge entered, black robes brushing the floor, quiet authority filling the room. Silver-rimmed glasses caught the light, her gaze keen but not unkind as it swept the room before landing on Anna.

"Ms. Buchman," the judge said, her words commanding yet not unkind, each one echoing in the silence. "You're requesting full guardianship of your younger brother, Samuel Buchman. Do you understand the responsibilities this entails?"

Anna rose, her hand grazing her mother's bracelet, her voice firm despite the tremor in her heart. "Yes, Your Honor."

The social worker spoke next, her words warm and affirming, wrapping around Anna like a cozy scarf on a chilly day. "Ms. Buchman has shown unwavering commitment to Samuel's well-being, providing a stable environment since their mother's passing."

Beside her, Sam visibly relaxed, tension easing from his small frame. But then, the opposing attorney stood, his sharp suit a stark contrast to the warmth of the season.

"She's nineteen, with no career—just a bakery job. Is that stability for a child?"

Sam's heart raced, fists clenching in defiance.

The judge turned her gaze back to Anna.

"Ms. Buchman, given your age and employment, how do you plan to provide long-term stability for Samuel?"

Anna's chin lifted, determination flooding her veins. She glanced at Sam, his wide eyes fixed on her, drawing strength from his unwavering belief.

"Yes, Your Honor. I've been Sam's caregiver since our mother passed. I've built a stable home for him."

Taking a breath, she continued, "Our house is paid off, and I have a steady job at the bakery. Sam is thriving. I promise to remain not just his sister, but his guardian and family."

The judge leaned in, requesting documents to support her claims. Anna handed the deed to their home and a letter of employment from the bakery. She felt the judge's familiarity with the bakery, a nod of recognition sparking hope within her.

The judge nodded, thoughtful, her fingers drumming lightly against the wooden surface. Then she turned to Sophia.

"Ms. Buchman, do you believe your granddaughter can take on this role?"

Sophia crossed the room, resting her hands on Anna's shoulders. "She's the reason Sam still smiles, Your Honor. My daughter would have wanted this."

Sam's throat tightened. He stood, fists clenched at his sides. "I want to be with Anna." His small voice broke in the silence of the courtroom. "Please."

The courtroom fell silent, as if the whole room held its breath with him. Anna's hand slipped into his, a tight squeeze of reassurance. The judge studied them, then turned to the back where Mrs. Lewis sat, hands folded. After a long pause, the judge nodded, fingers tapping against the desk, her expression unreadable.

"This court finds that Anna Buchman is a fit guardian and grants her full custody of Samuel."

Church bells chimed in the distance—full of promise. Tears blurred Anna's eyes as she turned to Sam. "We did it!"

They were a family, bound not just by blood but by love—and that would carry them through, whatever life threw their way.

A quiet peace settled in Anna's chest—along with the first fragile ember of hope she'd felt in months.

Together, they would shape the path ahead—and it would be bright.

With trembling hands, Grandma hugged them both. "You did it, sweetheart," she said into Anna's hair.

Anna sniffled, her heart swelling. "Yes, we did, Grandma."

As they gathered their things, the judge called them back, her tone a gentle reminder of the moment they had just experienced.

"Oh, and Samuel."

Sam turned, blinking up at her, uncertainty mingling with curiosity.

The judge's expression softened. She leaned forward, silver glasses glinting, eyes focused yet kind as she turned to Sam. "You don't have to call me 'Your Honor.' That's just for TV."

Sam blinked, caught off guard, then gave a tiny nod. The room, heavy with formality, suddenly felt lighter—as if even the judge wanted him to feel safe. Anna exhaled, believing, at last, they might be all right. Anna and Sam stepped into a gentle snowfall. Holiday wreaths curled around lamp posts, and laughter echoed from the town square, where a towering Christmas tree glittered with colored lights.

Chapter 14

21 going on 31

Yellow buses rumbled along the asphalt, engines thrumming as CreeksVille's streets filled with the first rush of autumn mornings.

From behind the bakery counter, Anna inhaled the warm, sugary scent of fresh pastries drifting through the crisp autumn air. Parents hurried in and out, arms full of cookie boxes bound for class parties, laughter spilling with the chime of the bell.

Watching them, Anna smiled. Twenty-one today—old enough to have lived too much but finally learning to live for herself.

Today marked Sam's first day of middle school, and Anna worked the dough with steady hands, though her thoughts drifted elsewhere. The new bus route, the lunch she'd packed, the PTA meeting that evening—her mind turned them over like dough beneath her palms, stretching and folding, never at rest.

When the rush finally eased, Lizzy slid into a cozy corner booth, pressing an envelope into Anna's hand.

"Happy birthday, Anna."

"Thank you," Anna smiled.

"Any big plans?" Lizzy asked.

"Not really. It's a school night. Maybe Sam and I will catch a movie Saturday." She said it lightly, but Lizzy caught the flicker of disappointment.

"That sounds nice," Lizzy teased. "Remember when we used to dream about turning twenty-one? We thought it was the gateway to everything exciting."

Anna chuckled, but her smile dimmed as she gazed out at the shifting autumn leaves. "Honestly, I've felt older than twenty-one for a while now."

She swirled her coffee, words tumbling out quieter. At seventeen, I was suddenly raising Sam. Some days I'd wondered what I missed out on."

Lizzy leaned in, warmth in her eyes.

"Whatever doubts you have, just remember—Sam sees you as his whole world."

A smile broke through Anna's heaviness. "I hope so. All I want is for him to feel safe. To have what I didn't."

The bustle of the bakery wrapped around them—laughter, clinking cups, the hiss of steam. For a moment, Anna let herself feel proud. She had made it this far. Twenty-one wasn't about wild nights out. It was proof of survival, of growth, of strength she never expected to find.

Lizzy lifted her cup. "Here's to you. To resilience, and to all the adventures ahead."

They toasted, porcelain clinking like a quiet celebration bell.

Just then, the door swung open.

"Is anybody here?" a man called.

Startled, Anna and Lizzy jumped, Lizzy spilling her coffee everywhere.

"Oh no!" Anna gasped.

A tall man with tousled dark hair stepped into view, concern and amusement flickering in his expression. His crisp white shirt and easy confidence made him seem both polished and at ease.

"Everything okay back there?" he asked, smooth voice cutting through the chaos.

Flustered, Anna scrambled to help, cookie trays rattling as crumbs scattered like confetti. Her cheeks burned as she scrambled to regain her composure, but the stranger's quiet laugh only deepened her mortification.

"I'm here for Pine Valley Hotel's order," he explained, offering a polite smile.

They handed over the boxes, cheeks still flushed. At the doorway, he paused, keys in hand.

"Paul Riley, by the way."

Anna's breath caught—part nerves, part curiosity—as she muttered a faint goodbye.

Moments later, Mrs. Lewis swept in, cheeks flushed with news. "Great job, girls—Pine Valley just renewed their order. Their new owner, Paul Riley, seems wonderful."

Anna froze. Lizzy blinked. "Wait—he's the nephew who's supposed to take over Pine Valley?" Mrs. Lewis nodded, oblivious to the cookie chaos she'd just missed. "That's right. And I have a feeling he'll be back often."

Anna felt heat rise to her cheeks. The words tumbled through her mind—fancy shoes and too much confidence. Lizzy's bakery gossip. She almost laughed, though her pulse betrayed her.

That night, in the mirror, she saw someone she hardly recognized— no longer the frightened seventeen-year-old, but a woman still piecing herself together.

Chapter 15

48 hours in CreeksVille

He hadn't planned on leaving New York. Then Monica happened—and everything unraveled.

He would've laughed if anyone had told him he'd trade the skyline for a rural town. Yet as he drove through CreeksVille, fresh air streamed through the open window and maple leaves blazed red and gold.

The feeling that rose in him was the one he trusted least—belonging. And belonging, after everything, felt dangerous.

They'd met at an agency party: Monica Fox—rising fashion blogger with a site everyone suddenly seemed to read—and he, a patent attorney who preferred schedules to spotlights.

For a year, their lives blurred—brand dinners, charity galas, a glossy piece that dubbed them "digital darlings." He'd been clear: no posting private images—no bed shots, no kissing.

On his twenty-seventh birthday in the Bahamas, she did it anyway: a homepage photo set of intimate moments—him asleep in the morning light, them kissing on the balcony—published on her blog. He ended it the next morning.

That afternoon, she posted again—this time a public update. By nightfall, the comments had rewritten him: commitment-phobe, bore, dead weight. By morning, his inbox was a tide of opinions from people who didn't know him.

So, when Aunt Emily called about Pine Valley, he said yes before she had a chance to finish the sentence. Memories of summers with his grandparents and Aunt Emily softened the edges of his return.

New York's chaos had driven him to Pine Valley. Running a hotel was never part of his plan.

Tucked away in the countryside, Pine Valley offered a serene escape. Its lush greenery and vibrant community stood in stark contrast to the relentless pace of city life. As Paul wandered the winding paths, he marveled at the quiet beauty around him, rediscovering a childhood love for hiking.

He bit into a cookie, buttery sweetness exploding on his palate. A sigh escaped—the same way it had when he was a boy. The familiar sweetness lingered, but his thoughts wandered elsewhere. Not to the cookies. To her. Anna.

He smiled, shaking his head at the memory of her flustered expression—the way she'd scrambled out of his path only to bump into Lizzy. Those sharp eyes that brightened when she laughed. The nervous bite of her lip. She had barely looked at him afterward, as if willing the whole scene to vanish.

After Monica, there was something almost refreshing about her unpolished honesty.

Paul smirked as he swallowed the last bite. CreeksVille, he thought, might hold more surprises than he expected.

Chapter 16

Paradise on Earth

Morning light spilled across Pine Valley's stone façade as Paul stepped onto the French terrace, coffee warming his hands. Below, the fountain murmured steadily, a sound that carried him back to boyhood summers—lugging trays for guests, the sting of pine needles on bare feet, his aunt Emily calling him in for supper.

From the terrace, the infinity pool shimmered as it spilled toward the mountains, where music would drift on summer nights and laughter lingered long after the lanterns went out.

At sunset, the river caught fire with color, guiding guests back to their rooms as though the land itself wanted to keep them close. Couples came for romance, artists for inspiration, families for the peace between the trees—each one leaving with Pine Valley stitched into their memory.

And now Paul stood here again, unsettled by how easily the place still felt like home.

For 125 years, the Riley family had tended Pine Valley. Paul's grandparents had grown it from a bed-and-breakfast into a hotel, and his aunt Emily later added the restaurant and bar. Now, at seventy-five, Emily was ready to hand it on.

Paul hadn't planned on returning to CreeksVille. New York—its briefs, deadlines, and endless nights—had been his world. But when Emily asked, he couldn't refuse. Family pulled, and so did the hotel: echoes of his own summers carrying trays, ringing up guests, learning its rhythms until they felt like his own.

Now he was back, giving the place a year before deciding its future. With Emily's staff around him and the longtime manager guiding him, he eased into the work more quickly than expected.

One morning, after unloading treats from the bakery onto the kitchen table, Paul indulged in a butter cookie with his coffee. Just then, James, the chef, entered and grabbed a cookie. After taking a bite, he nodded in approval.

"So, Paul, I take it you finally made it to the bakery?"

"Yeah. These are fantastic—we should keep them on," Paul said.

James chewed thoughtfully. "Good call. Always fresh, always top-notch."

"Exactly," Paul agreed. "Worth the partnership."

The road to Pine Valley Hotel wound between towering trees, their leaves blazing in autumn's palette. A crisp breeze rustled the branches as Anna rolled down her window, the cool air rushing in to greet her.

As she navigated the winding driveway, she glanced in the rearview mirror at the wedding cake sitting safely in the back. The scent of vanilla and buttercream filled the car, making her stomach grumble.

Ahead, the hotel emerged from the haze—stone walls radiant in sunlight, the fountain at its entrance veiling the air in a cool mist.

Under new ownership, it had quickly become the go-to venue for upscale events. Paul Riley had been polite in their few encounters, but Anna still cringed at the memory of her and Lizzy's disastrous first meeting with him three months ago.

Shaking it off, she parked by the kitchen entrance and wheeled the cake to the door.

The heavy door stuck, then gave way too fast, nearly sending her sprawling. "Hell no," she muttered. A low chuckle stopped her cold.

Paul leaned against the counter, coffee in hand.

Flushing, Anna straightened. "I'm from the bakery—here with the wedding cake."

He smirked. "Yes, Anna. We've crossed paths a few times."

Trying to recover, she asked where she could set up.

"This way.

Cake master, huh?" he teased.

"Only for today," she shot back with a smirk.

She couldn't help noticing how fit he looked—tall, broad-shouldered, the kind of strength that came from work, not a gym.

Paul led her to the banquet hall, then raised his cup in a casual farewell. Anna exhaled, relieved he didn't mention the earlier door debacle.

She centered the stand on the dessert table, lifted the cake, and set it carefully in place. The lemon-scented buttercream gleamed under the lights. A scatter of zest sparked against the creamy finish.

Fresh yellow roses circled the base, petals delicate and romantic. Stepping back, she adjusted a few blossoms until everything sat just right.

Finally, she set the topper in place, straight and secure, and lingered for a moment, admiring her work. A smile rose—then vanished as she collided with something solid behind her.

She spun around with a gasp—straight into Paul.

His coffee tipped, warm liquid splashing across his crisp white shirt. "Oh no!" Anna clapped her hands to her mouth. "I—I didn't see you!"

Paul glanced at the stain, then back at her, lips twitching as if fighting a laugh. "Well, I was going to enjoy this coffee. Apparently, my shirt had other plans."

Flustered, Anna grabbed a napkin and dabbed at the stain. Too late, she realized it carried frosting. Bright yellow streaks smeared across the fabric.

She flinched. "Oh no. No, no, no. I just made it worse."

Paul shook his head with an amused sigh. "You really are committed to this, huh?"

Anna groaned, lifting her hands in defeat. "I am so sorry. I swear I didn't mean to—

He cut her off with a smirk. "Didn't know this came with a frosting upgrade."

She blinked, caught between horror and laughter.

"Tell you what," he added, brushing at the streaks. "Instead of apologizing, why don't you make it up to me with cake—your treat, at the bakery?"

She shook her head, half-embarrassed, half-amused, and found herself smiling despite the mess. As he walked away, she pressed a hand to her apron, her heart racing faster than she wanted to admit. Outside, the fountain murmured on, constant as ever, as if Pine Valley itself had witnessed the collision and decided not to judge. Maybe this year wouldn't be as simple as she'd planned.

Chapter 17

Winds of change

Meanwhile, Anna returned to a cozy space infused with the soothing scents of vanilla and chamomile tea. She sank into the floral couch, the faint scent of lavender from her grandmother's sweater grounding her. Across the room, Grandma Sophia sat with her knitting needles, the lamplight catching the steady rhythm of her hands.

"Come sit with me, sweetheart," Sophia said, patting the chair beside her. When Anna settled near, she reached over and smoothed a strand of hair from her face. "How was your day?"

Anna offered a small smile, shrugging. "Busy."

Sophia's eyes softened. "And have you chosen your dress for the wedding reception?"

Anna shook her head, a laugh slipping out. "Not yet."

"Wear the blue one," Sophia said gently, a mischievous sparkle in her eye. "It makes you look sexy."

"Grandma." Anna's voice carried an amused protest, but her eyes glowed with affection.

Sophia pressed a kiss to Anna's forehead, then did the same for Sam. "Now, don't wait up too long, you two," she said, pushing herself up with a light groan. "My Bingo club awaits."

Anna chuckled as she watched her grandmother gather her shawl. Her movements were graceful despite her frail frame, and the scent of her light rose perfume trailed in the air as she walked toward the door.

"Have fun, Grandma," Anna called, waving as Sophia opened the door and climbed into the car.

Anna glanced at Sam, who was buzzing with excitement as he dashed toward his room to get ready. His footsteps thudded lightly down the hall, followed by the shuffle of drawers opening and closing.

Anna smiled, pushing herself off the couch to follow him.

A cool draft slipped in through the window, carrying the faint scent of fallen leaves and woodsmoke—a quiet reminder that autumn had truly settled in.

She entered her tidy bedroom, where her dress hung neatly on the door. The midnight-blue fabric shimmered subtly under the warm lighting.

She let the warm shower wash away the exhaustion. Steam wrapped her in a cocoon, and at last, she could breathe.

Draping herself in a towel, she stood before the mirror. Her long, damp chestnut hair fell over her shoulders in soft waves, accentuating her rosy complexion. She applied just a hint of pink lip gloss.

Slipping into the midnight-blue dress, she admired how it gracefully hugged her curves—a subtle rebellion against society's obsession with thinness. The sapphire pendant rested lightly against her collarbone, a striking contrast to her skin.

Finally ready, she slipped into her elegant pumps, draped a shawl over her shoulders, and took a deep breath.

Sam stepped out of his room, adjusting the sleeves of his neatly pressed shirt.

For a moment, Anna blinked.

Her little brother had grown somewhere between late-night homework sessions, scraped knees, and laughing over burnt pancakes.

His hair, still damp from his quick shower, was neatly combed, and though he was slightly gangly, there was an ease to his stance—a quiet confidence she hadn't noticed before.

Noticing Anna staring, Sam flushed. "What? Is it too much?"

"No. You look good," Anna assured, laughing.

They stepped into the cool evening, and the crisp fall air immediately embraced them, carrying the faint scent of burning wood, damp leaves, and lingering summer warmth.

The night was alive in its own quiet way—distant laughter from passing neighbors, rustling trees, and the occasional hoot of an owl.

Anna glanced back at the house, the light from the living room spilling onto the porch—a beacon of warmth and familiarity.

She smiled and turned toward the evening.

Stacy's face lit up when she saw Sam and Anna entering the banquet hall. She rushed toward them, her excitement evident.

"You look dapper, Sam!" Stacy beamed, giving him an approving nod before turning to Anna. "And you, Anna, look absolutely ravishing!"

Before Anna could respond, a familiar voice chimed in from behind her.

"I agree."

Anna stiffened slightly before turning around.

Paul stood just a step behind her, looking sharp in a well-fitted suit. His usual laid-back demeanor remained intact, but his expression was different as he looked at her. His eyes flickered with surprise before settling into amusement.

"Well, this is unexpected," he said, a smirk playing on his lips. "I'm used to seeing you covered in flour and frosting."

Anna narrowed her eyes, folding her arms. "And I'm used to seeing you with coffee stains on your shirt. Yet here we are, both defying expectations."

Paul smiled. "Touché."

Stacy glanced between them with interest before stepping in. "Oh, Paul, have you met my high school friend Anna?"

Paul gave an easy shrug. "We've crossed paths." He skipped over the awkward details.

"Small world," Stacy mused before gesturing toward Sam. "And this is Sam, Anna's little brother."

Paul turned to Sam and gave him a firm handshake. Then, stepping back, he sized him up with an amused expression.

"You're pretty tall—do you play basketball?"

Sam grinned. "A little, but I'm more into soccer."

Paul nodded approvingly. "Nice. You got the height for basketball, but soccer's a solid choice. What position do you play?"

"Midfielder," Sam said, puffing up slightly, clearly pleased by the attention.

Paul smirked. "Good spot. It takes skill and endurance. You'll have to show me some moves sometime."

Sam beamed, and Anna watched, surprised by Paul's easy effort with her brother.

At dinner, Anna was seated across from Paul, who appeared to be in deep conversation with a gentleman. She focused on the chicken on her plate, making a conscious effort not to stare at Paul. A few times, their eyes met, and she offered a polite smile.

As the speeches concluded and the dancing began, Anna glanced around for Sam, who was preoccupied with his friends.

As the lights dimmed and gentle music played, Paul approached her, extending his hand.

"Would you like to dance?" he asked, his words gentle but firm.

Anna instinctively placed her hand in his; it felt as though it were magnetically drawn to him. Almost immediately, she regretted her decision—not because she didn't want to dance with Paul, but because she had only danced once before at her prom.

She nervously looked at Paul, who asked, "Is something wrong?"

"I don't know how to dance," Anna admitted.

Paul threw his head back and laughed. "That makes two of us."

For a beat, they just stood there, unsure, smiling like two kids at their first school dance.

They swayed slowly to the music, their bodies moving in sync. Anna could feel Paul relax, and in turn, she began to unwind.

"See? You're a natural," Paul teased.

Anna laughed. "You're just saying that because I still didn't step on your toes."

"Maybe," he admitted, a playful glint in his eyes.

From a distance, Sam watched his sister and Paul, noticing just how beautiful she truly was.

As the song ended, Paul stepped back, his hand lingering in hers for a moment longer than necessary.

"Thank you," Anna said, her words barely above a whisper.

"Anytime," Paul replied.

As they parted ways, Anna couldn't help but feel a shift—something unspoken but undeniably real.

She hadn't known a touch could feel that gentle—unrushed and sure.

Chapter 18

My heart is beating again

The last notes of music clung faintly to Paul's ears while the reception thinned, laughter and glassware carrying across the hall. One dance with Anna had left its mark, slipping beneath his skin with a warmth he hadn't expected.

She had surprised him—stronger, gentler, far more complicated than he'd first assumed. After Monica, he had promised himself no more entanglements, no more mess. Order, control, solitude—that was safer. Yet when Anna's hand had rested in his, he had felt something dangerously close to belonging.

"Careful," someone called.

Stacy, who saw Paul as a brother, pulled him aside as the reception wound down, her tone low but firm.

"I see how you look at her," she said, crossing her arms. "If you're just looking for a distraction, walk away now. She doesn't need a broken heart after everything she's been through. You know she's practically raising her little brother alone, running a bakery, caring for her grandmother—trying to keep everything together?"

Paul kept his thoughts to himself. He had seen glimpses of Anna's resilience but hadn't known the full extent.

"I just..." he started, then sighed. "I don't know. I'm not sure."

"Then figure it out before she thinks you do," she warned, squeezing his shoulder before walking away.

The next morning, the dance still lingered in his mind. So did Stacy's warning.

Paul had expected New York to clear his head. It should have been easy.

His office, perched high above the skyline, glittered like a thousand distractions. A meeting with a client loomed that evening, yet as he swirled a glass of bourbon across from his associate, his mind slipped elsewhere.

The bakery. The warm rush of cream and coffee each time he walked in. The dance. Anna's laugh when she stumbled, the instinctive way he caught her, how natural she'd felt in his arms. And Stacy's words, sharp as glass, *"Figure it out before you make her believe you do."*

He closed his eyes briefly, slipping his phone back into his pocket before the urge to call overtook him. *Not yet,* he told himself.

That night at dinner, his parents noticed immediately. His mother, always attuned, set her fork down and studied him. "Paul, is everything all right?"

He barely heard her. The food sat untouched, pushed around his plate. "Yeah, just tired," he muttered.

His father let it pass, but his mother's gaze lingered, unconvinced.

Abruptly, Paul stood, muttering something about fresh air. Out on the terrace, the night air hit sharp against his skin, brisk but grounding. Below, the city pulsed with life, but his thoughts drifted far from it.

He hadn't expected to remember the dance so vividly—the fit of her hand in his, hesitant at first, then confident.

The scent of vanilla and citrus—maybe lemon—clung to her. Anna laughed when she nearly stepped on his foot, then apologized as if it mattered.

It didn't. Not to him.

What lingered was calm, the world gone quiet for a moment. Just music. Just the two of them.

That night as he dozed off to sleep, he thought of a small bakery in CreeksVille, where warm cinnamon lingered in the air, and a woman with chestnut hair and deep blue eyes worked tirelessly to keep her world together.

He tried to drown the memory in bourbon and the city's hum, but miles away, Anna held it close—a fragile secret she wasn't ready to release.

Anna tried to treat the dance as nothing more than a dream. She had lived through this before—moments of warmth, fleeting interest, and then the emptiness that followed.

Men tended to vanish when they sensed responsibility. None of them had ever called her back after the first date.

And even though what she had shared with Paul hadn't been exactly a date, she still hoped he would be different. She had hoped he would call. She had hoped he would at least stop by the bakery. But to her quiet dismay, neither happened.

The next morning, when she saw the hotel's van pull up, she felt her breath catch.

Paul?

But when Jo stepped out instead, Anna's heart gave a dull thud of disappointment.

She forced a smile as she handed over the neatly packed cookies. Jo, unaware of her expectations, simply thanked her and left.

Anna told herself it didn't matter.

She had work to do. The bakery needed her. Still, later that afternoon, when she checked her phone, her thumb lingered on the unlock button, as if the screen might light up on its own.

Nothing.

No missed calls.

No messages.

Just silence.

Leaning against the counter, Lizzy caught the way Anna's lips pressed together.

"Expecting someone?" she teased, raising an eyebrow.

Anna quickly slipped her phone into her pocket. "Not really," she said, forcing a laugh.

Lizzy smirked knowingly but didn't press.

Anna returned to the dough, focusing on the rhythm of kneading, stretching, and folding. The bakery smelled of warm bread—a scent that should have brought comfort. And in a way, it did. She found peace in baking.

But a quiet disappointment lingered as she moved through the motions, shaping the loaves and watching the golden crusts rise in the oven.

Maybe she had been foolish to think this time would be different. But still, part of her wasn't ready to stop hoping—not yet.

Chapter 19

The silence between us

Evening settled over CreeksVille, the crisp air carrying autumn's bite and the faint perfume of smoke. Streetlights cast long shadows across the empty street, their glow sliding over the bakery's windows. Inside, warmth clung to the air—thick with the scent of bread and sugar.

Anna wiped the counters in slow, absent circles, her heart far from her hands.

Then she noticed the headlights.

A car pulled up across the street, its engine humming before cutting off.

Paul.

Her breath hitched briefly, but she quickly turned away, pretending not to notice.

The doorbell jingled, the sound almost too loud in the quiet bakery.

Anna didn't look up.

Paul stood near the entrance, hands stuffed in his pockets, scanning the space before settling his gaze on her.

"Hi, Anna." He hesitated.

Anna finally turned, keeping her expression neutral. "Hi, Paul."

A brief pause stretched between them, thick with unspoken words.

Paul exhaled, tilting his head slightly as he studied her. "How are you doing?"

The question caught her off guard—not just a polite greeting, but a genuine inquiry. Something in his tone made her hesitate, but she quickly masked it.

"I'm fine," she said, steadying herself.

Paul gave a slight nod, his expression unreadable. A heavy pause stretched between them before he finally spoke.

I was hoping … maybe we could get a cup of coffee?

Anna glanced at the clock and then back at him. "Sorry, we're closed for the day," she replied smoothly, returning to her work.

Paul let out an amused breath as if he had expected her to say that.

"I know a place that's open late," he offered. "Would you join me?"

She busied herself by securing the lids on the sugar canisters, avoiding his gaze.

"I need to get home soon," she said, thinking of Sam.

Paul nodded, stepping aside slightly as if to give her space, though his expression remained patient.

"Of course," he said. Then, after a brief hesitation, "Can we meet for dinner tomorrow?"

His tone was careful, hopeful.

Anna's heart thudded, but she kept her composure, shaking her head lightly. "I can't do dinner."

Paul studied her, then asked. "How about lunch?"

Anna finally met his gaze, a playful smirk appearing on her lips.

"I have a date," she said, letting the words hang—not quite a lie, not quite the truth.

Paul blinked.

For a moment, he didn't react. Then, a slow, lopsided smile tugged at the corner of his mouth, though she didn't miss the flicker of disappointment in his eyes.

Anna grabbed her bag, threw one last glance at him, and walked past, her pulse thrumming as she stepped into the cool night air.

Paul remained standing inside the bakery, hands resting on his hips as he exhaled quietly.

The door shut behind her with a click, the small bell jingling once more.

She stepped into the night, the air crisp with the scent of leaves and the faint smoke of early fires. As the bakery door clicked shut behind her, she didn't look back.

But God, she had wanted to.

By the time she slid into the driver's seat and started the engine, her hands still trembled, anger and disappointment tangled into hurt. She barely noticed the streets rushing past. Her mind stayed locked in the bakery—on the careful way he'd asked her to coffee.

It wasn't just the invitation—it was him, showing up out of nowhere, after all this time. After so much silence.

And her heart—traitorous and hopeful—had leapt the moment she saw him.

Why did she care? Why did his presence still crack something open inside her?

Her fingers tightened around the wheel, as if she could hold herself by force.

She should have said yes. Just coffee, just a simple conversation. She'd wanted it—she couldn't lie to herself about that.

But something in her—pride, fear, maybe both—had kept the words from forming.

As her house came into view, Anna slowed to a crawl. The porch lights glowed warm against the dark, but inside, she wavered still.

The next morning, Anna woke to bright sunlight streaming through her window. It was her day off, and she tried to pull the covers over her head for a few more minutes of rest. But the events of the previous evening played on a loop in her mind.

Downstairs, she found Sam helping himself to cereal.

"Good morning, Sis!" he said cheerfully, his energy lighting up the room.

"Morning," Anna replied, reaching for her coffee.

As they sat together at the table, Sam chattered about his upcoming school play, his excitement spilling into every gesture. Anna listened with a fond smile, feeling a swell of pride. Despite everything, Sam remained resilient and full of hope.

"You're going to be amazing," Anna assured him, ruffling his hair affectionately.

"Thanks," Sam replied, his cheeks turning pink. "I just wish Mom could see it."

Anna's chest tightened at his words, but she maintained her composure. "She'd be so proud of you," she said. "Just like I am."

Sam had grown to understand that Anna and Grandma Sophia did everything they could to protect him. The grief counselor had helped, but a profound emptiness lingered.

He struggled to understand why their father had gone—not taken by death, but by choice. The absence carved a hole that even Anna's laughter and warmth could never fully mend.

Still, Sam clung to the joy of baking with Anna on weekends; the smell of fresh bread and pastries wrapped around him like comfort. He threw himself into schoolwork, knowing how much it would mean to her. Life, once fragile and uncertain, now carried a rhythm that felt almost safe.

Chapter 20

Our next meeting

She had promised Sam and Grandma Sophia a morning at the Apple Festival—an annual tradition that felt like a warm thread tying past to present.

After breakfast, they'd stroll through rows of food stalls and laughter-filled rides, chasing sticky-fingered joy and the sweet tang of cider in the air.

Memories of going with her mother—her laughter, the way she always tucked a stray curl behind Anna's ear, and the caramel-dipped apples that stuck to her chin and her heart—rose gently, wrapping her in a quiet nostalgia.

The enticing aroma of caramel apples and kettle corn greeted them, warming the crisp autumn air. The festival's lively energy was infectious.

While wandering through the bustling stalls, Anna bumped into several old school friends who were home for fall break from their universities.

Their lively chatter, brimming with stories of campus life and ambitious plans for the future, filled the air. Anna smiled as she joined the conversation, though a pang of insecurity tugged at her heart.

Her ambition—like studying French baking—felt distant and unattainable. She could almost picture herself strolling along cobbled streets, inhaling the scent of fresh pastries, and learning from master bakers. But the vibrant dream faded as reality reminded her of her responsibilities.

Managing the household, ensuring Sam's education, and working at the bakery left little room for pursuing her passions. Living the dream in a different location seemed impossible.

Still, Anna had found a small piece of her dream in her job at the bakery.

Mrs. Lewis, a seasoned expert in French baking, had taken Anna under her wing. While the bakery was modest, it exuded an authentic charm. Mrs. Lewis, recognizing Anna's natural talent, gradually entrusted her with more responsibilities and shared her wealth of knowledge.

Under Mrs. Lewis's patient guidance, Anna mastered techniques like cracking eggs with one hand and crafting delicate soufflés. Each day felt like an intensive culinary lesson, and as Anna kneaded dough and whisked egg whites, her confidence grew.

Pouring her love for baking into her work, she found a sense of purpose that lightened the sting of her unfulfilled dreams.

"You know," Anna mused as she carefully folded butter into chilled dough, "I used to think I had to go to France to become a real baker."

Mrs. Lewis, standing beside her, chuckled as she watched Anna's technique. "And now?"

Anna exhaled, running her fingers over the dough's smooth surface. "Now, I think maybe I was romanticizing it too much. What difference does it make where I learn, as long as I learn from the best?"

Mrs. Lewis gave her a knowing look. "Flattery will get you extra pastries."

Anna laughed. "I'm serious. I've learned more here in one year than I ever could have in some fancy Parisian school. Besides," she smirked. "I hear French chefs are kind of rude."

Mrs. Lewis raised an eyebrow. "Oh, very rude. I worked in Paris once, you know."

Anna turned to her in surprise. "Wait—really?"

'For two years," Mrs. Lewis confirmed, eyes glinting with amusement. "Let's just say, after being yelled at in five different accents, I decided there are better ways to teach baking."

Anna grinned. "Well, I'd take CreeksVille over a kitchen full of angry French chefs any day."

Anna's thoughts were interrupted when Sophia suddenly waved at someone in the crowd. Turning, Anna saw Paul approaching, his smile broad as he hugged Sophia warmly. Startled, Anna asked if they knew each other.

"Of course!" Sophia said with a twinkle in her eye. "Our bingo nights at the Pine Valley Banquet Hall wouldn't be the same without Paul. He always takes good care of us."

She winked at Paul as Sam grinned and gave him a fist bump.

Paul joined their table after Sam invited him, and soon, the two were off to get hot dogs. Anna watched as Paul leaned down to hear Sam over the music, his attentiveness catching her off guard.

When they returned, they brought a feast—hot dogs, fries, chili, and drinks. Over their meal, the conversation flowed naturally. Anna couldn't help but notice how easily Paul connected with Sam. It dawned on her how much Sam missed having a male role model.

When Sam eagerly asked to go fishing with Paul, Anna hesitated but eventually agreed, reminding him to be home by six.

As she watched Paul and Sam interact, emotions swirled within her. Paul's warmth toward Sam was heartening, yet her curiosity about him lingered. His easygoing nature intrigued her, and even Sophia seemed to enjoy his company—a rare thing.

The festival bustled around them—families laughing, the air rich with caramel and roasted nuts, leaves crunching beneath hurried footsteps. Yet for a moment, time slowed. Sam, chatting with Paul, looked lighter than he had in months, his face bright with excitement.

She glanced at her grandmother, who sipped her warm cider, watching the scene with quiet amusement. Sophia had always been protective of Anna and Sam, yet she welcomed Paul effortlessly. And Sam? He had already decided that Paul was his friend.

Anna hesitated, her fingers tightening around her paper cup. Maybe she should have been more cautious, more guarded.

She exhaled, shaking off the flutter in her chest. This was just a simple afternoon at the festival. Nothing more.

But as Sam and Paul made their way toward the exit, Anna watched Paul a little longer than she meant to, a small smile tugging at her lips.

The autumn breeze wrapped around her, carrying the scent of apples and something else she couldn't name—like a loose thread she wasn't ready to pull.

Chapter 21

When the heart whispers

One morning, as Anna reached for a tray of scones at the bakery, a familiar greeting cut through the quiet.

"Morning, Anna." Paul stood by the counter, a steaming cup of coffee in hand.

She raised an eyebrow, masking her surprise. "Three visits in one week? We must be doing something right with our coffee."

Paul chuckled, glancing at the pastry display. "It's less about the coffee and more about the company."

Their easy banter was interrupted by Sam, who emerged from the back room, his face lighting up at the sight of Paul.

"You're here again!"

Paul grinned and gave him a fist bump. "Couldn't stay away. How's my favorite soccer player doing?"

"I'm actually playing on my school's basketball team now," Sam said proudly.

He launched into an animated recap of his practice, his enthusiasm infectious. Anna watched from behind the counter, her hands busy, but the effortless bond between Paul and Sam captured her attention.

As Paul chatted with Sam, Anna found herself smiling. Something about Paul's genuine nature warmed her heart and sparked a flicker of curiosity she couldn't ignore.

As she wiped her hands on her apron, she stole another glance at Paul. He was effortlessly engaged in Sam's stories, laughing at all the right moments, his expression filled with genuine interest.

Anna rarely dated; it was like watching a magician perform a vanishing act with the worst audience ever. The moment potential partners caught a glimpse of her responsibilities, they'd bolt faster than a cat at a dog show. Instead of pulling a rabbit out of a hat, she'd whip out a calendar packed with meetings, chores, and the occasional reminder to take Sam and Grandma to the doctor's appointments.

It was no wonder men were scared stiff—who wanted to date a woman whose idea of a good time involved balancing a kid and a senior citizen while navigating a schedule that would make a CEO weep?

Yet Paul was different. He didn't shy away—he leaned in, fully present, as if Sam's world mattered just as much as his own.

That realization made Anna pause.

She wasn't sure what to make of it.

Paul was charming, that much was obvious, but charm alone didn't impress her. What caught her off guard was the quiet sincerity with which he treated Sam, the ease with which he fit into their world without demanding space.

As the late autumn breeze drifted through the bakery's open window, it carried with it the crisp scent of fallen leaves and nutmeg from the morning's baking.

The street was alive with the golden hues of late fall, the town preparing for the colder months ahead.

And yet, at this moment, Anna felt something unfamiliar that made her heartbeat just a little faster.

Maybe, just maybe, Paul wasn't someone she needed to keep at arm's length after all.

Paul laughed again, entirely at ease with Sam.

Anna caught herself smiling, then looked away. What was she doing?

What did she really know about Paul? He was like a tourist passing through—friendly, easy to talk to, but with one foot already out the door. For all she knew, this was just a charming detour before he returned to whatever life he had before Pine Valley.

And she? She was the one buried in routines and obligations, not strolling through life like it was a farmer's market on a Sunday morning.

It was ridiculous, really—this flicker of hope, this heartbeat of curiosity.

She barely knew him—except that he owned Pine Valley. He was virtually a stranger.

She needed to stop acting like some desperate woman in a Hallmark movie, mistaking kindness for something deeper.

She turned back to the counter, busying her hands—anything to stay grounded.

Paul laughed, the sound rising to blend easily with Sam's chatter.
Maybe that's all it was.
A nice moment.
Nothing more.

Chapter 22

An untamed heart

Paul wanted to get to know Anna better. That much he knew.

But knowing and acting weren't the same.

She wasn't a casual decision. Anna came with roots—real ones. She had Sam to care for, a business to run, a life built in the quiet rhythms of CreeksVille. She wasn't the type to fall for someone passing through, and Paul hadn't exactly proven he was staying.

He hadn't even planned to. His original intention had been simple: oversee the hotel renovation, lease it out, and return to New York, where his real life waited. His work as a patent attorney, his clients, his apartment, his pace—it was all still there, ticking forward without him.

But now…there was Anna.

Her calm steadiness. Her quick wit. The way she moved through life like someone who had learned to carry the weight of others without making it look like a burden—he admired that more than he could say.

And yet.

What did he have to offer her? A half-lived presence? A maybe someday? That wasn't enough. Not for someone like her.

Still, wanting something didn't make it wise. She hadn't exactly made her feelings clear, and he respected her too much to assume anything.

So he hesitated—stuck in that fragile space between longing and logic.

The next morning, sunlight poured through his window in wide, golden sheets. Paul sat by the window with a cup of coffee, the steam curling lazily toward the ceiling, his laptop closed beside him.

Anna.

She made him feel something he hadn't in a long time—like maybe, just maybe, he could belong somewhere other than a glass-walled Manhattan office. But relocating for good? That was a decision he couldn't rush.

His parents were planning to retire in CreeksVille soon. That offered a sliver of permanence, a reason to stay. But still, balancing two very different lives felt more like splitting in half than settling down.

That afternoon, he picked up his phone and called her. When it went to voicemail, he hesitated for a second, then left a short message.

"Hey Anna, just wanted to say I'll be in New York this week—some things I need to take care of. I'll call you soon. Take care."

No grand declarations. No promises he couldn't keep.

Anna noticed the missed call just after the afternoon rush at the bakery. She leaned against the back counter, still wearing her flour-dusted apron, and pressed play.

His voice was calm. Kind. Distant.

A twinge of disappointment flared before she could stop it. But she smiled anyway, small and private.

At least he called.

She tucked the phone away and returned to work, hands busy kneading dough, heart stubbornly quiet. She didn't have time to miss someone who hadn't decided to stay. Still, that didn't stop the ache from curling into the space he'd left behind.

That week, she poured her energy into other things. Sam had extra basketball practice, and she made sure to be there—cheering from the bleachers, even when she had to sneak away from the bakery.

She tested new menu ideas, filling the kitchen with the scents of cinnamon and burnt sugar. She even started reading the novel she'd left on her nightstand for months, picking up the thread of someone else's story when hers felt suspended.

CreeksVille rolled on, unchanged as always.

But sometimes, in the quiet minutes before dawn, or just after Sam had gone to bed, Anna would glance at her phone… then set it face down without checking.

Chapter 23

Blast from the past

Another October rolled in, the air crisp and carrying the same scent of cider as the year before—hot dogs, laughter, and those first easy smiles that had once felt like the start of something.

Anna spotted her on the café porch before the name surfaced—glossy as a magazine spread, two friends in tow. CreeksVille saw travelers, but this one felt familiar. She checked her phone, and it clicked: Monica Fox. A famous influencer. And—more importantly—Paul's ex-girlfriend.

In person, Monica was even more dazzling than her photographs. Golden hair fell in effortless waves, her crop top and low-waisted jeans sculpting a body that seemed born for attention. She didn't have to try; people turned to look at her when she walked past.

A pang twisted in Anna's chest. Monica was the kind of woman who belonged in glossy spreads, not small-town cafés.

Later that evening, Anna and Lizzy scrolled through Monica's social media. The posts were relentless—sunlit smiles, curated perfection. One photo made Anna's stomach tighten—Monica at the edge of an infinity pool, a white bikini clinging to her flawless frame, a cotton scarf tied at her hips like a careless afterthought. Behind her, the sky was a firestorm of orange and pink, the water reflecting the blaze.

"Wow," Lizzy murmured, squinting at the screen. "She looks amazing. And that pool! It looks like it spills straight into the sunset."

Anna tried to smile, but the words cut deeper than they should have.

"Why would Paul leave this…" she gestured toward the screen, her jaw tightening. "…for this?" She pointed at herself.

Lizzy rolled her eyes, nudging her playfully. "Don't flatter yourself. Paul left *that* long before he even met you."

That night, unease refused to let Anna sleep. Monica was here in CreeksVille. And Paul hadn't said a word.

As she lay in bed, the shadows of tree branches stretched across her ceiling, swaying with every gust of wind. The low whir of the ceiling fan only magnified the quiet storm in her chest.

He didn't owe her anything—they weren't a couple. They hadn't even had a real conversation about what they were. Still, the thought lodged under her skin like a splinter.

Had they met up? Were they still in touch? Was Monica here... for him?

Her thoughts circled endlessly, each question sharper than the last. Anna hated how easily her mind fell into what-ifs. It wasn't like her to obsess—not over a man who had made no promises.

And yet.

Would it be crazy to ask him? Probably.

But saying nothing—swallowing her questions whole—felt worse.

The weight of the unspoken closed in, thick and suffocating. She shut her eyes and exhaled, the breath snagging in her throat. There was no rulebook for this. All she knew was that it hurt more than it should.

After pacing the room until her legs ached, Anna finally gave in. Her fingers trembled as she picked up her phone and dialed. Each ring thudded against her ribs.

"Hey, Anna!" Paul greeted her, warm—almost too cheerful.

"Hi, Paul. Can we talk?" she asked, struggling to catch her breath.

"Of course. Is everything okay?"

"Can we meet at the café tomorrow afternoon?"

A pause. Then his easy reply: "Sure. Two o'clock?"

Anna nodded, though he couldn't see her. Her grip tightened on the phone.

Tomorrow might bring answers—or more questions she wasn't ready to face.

Chapter 24

A matter of heart

The next day, sunlight poured across CreeksVille, painting the streets in warm tones. After the lunch rush, Anna slipped into a corner table by the café window, her hands restless against her cup. She told herself to breathe, but her chest still tightened every time the door swung open.

At precisely two, Paul stepped inside. His smile lit the room, easy and familiar, and when he leaned down to kiss her, Anna tried to return it—though her lips held more nerves than warmth.

"Let's take a walk," she suggested, standing before her courage had time to falter.

They strolled down Main Street, their footsteps falling into an unspoken rhythm. Finally, Anna broke the silence.

"Monica came into the café yesterday."

Paul's brow lifted, surprise flickering across his face.

"I didn't recognize her at first," Anna continued, her tone casual but edged. "Then I saw her posts. She's been in Pine Valley."

Paul exhaled, slowing his pace. "Yeah. She showed up at the property with a film crew. I wasn't expecting it. We didn't plan anything. It was… nothing."

Anna nodded, but the pause that followed pressed her forward. "It just caught me off guard. I didn't know if I should ask. I mean… we're not—"

"I know," Paul said firmly. "But there's nothing between me and Monica. Hasn't been for a long time. If it mattered, I would've told you. Honestly, I didn't want to drag something into our world that didn't belong here."

The words almost eased her—but not completely. "Then why not just tell me anyway?"

Paul turned. "Anna, I have a past—people I've known, mistakes I've made—but none of that changes how I feel about you. I stayed here for you. My heart is with you. What I need is for you to trust that."

Her chest loosened, the knot easing just slightly. "I'm sorry." His gaze held hers.

"Don't be. If it mattered to you, then I'm glad you said something."

Anna nodded, a breath slipping free. Not quite relief—but something close.

As they walked back, the night gathered around them in cool air. Overhead, stars glittered like scattered glass, and the world seemed to wait in stillness.

At the edge of the small park, they slowed. The lamppost light fell across Paul's face, tracing the curve of his smile, the calm in his eyes. Anna's pulse quickened.

"Thank you… for understanding. "Paul tilted his head, a faint grin touching his lips. "You cared enough to be jealous." His words came out quiet, threaded with warmth. "And I loved that."

Her breath caught—half a protest, half a laugh. The moment that followed shivered with something unspoken, fragile but real.

Their eyes met, and in that stillness the world receded. The cool breeze brushed against them, mingling with the warmth rising between their hearts.

Anna swallowed, feeling the gravity of what lingered unsaid.

Paul whispered—firm and unflinching—"I love you."

The words fell into the night like a vow, and when he smiled, the honesty in his eyes told her he meant every syllable.
She didn't trust her voice. Instead, she rose on her toes and kissed him—slow, sure, an answer without a single word.

Chapter 25

Blooming tulips

After that night in the park—their words dissolving into the cool air, his *I love you* certain as a promise, her kiss the only answer he needed—Paul didn't press for more. The next day, his message was simple, *Let's do this properly. Dinner? No rush—just us.* That was last week.

Anna had slipped into leadership at the bakery, Mrs. Lewis content to step back and let her steer the day-to-day. With Lizzy's help, constant and reliable, the kitchen carried on with ease—even in the thick of the rush.

The delightful scents of freshly baked bread and pastries enveloped the space, a gentle embrace—warm and comforting, like a loaf of sourdough fresh from the oven.

Beyond the bakery, Anna's personal life was flourishing; her relationship with Paul was blossoming.

Friends, especially Lizzy, were abuzz with curiosity about their romance. Lizzy, in particular, was eager to help Anna find the perfect dress for their next date.

Lizzy's eyes gleamed with excitement as she sifted through the clothing racks.

"We need to find you something absolutely stunning for your date," she declared, flipping through dresses with the enthusiasm of a seasoned stylist.

Anna chuckled. "It's just dinner, Lizzy. Not the Met Gala."

Lizzy shot her a knowing look. "Yes, but it's dinner with Paul, which means we need to strike the perfect balance between elegant and effortlessly beautiful."

After trying on an array of styles, they finally settled on a breathtaking deep blue dress that accentuated Anna's eyes.

"Now this," Lizzy said, stepping back to admire the choice, "is what I call the perfect date dress. Classy, flattering, and completely spill-proof—just in case dessert gets too exciting."

Anna rolled her eyes but smiled as she ran her hands over the fabric.

For a brief moment, her mind wandered to Paul. She wondered how he would react when he saw her in it—and the thought made her heart flutter.

On the night of their date at Pine Valley Restaurant, Anna felt a restless mix of nerves and excitement that made her heart feel unsteady.

She took her time styling her hair and perfecting her makeup, glancing in the mirror to ensure everything was just right.

Beneath the moonlight sky, they enjoyed a meal together.

Paul's childhood tales kept the conversation flowing. One in particular—when he and his friends stole beer and ended up chased by a bear through the muddy valley—had Anna laughing until her cheeks hurt.

As the evening came to a close, Paul leaned in, kissing her cheek and enveloping her in a warm embrace.

The tenderness of the moment filled Anna with hope and anticipation for what lay ahead.

She couldn't help but secretly wish he wouldn't suggest trying his grandma's infamous meatloaf on their next outing.

The following morning, Lizzy burst into the bakery, her excitement palpable.

"How did it go?" she asked eagerly, her eyes sparkling with curiosity as if she were waiting for the latest juicy gossip.

"It was nice," Anna replied, a blush creeping onto her cheeks as memories of the evening washed over her.

She felt both flustered and excited, like a dancer stepping onto the stage a beat before the music started.

"Nice? You guys kissed, right?" Lizzy pressed, waving a stack of papers in her hands, eager for every detail like a detective in a romantic comedy.

"Just a goodbye kiss on the cheek," Anna mumbled, a nervous laugh escaping her lips.

Lizzy's playful teasing about future romantic encounters left her feeling flattered yet shy.

Meanwhile, Paul found himself deep in thought, reflecting on Anna's kindness.

The prospect of a long-distance relationship seemed daunting, but he allowed himself to dream about the possibilities—like waking up to the smell of pancakes instead of the emptiness of heartbreak.

Later that day, Paul shared breakfast with his parents, who quickly noticed his distracted demeanor.

"What's on your mind?" Richard asked, noticing the distracted look on Paul's face.

"I've been thinking about Anna a lot lately. You know, ever since we started seeing each other," Paul said, his brow furrowing.

"It's just… I'm not sure what to do about my plans to go back to New York. I thought I had everything figured out, but now…"

"Now you're feeling torn, right?" Richard interjected, leaning forward slightly.

"Exactly! It's like… do I stick with what I know? Or do I take a leap of faith for something that might be really special?"

"You don't have to rush," Margret reassured him, giving him a warm smile.

"Just take your time and see where things go with Anna. You might find that future you're dreaming about."

Paul smiled faintly at his mother's words, but later, alone with his coffee, the warmth faded. Time was exactly what he didn't have. New York was calling, and so was Anna—and he wasn't sure how long he could stand in both worlds without breaking one of them.

Chapter 26

A promise to the stars

That weekend, Paul invited Anna to meet his parents.

On the drive over, Anna still couldn't shake the memory of their last conversation—when Paul had stood outside the bakery, gently taking her hand. "My heart belongs to you. I need you to trust me."

He'd paused, letting the words settle between them.

"I've decided to move to CreeksVille. I'll travel to New York when I need to, but this… this is where I want to build something. With you."

Anna hadn't responded right away. She'd just looked at him, her heart brimming with love, surprise, and gratitude.

Now, as she crossed the threshold of the Rileys warm, wood-paneled home, the truth of his decision settled inside her like an anchor, giving her courage.

At first, Paul's father, Mr. Riley, seemed intimidating with his tall stature and commanding presence. However, Anna quickly discovered he was a gentle soul with a warm sense of humor. His mother, an elegant and gracious woman, immediately put Anna at ease with her lighthearted laughter and engaging conversation.

During dinner, Mr. Riley playfully asked if Anna had made the pastries on the table. When she replied no, he exaggerated his disappointment, earning laughs from everyone.

The Rileys also asked about Sam, his school, and Grandma, showing how much they already knew about Anna's life through Paul. Before the evening ended, they extended an invitation for Anna, Sam, and Grandma to visit their home in New York.

As Paul walked Anna to her car, his hands rested gently at her waist. He kissed her and promised to call later. Just as she settled into the driver's seat, he rushed back, leaned in, and kissed her again.

"I love you," he said, low and quick, disappearing before Anna could respond.

She smiled to herself, the words catching in her throat as she pulled away.

"I love you too," she whispered to the quiet.

The evening at the Riley home had left a warmth in Anna's heart that she couldn't shake. As she drove home, she replayed the laughter and stories shared over dinner, the cozy atmosphere, and the way Paul looked at her—like she was the only person in the world.

It was a night filled with connection, acceptance, and a budding sense of belonging that both thrilled and terrified her.

The streetlights illuminated her path as she navigated through the quiet, snow-covered streets. Each flake that danced against her windshield felt like a whisper of something magical, something that hinted at what was to come. The warmth of Paul's kiss lingered on her lips, igniting a spark of hope within her.

Weeks slipped into months, and still that night at the Riley home remained a beginning—an anchor and a promise quietly growing between them.

Anna felt it in the small things: the afternoon Paul fixed Sam's bike while she watched from the porch, her apron still dusted with flour. It was in moments like that—ordinary yet tender—that she realized how naturally he had become part of her world.

With every thoughtful gesture, effortless moment, Paul wove himself deeper into her life until she could no longer imagine her days without him.

Chapter 27

More than a birthday

As Anna stood in front of the mirror, adjusting her hunter-green dress, she felt a mixture of nervousness and exhilaration. The night was not just about celebrating another year of life; it felt like a prelude to an important moment, a turning point that might lead them further down a path of commitment and love.

Since Sam was running late, Grandma reassured Anna that they would join her soon and encouraged her to go ahead, knowing Paul was waiting.

The host guided her to the balcony, and as she stepped onto it, she stopped short.

The scene before her was breathtaking. Twinkling fairy lights hung overhead, softening the evening with their glow. A small table adorned with fresh wildflowers awaited her, and the warm scent of jasmine drifted through the air, mingling with the melody floating from the restaurant.

It felt like a dream—one she never wanted to wake from.

From behind, Paul's voice broke through her awe. "Happy birthday, Anna," he said, stepping forward with a smile.

Anna turned, her eyes wide with delight. "Oh my God, Paul! This is beautiful!" she exclaimed, joy brimming in her tone.

For someone who had always marked birthdays with simple dinners or movies, this felt like a fairy tale. The sight of a table for two, adorned with her favorite flowers, made her heart swell with gratitude.

"This is the most thoughtful thing anyone has ever done for me," Anna said, squeezing Paul's hand.

Paul picked up the bouquet from the table and handed it to her. "Do you like these?" he asked.

Before Anna could respond, Paul dropped to one knee, the flowers still in his hand.

She laughed at first, thinking he was being playful. But then she saw the depth in his eyes—the way he looked at her, not with mischief but with certainty—and her laughter stilled into silence.

"Anna Maria Buchman," Paul began, his voice breaking with love, "will you marry me?"

For a moment, Anna stood frozen, joy tightening in her chest. Paul looked up at her, his eyes searching hers.

"Anna?" he repeated gently.

Tears welled in her eyes as she nodded fervently. "Yes! Yes!" she exclaimed, her voice thick with emotion. Her fingers brushed the sapphire pendant at her neck—a quiet tribute to the memory of her mother. In that instant, she felt her mother's presence: steady, proud, and with her as always.

Paul slipped a sparkling solitaire ring onto her finger, then rose and swept her into his arms. Their lips met in a kiss that felt like it lasted an eternity, the world around them melting away.

Above them, the stars seemed to shine even brighter, as if they, too, were celebrating this perfect moment.

When they finally pulled apart, Anna gazed into Paul's eyes, her heart overflowing with joy.

Paul drew her in, his breath warm against her ear. "I can't wait to spend the rest of my life with you."

"Me too," Anna replied, her smile radiant.

Just then, Sam and Grandma appeared as if on cue.

Sam ran to Anna and Paul, his excitement uncontainable. "Congratulations!" he shouted, throwing his arms around them.

Grandma Sophia followed, her eyes glistening with tears of happiness. She embraced them both tightly. "I'm so happy for you," she said, her tears carrying the fullness of her joy.

Paul grinned as he shared a secret. "I had Sam and Grandma's permission before I asked you to marry me."

Anna laughed through her tears. "Who else knew about this?"

"Well, Lizzy, Bob, Mrs. Lewis, and my parents," Paul admitted with a wink.

Anna shook her head, laughing. "This is truly an amazing surprise."

Paul turned to Sam, Grandma, and the others, a wide grin stretching across his face. He lifted the champagne bottle with a flourish.

"Ladies and gentlemen," he said, pausing just long enough for effect, "meet my fiancée, Anna Maria Buchman!"

It was a celebration not just of her birthday but of their love story—a story that was just beginning.

As they embraced, the universe seemed to align, celebrating their union with shimmering stars and the gentle rustle of the breeze. The laughter of family and friends echoed in the background, a joyful reminder that they were embarking on this journey together, surrounded by love and support.

In that magical moment, Anna knew that this was the beginning of a beautiful chapter in her life—a chapter filled with love, laughter, and a promise of forever.

Life has a way of shifting, transforming us in ways we never anticipated. As Anna stood on the precipice of her future, she could feel the vibrant energy of possibility coursing through her.

In that fleeting moment of clarity, she recalled her mom's gentle words echoing through her heart.

"Darling, just like the tulips, you too will bloom beautifully, and I will always be here to watch you thrive."

Chapter 28

To have and to hold

At last, the wedding day arrived—woven with joy, love, and tender memories. Autumn's crisp air smelled of woodsmoke and pine, the world itself leaning close to witness.

Sam stood proudly as he escorted Anna toward the altar. Radiant in her lace gown, she looked like she'd stepped out of a fairy tale, adorned with her mother's cherished blue pumps and her grandmother's sapphire jewelry.

Her bouquet—a delicate mix of white and yellow roses—cradled a small portrait of their mother, an intimate tribute weaving family history into her new beginning.

Lizzy, her loyal friend, stood beside her, a pillar of unwavering support.

The aisle, lit with lanterns and ivory blooms, shimmered with the promise of romance and new beginnings. Candlelight danced around them, casting a warm, expectant aura over the space.

The ceremony unfolded elegantly, attended by Paul's family, their faces alight with love as they watched Anna walk forward, her gown flowing like a gentle wave. In the front row, Grandma Sophia dabbed at her eyes, pride swelling in her heart, while Mrs. Riley leaned in to whisper admiration.

As Anna and Paul stood before their loved ones, hands intertwined, the officiant's words resonated through the still air.

"Marriage is more than the union of two hearts; it is the weaving of two families, their traditions and dreams entwining like threads in a timeless tapestry. It is not just love that binds, but the echoes of generations past, merging into one shared future."

Anna's gaze drifted toward the front row—where Sophia sat beside Mrs. Riley, their hands clasped in quiet understanding. Two families, once strangers, are now forever connected.

Paul's thumb brushed against her hand, and her heart rose to meet his gaze. Their promise was not theirs alone—it carried the legacies, traditions, and hopes of generations past.

With a calm voice, Paul said, "I do." The words echoed like a vow written in the stars.

Anna's response was just as calm, just as certain. "I do."

As the officiant pronounced them husband and wife, Paul lifted her veil, his eyes filled with warmth, before he leaned in and sealed their promise with a kiss.

Hand in hand, they walked back down the aisle as husband and wife, greeted by applause and cheers, their hearts intertwined.

The reception at the grand lodge welcomed guests with warmth and laughter. Candlelight shimmered across the room, wrapping the space in a cozy ambiance. By the fire, Sophia sat with Mrs. Riley, watching Anna and Paul dance, their silhouettes outlined in the flickering light.

Mrs. Riley chuckled. "We're officially family now."

Sophia nodded, her eyes shining. "I couldn't have asked for a better family for her."

Their cups clinked together in a quiet toast, hearts full of gratitude and connection.

As the night unfolded, laughter echoed, and love enveloped everyone. The first notes of *"Count on Me"* by Bruno Mars began to play.

Anna turned to Sam, who stood beside her in his sharp suit, suddenly appearing more mature than she recalled. His youthful features still carried traces of childhood, yet he exuded a quiet confidence that filled her heart with pride.

With a playful smile, he extended his hand. "Shall we, Sis?"

Anna laughed, blinking back tears. "You look fantastic, Sam."

He rolled his eyes, warmth shining through his teasing smirk. "I know."

The fireplace crackled in the background, adding a touch of coziness to the cool autumn evening. The aroma of apple cider and vanilla wafted from the dessert table, mingling with the crisp breeze drifting in through the open balcony doors.

Taking Sam's hand, Anna followed him onto the dance floor. The melody enveloped them, the lyrics embodying everything left unsaid between them.

The room filled with *"Count on Me,"* the lyrics drifting over them in memory rather than actual sound

The guests observed in quiet admiration as the siblings swayed in harmony, lost in the magic of the moment.

Sam spun Anna around, his movements charmingly awkward. Her laugh broke free, her heart overflowing with affection.

Grandma Sophia sat nearby, a tissue in hand, her proud gaze fixed on Anna and Sam. Mrs. Riley leaned in content, and Lizzy—always the sentimental one—wiped away a tear.

She leaned in, her words tender. "This is the sweetest moment ever."

As the song neared its end, Sam executed one last dramatic spin, prompting Anna to laugh through her tears.

"I love you, Sam," she murmured.

Sam, ever the tough one, cleared his throat and smirked. "Yeah, yeah. I love you too, but if you cry anymore, people might think I stepped on your foot."

A wave of laughter and applause erupted as Anna embraced him tightly. For a moment, brother and sister simply held on, their bond shining brighter than the lights above them.

As the dance floor filled again, Anna turned to Paul, their fingers naturally finding each other.

"Shall we?" he murmured.

She nodded, and together, they glided onto the floor, their first dance as husband and wife. Their movements were effortless, their love radiating through every step.

Paul pulled her close. "You are breathtaking."

Anna smiled. "You're not so bad yourself."

As their families mingled, the air filled with easy joy—stories exchanged, laughter carrying across generations.

As the festivities continued, Anna realized that this day was about more than just her and Paul; it marked the beautiful union of two families, their destinies now intertwined.

The dance floor shimmered under the golden light, joy echoing in the air and hearts overflowing in the purest celebration of love.

The tulips her mother had planted were already fading, their petals loosening into the night wind. Anna held fast to her mother's words: "Darling, bloom like a tulip."

Tonight's laughter and warmth—the way love gathered around her like armor—she would carry into every season ahead, even the hardest ones.

Chapter 29

Where the light settles

Their new home felt like something out of a dream—warm, inviting, and surrounded by quiet beauty. Paul's French-style house overlooked rolling meadows and a tranquil creek, its wraparound porch perfect for lazy mornings.

Inside, Anna blended her cozy charm with Paul's refined taste. Soft-hued walls, rustic furniture, and little details made the house theirs, filled with laughter, fresh coffee, and a comforting rhythm.

Anna's days at the bakery began early, the air rich with bread and coffee that wrapped her in warmth. Stephanie and Todd's playful banter brightened the mornings, while Lizzy's sure hand on the business side freed Anna to focus on her craft and experiment with new recipes.

Meanwhile, Sam, now fifteen, was thriving in his new life. He had grown taller and more confident, balancing advanced coursework with his passions for debate and basketball.

He rode his bike to school or the gym, embracing his independence.

Evenings by the dock with Paul became a cherished routine for Sam. The sun dipped low in the sky, painting the horizon with hues of orange and pink as they cast lines into the shimmering lake.

The gentle lapping of the creek against the wooden dock and the rustle of leaves in the evening breeze created a serene backdrop for their conversations. Bonding over fishing trips and stories from Paul's past, they created lasting memories.

For Anna, seeing Paul and Sam grow closer brought her immense happiness. With each passing day, she marveled at how far they had come—from the challenges they had faced to the new life they were building together.

One quiet evening, Anna stood on the porch as the sky blazed with sunset. In that stillness, she knew they could face anything together, surrounded by love and hope.

As the seasons changed, Sam became more settled in their new life. His days were filled with laughter, hard work, and the warmth of new friendships, turning Paul's house into a true home. He became a confident, self-assured teenager, idolizing Paul like a superhero.

Paul fully supported Anna's dream of growing her bakery and became her biggest cheerleader. He drove Sam to basketball games and debate contests, cheering so enthusiastically that he was banned from two games for being too disruptive.

Paul also had the honor of teaching Sam how to shave and having the important, albeit awkward, talk about relationships and responsibility. Their conversations, sometimes humorous and sometimes heartfelt, forged a bond that would carry them into adulthood.

Together, they often visited Grandma Sophia. Trips to New York—especially skating at Christmas under glittering lights—became a treasured family tradition.

Meanwhile, CreeksVille Bakery evolved into CreeksVille Café, renowned for its artisanal sourdough, rye bread, and pretzels. Under Anna and Lizzy's leadership, the menu expanded to include hot sandwiches, hearty soups, and vibrant salads.

The café's reputation soared, attracting both locals and visitors. What had once been a quiet bakery, bustling only during the morning rush, now thrived throughout the day, filled with the sounds of clinking dishes, laughter, and the chatter of patrons enjoying their meals.

Rustic wooden tables adorned the porch, inviting guests to enjoy the sunshine and fresh air. More than just a business, the café became a gathering place where neighbors mingled and new friendships blossomed—a haven of joy and connection.

Paul transformed Pine Valley Hotel into a Creekside resort of wooden cabins, glowing in winter with snowy rooftops and warm fireplaces.

Grateful for Mrs. Lewis's guidance, Anna felt a pull to give back. CreeksVille's local college offered a Diploma in Culinary Arts, but nothing devoted to Pastry Arts.

To fill that gap, she launched an internship at the café, giving aspiring bakers a place to learn through flour-dusted hands and the true rhythm of a working kitchen.

Her first group of interns came with varied dreams: Zac wanted to cater weddings, Mark longed to run a soup kitchen, and Melissa—a high schooler—was inspired by her family's love of cooking.

Under Anna's care, the café became a classroom where questions were encouraged and mistakes folded into lessons, the pans clattering as conversations wove through the space, wrapping it in warmth and possibility.

As the program progressed, the interns mastered basic techniques before delving into advanced skills like tempering chocolate and crafting delicate pastries.

To culminate the program, Anna organized a showcase event where the interns presented their own take on a classic Bundt cake challenge. The twist? Each cake had to be vegan—free of dairy and eggs.

Mark impressed all with a decadent chocolate Bundt infused with espresso, topped with a sharp raspberry glaze. Zac followed with a bright lemon Bundt, accented by rosemary and finished with a tangy lemon-mint icing.

But Melissa's spiced pumpkin Bundt cake stole the moment. Cinnamon, ginger, and nutmeg filled the room, the creamy cashew frosting gleaming under the lights and drawing an extra round of applause.

As the event wrapped up, the audience showered the interns with praise, treating them like stars. The room buzzed with excitement, a celebration of their hard work and creativity.

Sam, grinning from ear to ear, congratulated Melissa. "Your cake was amazing," he said, his boyish charm evident. Sam lingered a moment longer on her smile than he meant to, a flicker of something new tugging at him—light but undeniable.

Melissa smiled brightly. "Thanks, Sam! See you at school tomorrow."

Anna joined Sam, hugging Melissa warmly.

"You did an incredible job. Would you like to work here part-time?"

Melissa's eyes widened.

"For real?"

Anna nodded.

"Of course. Take your time to talk to your parents and let me know."

Her curls bounced as she beamed with excitement. As she hurried off, Sam caught the faint scent of cinnamon and sugar clinging to her—as if she carried the bakery's warmth with her.

"I'll let you know soon!" she promised.

In the glow of the café lights, it felt as though nothing could touch them. Yet, beyond the quiet meadows and cinnamon-scented air, the world was already shifting, clouds stirring just out of sight.

Chapter 30

Winds of change

As Sam and Anna walked home, the memory of the evening lingered between them. CreeksVille had blossomed in ways Anna never dreamed possible. With Paul beside her, Sam thriving, and the café flourishing, she carried a quiet fullness she hadn't known in years.

The stars above twinkled like diamonds, the night sky a vast expanse filled with promise. In that moment, Anna thought this was just the beginning.

She glanced at Sam walking beside her, marveling at how much he had changed.

Sharper angles now defined his once-boyish features. His jawline had set, and his dark brown hair—forever messy—had evolved into a style that made him look effortlessly cool.

He was confident, with an easy confidence that turned heads at school—much to his amusement. Over the past year, his height had shot up, making Paul grumble that he'd soon be looking up at him instead of the other way around.

Even Melissa, who had known him since he was twelve, had to admit: Sam Buchman wasn't a little kid anymore.

The early autumn air was crisp, tinged with the scent of fallen leaves and fresh-baked bread. A cool, gentle wind rustled through the trees, sending golden and amber leaves drifting across the road.

Inside the car, the scent of vanilla and pumpkin spice clung to Sam's hoodie—a lingering trace of the bakery. His sleeves were pushed up to his elbows, and his toned forearms rested on the passenger door as he watched the town pass by, the familiar sights filling him with a sense of belonging.

"Man, I can't wait till I don't have to sit in this seat anymore," he muttered, glancing at Melissa, who maneuvered the Jeep effortlessly down the winding road.

Melissa chuckled, tapping the steering wheel.

"Enjoy it while it lasts, Carter. Soon enough, you'll be dealing with bad drivers, construction detours, and pedestrians who think they're invincible."

Sam smirked, shaking his head.

"Yeah, but at least I won't have to deal with your terrible music choices."

Melissa gasped dramatically.

"Excuse me? This is a classic playlist."

She cranked up the volume, filling the car with an old rock ballad.

Sam groaned, slumping deeper into his seat.

"Remind me why I agreed to this again?"

"Because I'm your only ride until you pass your test," she said smugly.

Golden light settled on the red brick building as they neared the soup kitchen. The air carried the scent of simmering soup and fresh bread, guiding them toward the bustle inside.

Sam sat up, stretching before glancing at Melissa with a smirk.

"Alright, chauffeur. Let's get to work."

She rolled her eyes but smiled, watching as he jumped out of the Jeep effortlessly, his confidence evident in his movements.

As he grabbed a box of pastries, Melissa shook her head slightly.

His lack of a driver's license wasn't due to a lack of trying. For months, he had practiced with Paul and Anna, but neither was an ideal instructor.

With Anna, every session turned into a nerve-wracking ordeal. She gripped the passenger seat as if bracing for impact.

"Slow down, Sam!" she'd cry, even when he was barely crawling past the 20-mile-per-hour mark.

"You're driving like a lunatic!"

Sam groaned.

"Anna, a squirrel just overtook us."

Their last attempt ended in disaster when Sam misjudged a turn and backed into the garbage bins, sending them toppling like bowling pins. Anna had thrown up her hands.

"That's it! You're unfit for the road!"

Paul wasn't much better. His approach was all nerves and endless lectures. He'd spend forty minutes explaining the theory of a perfect three-point turn before letting Sam try it. The ten minutes of practice usually involved Paul gripping the seatbelt with white-knuckled terror.

Frustrated, Sam finally turned to Bob, who took a no-nonsense approach.

"You get in, you drive, and you don't kill anyone," he said.

That was the whole lesson.

And somehow, it worked.

On test day, Sam and Bob returned to the house triumphant, a freshly printed driver's license in hand.

Paul, arms crossed, tried to look unimpressed.

"Bob, I thought you said he wouldn't pass if he weren't ready."

Bob smirked.

"Turns out he was ready."

Paul sighed dramatically before pulling Sam into a bear hug.

"Welcome to adulthood, kid."

Sam grinned, holding up his license like a trophy. But as Paul clapped him on the back, a twinge of sadness flickered in his eyes—like a shadow at the edge of a bright day.

He'd miss driving Sam around.

Chapter 31

Dance me into the night

It was the kind of spring that smelled like change.

Senior year was winding down, and with it came the quiet pressure of choices that would shape the rest of Sam's life.

He had spent months poring over college applications, polishing essays late into the night, and juggling extracurriculars like puzzle pieces of a future he was still figuring out.

His top choices—NYU, Yale, and Stanford—represented vastly different versions of who he might become. Cities, climates, dreams—none of it felt real yet.

Paul and Anna offered steady support, guiding when needed but never pushing. And though the road ahead felt uncertain, Sam tried to stay anchored in the present. After all, it was his final year at CreeksVille High—and there were still memories left to make.

Melissa, too, was preparing for a big transition, though hers had far less uncertainty. Her passion for baking had been evident for years, and she had already secured early admission to several prestigious culinary schools. Unlike Sam, she had no hesitation about where she wanted to be—staying close to home and continuing her work at the café felt like the perfect path.

Despite the looming decisions about the future, high school life still carried its usual traditions—and that included prom.

Excitement buzzed through the halls of CreeksVille High as prom season approached. At dinner one evening, Sam casually mentioned needing a new suit, prompting playful teasing from Anna and Paul.

"Who are you taking to prom?" Paul asked, a mischievous glint in his eye.

Sam hesitated before replying, "Not sure yet. I'm deciding between three girls."

"Three?" Anna exclaimed, raising an eyebrow.

Sam shrugged. "Yeah, three."

Paul leaned in, his curiosity piqued. "Okay, who's on the list?"

Sam began listing, "One's from the debate team—she's smart and pretty. Another is in my class and is really nice. And then there's Melissa."

Paul's eyebrows shot up. "Melissa? From the café?"

Sam nodded. "I don't know why, but I just... like her."

Paul smiled knowingly. "When you can't explain why you like someone, it usually means they're special."

Later that evening, Sam mustered the courage to text Melissa.

Sam: Hi Melissa, are you still awake?

Melissa: Just about to sleep. What's up?

Sam: Are you planning to go to prom?

Melissa: Hope so.

Sam: Would you like to go with me?

Melissa, leaping onto her bed in excitement, quickly typed back:

Melissa: I would love to!

Sam: Awesome! I'll pick you up at 5 PM, okay?

Melissa: Sounds good. Good night!

Sam: Good night!

Sam switched off his lamp with a satisfied smile and drifted to sleep, the anticipation of the night ahead filling him with excitement.

When prom night arrived, excitement filled the house. The late spring air drifted through the open windows, carrying the scent of freshly cut grass and blooming lilacs.

Paul and Anna stood near the staircase, anticipation in their eyes. Anna had her phone in hand, ready to capture every moment, while Paul adjusted his camera settings to get the perfect shot. Grandma sat in her armchair, a tissue already in her grip, prepared for "a moment too precious not to cry over."

Then came the sound of polished dress shoes against the stairs.

Sam appeared at the top landing, standing tall in a classic black tuxedo tailored to fit him perfectly. The deep navy tie he wore subtly complemented his sharp suit, and his polished shoes gleamed.

His usual tousled hair was neatly styled, though a few strands stubbornly fell across his forehead—just enough to keep his signature charm intact.

Anna gasped, pressing the record on her phone. "Sam, you look incredible!"

Paul let out a low whistle, shaking his head. "Who is this young gentleman, and what has he done with my kid brother-in-law?"

Sam smirked, adjusting his cuffs. "I'm still me—just upgraded."

Grandma clapped her hands together, her eyes shimmering with pride. "Oh, sweetheart, you look like your grandfather on our first dance." She dabbed at her eyes. "He'd be so proud."

She swallowed a lump in her throat, remembering how Sarah had once done the same before Sam's first school performance.

Sam shifted slightly, a rare moment of shyness flickering across his face. But his confidence grew as he looked at his family—their joy and pride washing over him.

Anna stepped forward, smoothing a small wrinkle in his lapel. "You look perfect," she murmured before grinning and ruffling his hair.

"Anna!" Sam groaned, immediately smoothing it down again. "Do you have to?"

Paul chuckled. "It's a sibling's duty."

Just then, the honk of a car outside signaled that it was time.

Sam grabbed his keys and turned toward the door. "I'll see you all later."

Anna, ever the teasing sister, smirked. "Don't forget—we want pictures! Lots of them."

With a final eye roll and a smirk, Sam stepped out, the night air wrapping around him like a cloak of excitement.

Anna stood by the door long after the car disappeared down the street, the night air soft against her face. She remembered the first time Sam had begged her to take him to the middle school social, his tie crooked, his nerves barely hidden beneath bravado. She had laughed, fixing his collar, thinking he'd always be her little brother.

Now he was tall, confident, in a tuxedo that made him look too much like a man.

Grandma dabbed her eyes, her voice soft. "Sarah would've loved this. She always said Sam would outgrow us one day."

Anna smiled, not with sadness but with fondness. It wasn't sorrow she felt—it was pride, laced with memory. Just a quiet warmth in the room, like a laugh left behind.

The late spring sky had settled into a dusky blue as Sam pulled into Melissa's driveway. Melissa stood waiting.

When she stepped forward, Sam felt his breath hitch.

She wore an elegant, flowing dress in deep wine-red that shimmered softly. Her usually tousled curls were pinned back, a few loose strands framing her face. For a moment, she took his breath away.

Melissa smiled as she approached, her eyes bright. "Wow, Sam. You look really good."

Sam grinned, pretending to dust off his tux. "What can I say? I aim to impress."

She laughed, looping her arm through his as he led her to the car. "Well, mission accomplished."

As he opened the door for her, she slid into the passenger seat, glancing up at him. "Are you nervous?"

Sam shrugged as he slid behind the wheel. "I hope I don't trip over my feet on the dance floor."

Melissa smirked. "Lucky for you, I'm an excellent dance partner."

He turned to her, his smile warm. "Yeah, I think I lucked out tonight."

At the prom hall, when the music swelled and Sam nervously stepped onto the dance floor with Melissa, a memory flickered to life.

She'd laugh as his small bare feet rested on top of hers, swaying them gently around the living room like they were gliding across a grand ballroom.

The cassette player crackled softly in the corner, playing one of her favorite old tunes.

"You're a natural, Sam," she'd whisper, as he clung to her fingers, wobbling with every step.

And he believed her—because when you're little and standing on your mother's feet, the whole world moves with you.

Now, here on this polished floor under glittering lights, with Melissa's hand in his, Sam found their rhythm.

He exhaled, steady and smiling.

He wasn't nervous anymore. He was exactly where he was meant to be.

Chapter 32

The road awaits

With that, he pulled out of the driveway, headlights sweeping across the quiet road ahead. The night brimmed with laughter, music, and the promise of memories that would outlast high school.

The clock had barely struck midnight when Sam pulled into the driveway, the car engine fading into the quiet of the night.

As he stepped inside, still grinning, he found Anna, Paul, and Grandma sitting in the living room. Their expressions were brimming with excitement, barely contained.

"Uh... what's going on?" Sam asked, narrowing his eyes at their expectant faces.

Anna bounced on her toes with excitement. "We have news."

Sam raised an eyebrow. "Good news?"

Paul stepped forward, grinning ear to ear. "The best news."

Anna took a deep breath before practically shouting, "YOU GOT INTO YALE!"

For a moment, time seemed to freeze. The words echoed in his mind, their weight sinking deep into his chest.

Sam blinked, his heart hammering. "Wait... what?"

Grandma, teary-eyed, held up an envelope that had arrived earlier that evening. "Full scholarship, sweetheart," she added with pride.

The world tilted briefly as Sam reached for the letter, his fingers trembling. His eyes scanned the words, barely processing them, before reality hit him like a tidal wave.

"Yale?" he said, the word barely leaving his lips, like speaking it might make it vanish. "I got into Yale?"

Paul clapped him on the back, his grin impossibly wide. "You earned it, kid. Congratulations!"

A disbelieving laugh escaped Sam before a wide, unstoppable smile took over his face.

Anna threw her arms around him, squeezing tight. "I knew you'd do it," she said, beaming.

Grandma wiped at her eyes, pride radiating from every inch of her. "Your mother would be so proud," she murmured, emotion thick in her throat.

As the news sank in, a different kind of magic filled the room— one woven from love, resilience, and the promise of a future brimming with endless possibilities.

Sam took a step back, looking at his family—the people who raised him, fought for him, and believed in him. His heart swelled with gratitude and love. This was his moment. His best night ever.

"Okay," he finally said, breathless and still grinning. "This night just became legendary."

Laughter rang through the house as Anna grabbed the leftover cake from the fridge, slicing generous pieces while they all gathered around the kitchen table.

The wind drifted through the trees, fragrant with blossoms, and the stars seemed to burn a little brighter. Sitting among his family, Sam knew—wherever life led him, this night and this love would always anchor him.

Chapter 33

The wings

Sam's suitcase waited by the door. The late-afternoon sun wrapped Anna in warmth as the house filled with the scents of bread, pot pie, and Sophia's lavender perfume—a tapestry of cherished memories.

She felt a deep sense of fulfillment, knowing she had played a part in Sam's journey alongside Paul, who had been an unwavering presence in their lives. The bond between Sam and Paul had strengthened over the years, forged through road trips, fishing excursions, and long conversations beneath the stars.

Though Anna sometimes felt a pang of exclusion when Sam and Paul ventured off together, it comforted her to see how much Sam admired Paul. His guidance had been a beacon during the turbulent teenage years.

Their hard work at the café and restaurant had helped Sam save money, thanks in part to Paul's encouragement.

Together, they had transformed their old house into a cozy Airbnb—a project that ignited a sense of pride and responsibility in Sam. The thought of welcoming guests into the home they had lovingly restored filled him with excitement.

As the golden sunset painted the sky in hues of amber and lavender, laughter echoed around the dining table, the clinking of silverware punctuating the warmth of the evening.

Seated at the head of the table, Sam took in the moment, savoring the easy camaraderie. Paul and Bob bickered playfully over baseball scores, Lizzy teased him about living alone, and Anna quietly observed, committing every detail to memory.

The joy of the evening masked the undercurrent of sadness threatening to surface.

Anna passed the mashed potatoes to Sam, blinking back tears. For years, she had protected him. Now she had to let go.

Under the table, Paul's hand slipped into hers, his warmth grounding her. He leaned in, whispering words that steadied her.

Across from them, Grandma Sophia sat back in her chair, hands folded in her lap. Though her tea had gone cold, she paid no mind. Her gaze remained fixed on Sam—her grandson, her anchor.

For years, Sam and Anna had been Sophia's greatest joy. After losing her daughter, Sarah, their laughter and quiet determination had kept her going. But as she watched Sam joking with Paul and sneaking one last bite of pie, a bittersweet ache settled deep within her.

He had always been her little helper—fetching her sweater, making her tea. Tomorrow, that routine would change.

Sophia had faced many goodbyes—her husband, her daughter, and now, in a different way, her grandson. She knew he was leaving to build his future, just as life intended. But that knowledge offered little solace.

Anna must have sensed her thoughts. She placed a warm hand over Sophia's.

"Grandma?"

Sophia looked up, forcing a smile that didn't quite reach her eyes. "Just thinking, sweetheart."

Anna studied her for a moment before speaking. "It's going to be different without him, isn't it?"

Sophia nodded, her throat tight.

"Yes… very different."

That night, as Sophia lay in bed, she listened to the familiar sounds of the house—Sam's footsteps, Anna's laughter, the wind rustling outside.

Soon, those sounds would become memories.

She closed her eyes and offered a prayer for Sam's safety, his happiness, and for the house to still feel like home, even in its quietude.

As the night wore on, Sam wandered through the house one last time.

He lingered in the kitchen, where he had often stolen bites of Anna's baking, the faint scent of cinnamon still drifting from the morning.

He paused in the living room, where family photos lined the shelves—his childhood captured in time, each frame a reminder of love and belonging.

And finally, when it was time for bed, Anna wrapped her arms around him and pressed her face to his shoulder. "I'm so proud of you, Sam."

He smiled, though his heart clenched at the thought of leaving.

"Don't worry," he murmured. "I'll be back before you know it."

But they both knew things wouldn't be the same.

As the house settled, stillness gathered—wrapping them in the pull of change.

By dawn, the house seemed to hold its breath.

That morning, it felt unbearably still.

The breakfast table—usually cluttered with Sam's half-finished toast and coffee—was impeccably clean. Too clean.

Sophia wandered into his room, her fingers brushing the neatly made bed.

His scent lingered—soap, cologne, and the faintest trace of the vanilla candles Anna always bought him as a joke. A reminder of warmth, now absent.

She sank onto the mattress, exhaling slowly.

She had known this day would come, but nothing prepares a mother—or a grandmother—for the empty spaces left behind.

Paul tried to keep things light, making conversation over breakfast, but even he found himself glancing at the door, half expecting Sam to walk in with one of his usual jokes.

And Anna, usually strong, was quieter than usual. Her smile remained—but just a little more forced.

That evening, Sophia sat in her rocking chair by the window, knitting needles in hand. But she barely made it through a row.

The rhythmic clicks echoed her restless thoughts.

She missed him already.

She missed the boy who once begged her to teach him how to make her famous stew—only to turn the kitchen into a disaster. The boy who always made sure she had a throw before they sat down to watch TV.

A deep sigh escaped her lips, heavy with nostalgia.

Then, as if on cue, the phone rang.

Anna answered, her eyes lighting up at once.

"Sam! You made it okay?"

Sophia closed her eyes, listening to the sound of Anna's laughter. A small smile crept onto her lips.

The warmth of that laughter wrapped around her, reminding her that even though Sam wasn't physically present, his spirit still filled their lives.

Sam wasn't gone.

He was just away—living the life they had raised him to have.

When the door clicked shut, the house didn't just fall silent—it changed shape.

The house would adjust.

She would adjust.

And in the meantime, she would hold onto these quiet moments, finding comfort in the love they had built.

Chapter 34

When time turns back

One year after Sam left for college, Anna and Paul sat in Dr. Williams' office, the sterile scent of antiseptic clashing with memories of their warm, familiar home.

The waiting room buzzed with quiet conversations, the rhythmic tapping of the receptionist's nails against her keyboard filling the space.

Anna shifted in her seat, a clipboard resting on her lap. She had just finished writing her name and date of birth and was now hesitating over the line marked *Reason for Visit*. Paul, ever the jokester, leaned toward her and said, "Do we write that we're here because we need to get pregnant?"

Anna laughed. Still, she scribbled something vague—family planning consultation—then paused, staring at the words for a second longer than necessary.

Her hand hovered, as if handing it in would make the idea too real. With a quiet breath, she stood and gave the form to the receptionist.

At first, it was nothing more than an idea. A wistful someday. But in the quiet of their home—mornings over coffee, slow walks through the park—the thought found a rhythm. Anna caught herself watching young mothers push strollers, lingering longer than she meant to.

They weren't trying, not exactly. But the silence that followed each month began to feel like its own kind of answer.

And still, they hoped.

Hope, she had learned, often shared a room with fear. A whisper of a dream could stir up memories you thought you'd tucked away.

So, when Dr. Williams greeted them with a warm smile and opened Anna's chart, it didn't feel like a fresh beginning. It felt like turning a page on something unfinished.

She asked the usual questions—menstrual cycles, lifestyle, stress levels—before pausing, her brow furrowing slightly.

"I see there's a history of cancer in your family. Your mother's side?"

Anna nodded, her fingers curling in her lap.

"My mom… yes. And my grandfather."

Paul reached for her hand, his grip gentle, grounding her.

Dr. Williams made a note before continuing.

"It's good to be aware of family history. It doesn't necessarily mean anything, but we like to be thorough. For now, I'd recommend a few preliminary tests before we consider a fertility specialist."

Anna exhaled, forcing a smile.

"Okay. That sounds good."

But as they stepped out into the crisp afternoon air, her thoughts weren't on the tests or the possibility of pregnancy.

They were on her mother.

And now, on her grandfather—the man she had never met but whose name had been spoken in hushed tones throughout her childhood.

She had grown up hearing stories about him. How he was strong and full of life before the illness took hold. How her mother had spent her teenage years watching him fade.

The cancer had taken him long before Anna was born. She never knew him, yet in moments like this, he felt close—like a shadow in the background of her family's history.

She had never truly considered what that meant for her own body.

The thought wrapped around her chest, unfamiliar and unwelcome.

A chill crept through her despite the crisp afternoon sun.

Paul's question broke through her thoughts.

"Penny for your thoughts?"

Anna hesitated, then shook her head.

"Nothing. Just thinking about Mom. And Grandpa."

Paul gave her a knowing look but didn't press. He squeezed her hand as they walked toward the car.

The engine roared to life just as Anna's phone buzzed, sharp against her palm.

She glanced at the screen.

Grandma Sophia.

Frowning, she answered.

"Hi, Grandma."

There was a pause—a slight shakiness in her grandmother's voice.

"Anna...I'm heading to the hospital."

Anna sat up straighter, heart thudding.

"What? What happened?"

"I haven't been feeling well. The nurse here thought it would be best if I got checked out."

Anna tightened her grip on the phone.

"Are you in pain?"

"A little, sweetheart. It's nothing serious. Just some discomfort, and they want to run tests."

Paul was already starting the car.

Anna's pulse quickened, but she kept her calm.

"We're on our way."

Grandma Sophia exhaled.

"Drive safe, dear."

The call ended, but Anna still held the phone to her ear for a moment, as if that could stop the uncertainty from closing in.

She turned to Paul. "Let's hurry."

Chapter 35

Lavender perfume lingers

The room lay in stillness, pierced only by the beep of monitors and the drone of the ventilator. Antiseptic filled the air, carrying with it the faintest echo of Sophia's lavender lotion.

Her frail frame rested against the pillows; her silver hair fanned over them like a halo.

Anna and Paul stepped inside, their movements barely disturbing the stillness. The crisp white sheets, the IV line trailing from Sophia's arm, and the gentle rise and fall of her chest—all felt unbearably fragile.

Then, Sophia's eyes fluttered open.

A slow, knowing smile curled at her lips—the familiar, mischievous one Anna knew so well.

"Well, you two took your sweet time. I thought I'd have to put in a room service request."

Paul chuckled, stepping forward to kiss her forehead.

"You had us worried, Grandma."

Sophia gave him a weak but playful wink.

"I just needed a change of scenery."

Paul took her hand and squeezed gently.

"Anytime, my lady. Anytime you need a change, our home is yours."

Anna sat on the edge of the bed, forcing herself to match her grandmother's lightheartedness, but the lump in her throat made it difficult.

Sophia still had laughter in her eyes, but behind it lay something heavier—a deep weariness that even humor couldn't mask.

Anna reached for her hand, smoothing over the delicate skin, paper-thin and cool beneath her touch.

"You scared us," she admitted.

Sophia sighed, a ghost of a smile lingering.

"Sweetheart, I've lived long enough to know that worrying doesn't change a thing."

Anna pressed her lips together, swallowing down the ache.

"But I can't help it," she murmured. "Not when it comes to you."

Sophia's hand curled around Anna's, the touch light but firm.

"Then let's make a deal," she said, her voice laced with exhaustion. "You keep worrying a little, and I'll keep being stubborn a little longer."

Paul smirked.

"Sounds like a fair trade."

Sophia chuckled, though it was faint.

The room felt warm—not from the heat, but from something deeper.

Love.

It was filled with memories, stories, inside jokes, and the legacy of a woman who had held her family together through every storm.

Anna squeezed Sophia's hand just a little tighter, committing this moment to memory.

Anna stepped into the corridor, bracing against the sterile air.

Dr. Jones stood before her, his hands folded in front of him, his expression heavy with something unspoken. The man had once been her mother's physician, and now he carried the same burden of delivering news she wasn't ready to hear.

He inhaled slowly as if choosing his words carefully.

"Anna…" he began, then paused.

A flicker of hesitation crossed his face before he met her eyes again.

She swallowed hard.

"Just tell me."

Dr. Jones exhaled, his tone quieter now.

"Her body is shutting down," he said finally. "The decline is happening faster than we expected. It won't be long now—maybe hours."

The words hit her like a physical blow. The air felt too thick to breathe, and the walls of the hospital corridor suddenly too close.

"Is she in pain?" she asked, her words barely above a whisper.

Dr. Jones held her gaze.

"She's comfortable for now. We'll do everything we can to keep it that way."

Anna nodded numbly, unable to speak.

Dr. Jones rested a hand on her shoulder.

"I know how much she means to you. Spend as much time with her as you can."

She forced herself to respond.

"Thank you, Doctor."

Anna returned to Sophia's room, not bothering to wipe away the tears that blurred her vision.

She stopped at the doorway, taking in the gentle rise and fall of her grandmother's chest, the scent of lavender that still lingered in the air.

Paul turned at the sound of the door, his eyes immediately locking onto hers.

He didn't ask. He didn't need to.

Without hesitation, he crossed the room and wrapped her in his arms.

Anna buried her face in his chest, gripping the fabric of his shirt as if it could hold her together. His warmth—it was the only thing keeping her grounded.

The faint crunch of leaves drifted through the quiet, a reminder that the world was still turning, even now. But in this room, time had slowed. Sophia stirred in her sleep, murmuring something Anna couldn't understand.

Anna watched her, heart aching, knowing this was one of the last moments she would have.

What could she possibly offer this woman, who had sheltered her from the storm that had once threatened to engulf them?

What could she give in return for a lifetime of love, of sacrifice, of unwavering strength?

Nothing—except a grateful heart.

Paul tightened his arms around her as if shielding her from the heartbreak that loomed ahead.

Anna exhaled shakily and pressed a kiss to his shoulder, seeking solace in his unwavering strength.

She wasn't ready—and knew she never would be.

But for now, she would hold onto every last moment in this quiet space between love and goodbye.

Sam arrived early, his presence a beacon of light in the heavy air.

The moment he stepped into the room, his eyes met Anna's, and without a word, he pulled her into a tight hug.

Lizzy and her husband followed soon after, their laughter and easy chatter bringing warmth to the room, a stark contrast to the solemnity that had settled over them.

For hours, they sat together, sharing stories and reminiscing about Sophia's sharp wit and boundless love.

Sophia, though weak, smiled as she listened, her tired eyes filled with quiet peace.

That night, when CreeksVille went quiet and the streets lay still and the conversations faded, Sophia drifted to sleep.

And in the stillness of the early morning, she slipped away.

Peaceful.

Loved.

Surrounded by the family she had protected and cherished for so many years.

The day of Sophia's funeral was overcast, a gentle breeze whispering through the trees. The small chapel brimmed with family and friends, each holding cherished memories of Sophia, the air thick with the sweet scent of flowers and the weight of grief.

Anna stepped forward to speak, her hands trembling slightly.

"Grandma Sophia was more than just a grandmother. She was our mother, father, and protector.

From a young age, she taught Sam and me the importance of kindness, resilience, and love. She showed us that even in the darkest times, there is always hope, and for us, she was that light.

Even after all she had lost, she never let it dim her kindness, giving Sam and me a home filled with love, laughter, and resilience.

She taught me how to braid my hair and held me when life got hard. Her strength was incredible, and her love was unconditional.

I promise to carry her legacy forward.

Thank you, Grandma, for being our everything."

She took a step back, her fingers tightening around the edges of the podium, blinking away the sting of tears.

Her fingers were trembling as she met Sam's eyes in the front row. For a moment, neither moved—then Sam rose and crossed the small space between them.

Anna folded into his embrace, the two of them holding on as tears slipped silently down her cheeks

When Anna finally released him, she gave a slight nod, and Sam took her place at the podium.

"When I think of Grandma, I think of warmth and comfort—like sunlight streaming through the kitchen window. She made everyone feel safe. Sure, we missed out on having our parents, but she gave us so much love that we never felt lacking.

I'll always treasure her stories, her hugs, and the way she believed in us.

I miss her, but I know she's watching over us, cheering us on like she always did.

We love you, Grandma."

Sam's voice cracked slightly on the last word, and he exhaled, running a hand through his hair as he stepped down.

The chapel fell quiet for a moment, the weight of their words settling like dust in the air.

As the service concluded, Anna felt goodbye press heavy in her heart. Yet as she stepped out of the chapel, she realized Sophia's love hadn't left—it lived on in them.

In the days that followed, grief ebbed, making way for something else—a quiet strength woven from all the love and resilience Sophia had left behind.

Anna and Sam often reminisced about their grandmother, sharing stories that brought warmth and laughter, celebrating her spirit rather than mourning her absence. They gathered in the kitchen, where the familiar scents of home-cooked meals filled the air, and felt her presence in every corner of the house.

Anna took comfort in continuing the traditions Sophia had instilled in them—baking her famous pot pie, hosting Sunday dinners, and sharing stories around the table. Each moment became a tribute, a way to honor her grandmother's memory.

One evening, as Anna and Paul sat on the porch watching the sun slip beneath the horizon, a quiet peace settled over her.

"We'll be okay, won't we?" she asked.

Paul took her hand and squeezed it gently.

"We will. We have each other—and we'll always carry her in our hearts."

In that moment, Anna realized that while the nest had changed, the love within it remained unwavering. They were embarking on a new chapter—not defined by loss but by the strength, resilience, and love that Sophia had instilled in them.

As the stars began to twinkle in the evening sky, Anna looked up, a smile breaking through her tears.

"Thank you, Grandma." She closed her eyes for a moment, letting the warmth of love settle in.

"We'll keep your spirit alive in everything we do."

Chapter 36

The unwelcome name

Sam arrived home from Yale, shoulders sagging under a burden heavier than the duffel bag on his back.

He had told Anna and Paul he had something important to discuss, but had refused to elaborate over the phone.

As he stepped into the dimly lit living room, the familiar scents of home enveloped him—wood smoke from the fireplace and the faint aroma of baked goods lingering from earlier in the day. Anna and Paul exchanged glances, their expressions a mix of concern and anticipation.

Perhaps he had good news about a summer legal internship or a major fellowship.

Life had changed in many ways since Sophia died—more than a year—yet the life growing inside her was a quiet, surprising mercy.

The morning sun streamed through the kitchen window. The smell of coffee lingered, but something unspoken pressed in, making the room feel too small for what needed to be said.

Paul and Sam sat at the kitchen table, stiff and tense, exchanging furtive glances like two boys caught sneaking out past curfew—clearly hiding something.

She noticed the way his hand tightened around the cup. Something told her this wasn't about law school at all.

Standing at the counter, Anna eyed them suspiciously as she poured herself a glass of orange juice, the citrus scent sharp and refreshing.

"Alright, what's wrong with you two?" she asked, setting the glass down with a thud. "You two look like you've been caught committing a crime."

Sam straightened and stood, pulling out a chair for her. "Sit down first," he said, his tone serious.

Anna narrowed her eyes but complied, resting a hand on her belly. "What's with the cat-that-ate-the-cream expressions?"

The room fell quiet, save for the clink of Paul's spoon against his cup.

Sam took a breath.

"Dad is back in town."

Anna blinked.

"Whose dad? Paul's?"

Paul gently took her hand.

"Your father."

"Jake Buchman?" Her eyes widened, disbelief flashing across her face. "Where? How? When?"

Sam shifted uncomfortably. "He called me yesterday," he admitted, voice low. "Said he was back in town and wanted to meet us."

"Who told him where we are?"

"It's my fault," Sam said.

Paul rose quickly to get her water. "What do you mean, your fault?" Anna asked, tension rising like steam.

Sam rubbed his hands together.

"When I went to clean out Grandma's things, I found a postcard—from him. From years ago. He wrote that he was sorry, that he'd come back someday, and that he needed money."

Anna's eyes narrowed.

"And?"

"There was a return address. I sent a letter. I told him who I was and asked if he wanted to meet us. I didn't think he'd reply—it was just an impulse."

Anna rose, her chair screeching. "You did WHAT?"

"Please, Sis. I didn't mean to hurt you. I never expected him to show up."

Anna shook her head.

"You are my only family, Sam. And this—this feels like betrayal."

Sam's eyes pleaded.

"I didn't mean it that way. I swear."

The silence that followed was thick and final, broken only by the faint hum of the refrigerator and the clatter of her own heartbeat in her ears.

The postcard—a ghost long buried—now stood before her, demanding to be faced.

The light of morning, the smell of coffee, the comfort of home—all of it blurred as Sam's words landed like a stone.

That same bitter scent had filled the kitchen years ago, when she clutched the phone with shaking hands, dialing a number she barely remembered. "This is Anna. Dad... Mom died. The social worker said they might have to put Sam in foster care. If you came, they wouldn't take him away. Please..." Her voice cracked with desperation. She left the message and waited by the window until night fell, but he never came.

That same abandonment rose up in her chest, burning fresh, hardening her resolve. "If you want to reconnect with him, that's your choice. But I want nothing to do with him."

She left, her anger trailing behind her like a shadow.
"Anna, please—" Sam's voice cracked behind her, but she didn't look back.

Chapter 37

Forgiveness is overrated

The café buzzed with espresso and sugar, but Anna couldn't taste any of it today.

She moved through the space with clipped motions, her usual rhythm lost. Trays clattered, parchment snapped, and cups clinked—each sound sharp, like it might crack something inside her.

Behind the counter, Lizzy paused mid-wipe on the espresso machine, raising an eyebrow just as Anna slammed a tray of cookies onto the counter. A few bounced off, landing on the floor with thuds. The scent of chocolate rose in the air.

Lizzy's brow lifted. "Well, that's one way to test gravity."

Anna leaned on the counter, palms pressed flat, her jaw tight. "I just—"

She let out a breath. "I can't deal with this today."

Lizzy rounded the counter and gently nudged her shoulder. "Talk to me. What's got you baking with rage?"

Anna didn't answer at first. She rubbed her temple, steam hissing behind her as the espresso machine whirred to life again.

Lizzy folded her arms, watching her. "If I had to guess, I'd say this isn't about cookies."

Anna's shoulders tensed. She leaned closer, her words barely audible. "Jake's back."

Lizzy froze. "Jake as in...your dad?"

Anna nodded, the name bitter on her tongue.

Lizzy gave a low whistle. "Damn. No wonder you're hurling baked goods."

A short, humorless laugh escaped Anna.

Lizzy squeezed her arm.

"Alright, babe. Let's leave the cookies alone and go clear your head. You want to walk to the ice cream shop?"

Anna hesitated, then yanked off her apron. "Let's go."

The bell above the ice cream shop door chimed as they entered. The air was cooler here, tinged with fresh strawberries, and the buttery sweetness of waffle cones baking in the back. The buzz of a blender rose behind the counter, mixing milk and chocolate into something smooth and numbing.

They found a corner booth by the window. Anna sat heavily, shoulders hunched, eyes distant.

Lizzy drummed her fingers lightly on the cold tabletop, watching Anna stare at a crumpled napkin in her hand.

"Still mad at the world?" Lizzy asked.

Anna shook her head slowly.

"Not mad. Just...tired."

Lizzy studied her.

"So… are you even thinking of seeing that jerk?"

Before Anna could answer, a teenage server approached with two towering sundaes. His apron hung crooked, and his messy hair looked like he'd combed it with his fingers.

He slowed as he neared them, reading the tension like a book. Still, he forced a smile and gave a goofy little bow. "Enjoy, ladies," he chirped, and then vanished as quickly as he came.

Lizzy chuckled. "At least someone's having a good day."

Anna smirked faintly and scooped up a bite of ice cream, letting it melt on her tongue. The cold sweetness offered the first real comfort she'd felt all day.

After a long pause, Lizzy asked, "Can you forgive him?"

Anna didn't hesitate. Her head moved once—a hard no, her mouth tightening into a grim line.

Lizzy tilted her head. "Why?"

Anna's eyes stayed on her spoon. The swirl of melting cream blurred, pulling her backward—

The living room was dressed for celebration—balloons bobbing, party poppers scattered, the smell of dinner drifting in from the kitchen. From her stool, she watched her mom hang streamers and call out,

"Jake, it's getting late. Can you pick up the cake?"

He didn't move, eyes glued to the game. The second time, he only shifted in his chair. The third, the TV went black as he hurled the remote onto the table.

"Stop nagging me! It's just a cake, woman!"

He stormed out. The door slammed, rattling the balloons on their ribbons. She ran after him, but the driveway was already empty.

Minutes later, tires crunched on gravel. She ran to the porch—only to see her grandmother step out, cake box in hand.

That slam of disappointment stayed with her, louder than his shouting ever had.

The memory snapped away, leaving only a cold hollow in her chest. She was back in the ice cream shop, her sundae half-melted in front of her.

"He abandoned us. He left our mom to raise two kids alone and never came back—not when she was sick, not even after she died." She stirred the melting cream in her bowl.

"Forgiveness assumes the person cares. They've earned it. He hasn't even said sorry."

Lizzy said nothing.

Anna's tone sharpened, rougher now. "He walked away from being a father. And the man I've seen—he didn't just make a mistake. He was never meant to be a father."

She stopped, breathing hard, her throat tight.

Lizzy reached over and gently rubbed her back. "Every time a man over sixty walks in, you look at the door, like you're bracing for him."

Anna blinked, caught off guard. She hadn't even noticed. "I guess...part of me hoped he might try," she said quietly. "But hope's not the same as forgiveness."

Dusk pressed gently against the windows, but inside, neon lights and a sugary haze wrapped the shop in warmth—a fragile pause between moments.

They ate the rest of their ice cream heavy with everything unsaid. Forgiveness, she thought, was overrated. All she'd ever wanted was a father who stayed. And even now, part of her still caught herself looking at the door.

Chapter 38

A new moon

Past midnight, Sam pushed open the birthing-room door.

The air was sharp with antiseptic, softened by the faint trace of floral air freshener. Light washed over Anna, where she lay against the pillows, her fingers gripping Paul's hand.

Monitors beeped steadily, nurses spoke in low tones, and the room shifted with the quiet rustle of fabric and the shuffle of footsteps.

Balancing two steaming cups of coffee, Sam stepped inside, the rich aroma cutting through the clinical atmosphere. When Paul had called to say Anna's water had broken, Sam had dropped everything and rushed to the hospital, his heart pounding with the thrill of becoming an uncle.

For Sam, this moment wasn't just about welcoming his niece—it marked the healing of the strained bond between him and Anna. The past months had been tense; their once-close relationship reduced to polite, hollow conversations.

Paul, ever the peacemaker, had worked tirelessly to mend their connection. The baby shower had been a turning point—apologies exchanged, heartfelt conversations unfolded, forgiveness extended. From that day on, no one mentioned Jake again.

Eight grueling hours passed in a blur of laughter, tears, and the primal sounds of childbirth. Each contraction brought a chaotic mix of pain and joy, filling the room with an energy unlike anything Sam had ever experienced.

"Coffee," Sam announced, his throat hoarse with excitement, as he handed Paul a cup.

Paul accepted it with a grateful nod, never letting go of Anna's hand.

Anna, her skin glistening with sweat, managed a breathless smile between contractions.

"You better be ready for uncle duties, Sam," she teased, her smile tight, her words pushed out through the strain but edged with determination.

Grinning, Sam pulled up a chair.

"I was born ready," he joked.

The lights cast a golden hue over the scene, creating an oddly peaceful moment amidst the chaos. But as the time neared, the atmosphere shifted.

A nurse moved swiftly to the control panel, and in an instant, the room shifted—soft light replaced by the stark glare of surgical lamps overhead.

Paul tensed beside Anna, his grip tightening around hers. The warmth of his hand was a tether in the whirlwind of emotions as nurses moved with practiced precision.

The doctor stepped forward, and the rhythmic beeping of the fetal heart monitor became the pulse of the moment.

Sam tightened his grip on his coffee cup, its warmth seeping into his palms as he braced himself. Then came a muffled cry from beyond the door—a sound that sent him racing down the hall.

In the waiting room, the air was thick with coffee and flowers, balloon ribbons bobbing, laughter too nervous to last.

Across the room, Lizzy tapped her foot absently, clutching a "Welcome, Baby!" balloon that bobbed with her movements. Beside her, Mrs. Riley smoothed the ribbon on a beautifully wrapped gift, fingers tracing the bow with careful precision.

A distant chime signaled the opening of a door.

All heads turned in unison.

A nurse emerged, clipboard in hand, scanning the room before offering a reassuring smile.

The collective breath of the waiting family hitched, bodies leaning forward as if to close the space between them and the long-awaited news.

Moments later, the doors swung open, and Sam's grin said it all before the words left his mouth. "It's a girl!" he shouted. "I'm officially an uncle!"

Cheers and laughter erupted, bouncing off the walls like a sweet symphony of celebration.

Back in the birthing room, Paul's hands trembled as he prepared to cut the umbilical cord. The enormity of the moment bore down on him. The nurse laid a steadying hand on his arm.

"You won't hurt them," she reassured gently.

Then, as dawn thinned the dark along the blinds, their newborn's first cry filled the room—like a melody breaking through stillness. The sound resonated deeply, bringing tears to Paul's eyes. Overcome with emotion, he turned to Anna. They held each other, their shared joy washing over them in a wave of love.

"Thank you," Paul murmured to the doctors and nurses, gratitude overflowing. He held Anna's hand as they both gazed at their tiny miracle, the cooing of their baby filling the space with a profound sense of wonder and completeness.

Sam, standing nearby, felt his throat tighten. Watching his sister step into motherhood stirred something deep within him. Stepping forward, he wrapped his arms around Anna and Paul. "I love you, Sis. I love you, Paul." A wide smile lit his face—he couldn't have been happier.

Bathed now in early light, the room pulsed with quiet joy, the air ripe with the magic of beginnings.

The nurse carefully swaddled the baby in a pastel blanket, the soft fabric cradling her tiny form. "Congratulations, Mom," she said warmly, placing the bundle into Anna's waiting arms.

Paul's parents stood nearby, faces alight with pride as they prepared to meet their granddaughter.

The door swung open, and Lizzy entered, carrying vibrant balloons and a bouquet of fragrant flowers, her presence enveloping the family in celebration.

The nurse smiled.

"Do you have a name for the baby?"

The room quieted, all eyes on Anna and Paul.

Paul looked at Anna, his smile brimming with love and pride. She nodded, joy radiating like sunshine.

Paul cradled their daughter in his hands, holding her like something sacred, fragile, and entirely his.

Slowly, he lowered himself onto the bed beside Anna, placing their daughter in her arms. Anna, still exhausted, gasped as she embraced their baby.

She felt impossibly light, yet in that moment, she carried the world.

Her voice, laced with deep emotion, carried across the room.

"Emma Sophia Riley."

The name rippled through the room—a tribute to love, legacy, and family. Cheers erupted once more, tears mingling with laughter as they celebrated the beginning of a new journey.

Later that morning, after the visitors had left, the nurse informed Anna that Emma would spend a little while in the nursery so she could rest.

Exhausted yet blissfully content, Anna drifted off to sleep, the beeping of monitors a lullaby in the background.

Paul drew Anna closer, his words trembling. "Emma Sophia Riley," he whispered, and then, with an unspoken vow: *I will show up every day. Not perfectly—faithfully.*

Above CreeksVille, the sky paled to morning light—a quiet promise of a bright future, a new chapter waiting to unfold in love and joy.

Chapter 39

Whispers before fall

Emma was one year old now, and life had never been busier—or more beautiful.

They marked her first birthday with balloons, cake, and the kind of laughter only a toddler can spark. Sam, back from his new life for the weekend, had insisted on an over-the-top display of streamers, and the little house rang with giggles and candlelight.

Anna never thought she could love someone so much. Emma was a whirlwind of curiosity, toddling on tottering steps, eyes wide, gummy grin flashing. Every day brought a new first—her first word, her first wobbly step, her first bite of cake.

She had smeared frosting across her cheeks, declared it "Mmm!" and sent Anna into such helpless laughter that tears had spilled down her face.

The rooms echoed with baby footsteps and the steady cadence of routine; a family wrapped in the comfort of its new rhythm. But beneath the joy, a change was moving—winds slipping through CreeksVille, unseen yet undeniable.

Flour dusted the counter as Anna rolled the dough, the warm smell of cinnamon filling the air—when the phone rang.

The call from Dr. Williams' office came on a Tuesday morning, right as Anna was rolling out the dough for the bakery's morning pastries.

The receptionist spoke with a politeness that carried a firm edge.

"Anna, it's time to schedule your annual check-up."

Anna glanced at the clock, sighing.

"You mean the one where you poke me with instruments in places I'd rather not talk about?" she deadpanned, wiping her flour-covered hands on her apron.

The receptionist chuckled. "That's the one."

Lizzy, overhearing from the counter, smirked.

"Yeah, Anna, sounds fun. Sign me up, too," she teased.

Anna rolled her eyes but reluctantly agreed to the appointment.

When the call ended, she muttered, "Maybe I should just ask for some stamina boosters and a magic elixir so I don't feel tired all the time."

Lizzy smirked. "I mean, if they're handing out energy potions, grab me one too."

Anna chuckled, but the humor faded almost as quickly as it came.

But hadn't she been feeling off lately?

Not in a way she could put into words—just a heaviness, a tiredness that stretched beyond sleepless nights and long workdays.

But sometimes, in the quiet before dawn, she felt as if her body was trying to whisper a secret she wasn't ready to hear.

Still, the wheels of time turned—slow, steady—carrying Anna toward something she could not yet see.

Chapter 40

Back in the memory lane

Anna followed the medical assistant into the exam room. Dr. Williams greeted her with a reassuring smile.

"How's little Emma?" Dr. Williams asked, beginning the routine pap smear.

Anna's face lit up. "She's almost walking now. Always on the move."

The thought made her smile, briefly cutting through her fatigue.

"Still breastfeeding?" the doctor asked, her hands gentle during the breast exam.

"No, she switched to formula a few months ago." Anna shifted. Her blouse clung lightly to her skin, but it was the pain in her limbs that concerned her most. "I've been so tired lately—but I guess that's motherhood, right?"

Dr. Williams nodded thoughtfully. "Let's check your iron and thyroid levels. I'll also schedule a mammogram, just to be safe."

The rustle of paper and the quiet ticking clock filled the space, echoing the unease in Anna's chest.

Anna stepped out of the clinic into the cool morning air. For a moment, the day looked ordinary—sunlight, traffic, the faint sound of children playing—but beneath it all, tomorrow's results pressed at her chest like a weight she couldn't shake.

Maybe it was nothing. Maybe vitamins. Or sleep.

By the time morning came, she clung to Emma's laughter as though it could steady her while the doctor's words still lingered.

The next day, golden light bathed the park as Anna pushed Emma gently on the swing, each arc sending a ripple of laughter into the air.

Paul stood nearby, camera ready. Just as he lifted it, Anna's phone buzzed in her bag. His rang too.

Paul checked the screen. Dr. Williams. His chest tightened.

"Hello?" he said, forcing himself to stay calm.

"Hi, this is the nurse from Dr. Williams' office. The doctor would like to review Anna's results—in person."

Paul's gaze shifted to Anna, still laughing as the sun streaked her hair. He forced a smile.

"Is everything okay?" he asked.

"We'll go over everything at the appointment."

He ended the call and crossed to her.

She caught the look on his face. "What's wrong?"

"The doctor wants to see you in person."

Anna's smile faltered. She wiped her palms on her jeans. "It's probably just my iron or thyroid. I've been tired for months."

Paul nodded, but unease pressed in like fog.

The next morning, the waiting room offered its usual illusion of comfort—pastel walls, faded parenting magazines, a play corner with tired toys. Antiseptic hung beneath hints of baby powder.

Expectant mothers rubbed their bellies. A young woman rocked a dozing infant. A toddler darted across the room, trailing giggles and her mother's sigh.

Paul sat beside Anna, tracing circles on the back of her hand. Overhead, an acoustic version of *"Can You Feel the Love Tonight"* gave way to *"Unchained Melody."*

He tilted his head. "Are lullabies for adults supposed to be soothing?"

Anna cracked a smile. "Someone's clinging to their 90s playlist."

Their laughter was brief—a pinhole of light in thickening tension.

Then the nurse stepped in and called her name.

It was time.

Dr. Williams welcomed them with a smile. She gestured for them to sit. "Anna, I wanted to go over your results personally."

Anna's fingers curled into her dress. Paul sat straighter beside her.

Dr. Williams exhaled.

"Your mammogram showed lumps in both breasts."

The words didn't crash down. They simply settled, heavy and final, stealing the air from her lungs.

Paul's thumb trembled against her hand, betraying the fear he could not hide.

Dr. Williams remained calm.

"Lumps like these are often harmless. This doesn't mean cancer, but with your background, we can't take chances. We need answers."

Anna blinked, the words hanging in the air, impossible to gather. The room seemed to fold in on itself, shrinking around her. Her hands knotted in her lap, as if holding herself together.

She nodded, though the motion felt distant, automatic—her body answering while her mind reeled.

Beside her, Paul cleared his throat. "What happens next?"

"First, a core-needle biopsy to confirm what we're seeing," Dr. Williams said. "If it's cancer, the lab will test the tissue for estrogen and progesterone receptors and HER2. Given your family history, I'll also refer you for genetic counseling and testing. I'll coordinate with the breast surgeon—we'll move quickly."

Anna managed another nod, but the air felt thinner now, the walls pressing in. Her chest rose shallow and uneven, each breath a reminder that nothing would ever feel routine again.

The lavender-scented calm was no match for the storm gathering inside her—one that threatened the rhythm of love, laughter, and ordinary days she had fought so hard to create.

Chapter 41

The beginning of fall

The following weeks blurred as Anna threw herself into the busyness of life, trying to outrun the fear gnawing at her from within. Paul buried himself in legal work, but his thoughts kept circling back to Anna—worry trailing him like a fog he couldn't shake.

Emma remained their anchor. Her laughter bounced off the walls, her toddling footsteps a melody of joy and distraction. In her innocence, she tethered them to the present, offering small, luminous moments of stillness in the growing chaos.

Three days after the biopsy, the waiting became unbearable. Every ring of the phone set their nerves on edge.

When the landline finally rang, they both flinched. Paul answered.

"Hi, Nurse Adams. Yes, speaking."

A pause.

"Okay. Sure, we'll be there… Do you have the results?"

"Alright. Thank you. We'll see you at 11 a.m."

Anna looked up, her stomach twisting.

"Well?"

"They want us to come in." Her whisper trembled. "If it were good news, they would've just told us." Paul pulled her into his arms. "Hey, let's not assume the worst," he said, though even he couldn't hide the catch in his throat.

That evening, he called Sam.

Sam arrived four hours later. They tried to act normal—passing around pizza, playing with Emma—but no one tasted anything. Conversations started and stalled. At one point, Sam reached for his drink only to realize his hands were clenched.

Anna sat nearby, motionless and still. The golden light of sunset stretched long shadows across the floor, but the warmth couldn't reach them.

The hospital air carried a faint medicinal crispness, the kind that settled in the lungs. A coffee machine whirred in the corner, and the front desk echoed with rhythmic typing.

Anna, Paul, and Sam walked slowly toward Dr. Williams' office. Anna's fingers were laced tightly through Paul's. Sam walked with his shoulders hunched. At the front desk, the receptionist glanced up. "Dr. Williams will see you in just a moment. Please have a seat."

The chairs lining the wall were stiff, designed more for waiting than comfort. Across from them, a father bounced a toddler on his knee. A soft-rock tune murmured from the speakers, blurring into background static.

Anna checked the clock. The second hand ticked forward, indifferent to the heaviness in her chest. Paul rubbed slow circles across the back of her hand.

Then the door opened.

"Anna," Dr. Williams said, stepping into the hallway with a calm, unreadable expression. Her gaze flicked to Paul and Sam, noting their tension.

"Come in."

The office smelled faintly of lavender. Sunlight streamed through the blinds, casting shadows across the polished desk. A closed folder waited between them.

Dr. Williams folded her hands, then looked up.

"I have your biopsy results."

Anna's grip on Paul's hand tightened. Sam leaned forward slightly, his jaw tense.

"The lumps are..." she paused. "They are cancerous."

The word dropped like a stone.

Anna didn't move.

Paul froze, as if his body didn't know how to process the word.

His grip on Anna tightened instinctively, but his wide eyes stayed fixed on Dr. Williams, searching for something in her face. There was none.

Sam inhaled sharply, the sound too loud in the quiet room. A flash of memory jolted through him—his mother's hospital bed, the beep of machines, the helplessness. He reached for Anna's hand, but stopped halfway, stunned.

No. Not Anna.

His hand hovered, unsure. She felt solid. Alive. But the fear of déjà vu slammed into him too hard to ignore.

He blinked, forcing himself back into the moment.

Dr. Williams turned gently toward him.

"Do you have any questions?"

He shook his head too quickly.

Paul still hadn't spoken.

Dr. Williams grew calm. "I know this is overwhelming. But you're not alone in this, Anna. We have a plan—and we'll walk through it together."

Anna stepped out of the clinic with Paul at her side, the world outside jarringly unchanged—cars rushing past, a mother pushing a stroller, a teenager laughing into her phone.

Everything looked normal, but inside, nothing was. She walked slowly toward the car, her arms folded tight across her chest, as if holding herself together.

Neither she nor Paul spoke on the drive home. The silence between them was heavy, but not empty—it was filled with all the words they couldn't bring themselves to say.

By the time they pulled into the driveway, Anna had already decided: she couldn't let Emma see her fear, couldn't let Sam or Lizzy feel it yet. She needed to breathe first. To sit. To find her footing.

Chapter 42

The weight of knowing

The following three months unfolded like a chaotic storm of medical appointments and evaluations. Each day brought a flurry of tests—blood draws, scans, and consultations with a team of specialists. The uncertainty of the prognosis hung like a dark cloud over any lingering optimism.

Yet, amidst the daunting news, the realm of cancer treatment showcased remarkable innovations, offering a faint yet persistent glimmer of hope that fueled their determination to fight.

Anna chose Dr. Barry, a renowned specialist in breast cancer, to oversee her treatment. After further tests, his expression remained calm but serious as he delivered the results.

"The cancer has spread to your lymph nodes."

Anna barely reacted. It was as if her mind had already braced for the worst.

Paul, however, stiffened beside her, his jaw clenching for just a moment before he exhaled, the news pressing down between them.

Dr. Barry outlined treatment options, weighing benefits against risks.

He spoke confidently, detailing how each approach could impact Anna's health journey.

But as the doctor spoke, Paul felt a growing sense of unease. Despite the thorough presentation, he couldn't shake the feeling that they needed another opinion—one more perspective, one more path not yet explored.

His mind raced with quiet questions. Were these truly the best options? Was there something they were missing?

Determined to leave no stone unturned, they agreed to seek a second opinion. They owed it to themselves—and to Emma—to be absolutely sure.

So, they flew to New York, chasing both clarity and the faint hope that maybe—just maybe—Dr. Barry had been wrong.

Even Sam had flown in for the appointment. His presence was quiet but solid, a reassuring force beside them.

He didn't speak much, but just having him there steadied something in Anna, like an anchor dropped deep into a shifting tide.

A week later, they arrived at Mount Sinai Hospital. The stark white walls and distant machinery felt both eerily familiar and entirely foreign.

The sterile air carried the faint aroma of coffee from a nearby café cart—a bitter reminder of the long hours spent waiting.

The waiting room buzzed—voices low, names called, nurses' shoes clicking on polished floors.

Finally, a medical assistant called Anna's name and guided them into a consultation room.

The doctors reviewed her case and confirmed what Dr. Barry had already told them.

Stage three cancer.

Stage three cancer. The words fell like an anchor, settling heavily in the silence that followed.

Anna sat perfectly still. Her fingers tightened slightly around the armrest of her chair. She had prepared herself, but hearing it again made it painfully real.

Paul reached over, resting his hand protectively on hers. He asked a few questions, as if breaking the diagnosis into manageable pieces could somehow ease its edge.

The doctors outlined a comprehensive treatment plan—chemotherapy, surgery, and radiation. A grueling road. Each step necessary. Each one fraught with uncertainty.

When they left the hospital, the New York air felt heavier than before. The city moved around them with its usual pace—taxis honking, pedestrians rushing, sirens wailing—oblivious to the upheaval that had just shifted their world.

Anna exhaled, watching her breath vanish in the crisp air, as though even the world was stealing pieces of her. The chill sank deep, a physical echo of the news now resting on her shoulders.

In the backseat of the cab, she lifted a hand to her collarbone. The lump in her throat had passed, but the phantom weight of it lingered, like a bruise beneath the skin.

Paul cut through her thoughts.

"We'll take it one day at a time," he said, gently squeezing her hand. "We'll get through this together."

Anna turned to him, searching his face. There was no hesitation, no fear—just love, solid and unwavering.

Sam nodded from the other side. "You're not alone, Anna. We've got this."

His words lit a quiet flame inside her—small, flickering, but real. Despite the fear, despite the unknown, something shifted. A thread of resolve tightened between them, invisible yet unbreakable.

Chapter 43

Déjà vu

The drive back home felt longer than ever, though Sam knew it was just his mind playing tricks on him. The road stretched ahead in muted colors—faded yellows, deep oranges, and stubborn patches of green refusing to surrender to the season.

The sky hung low and gray, the fading afternoon light fragile as glass. Along the roadside, leaves lay decaying—autumn giving way to winter, just as his own certainty gave way to fear.

His hands tightened on the wheel, the leather cold against his palms. He remembered Paul's call—the composure in his brother-in-law's tone even as the word cancer lodged in Sam's chest like stone.

Their mother's battle had shaped so much of his childhood, and now history was repeating itself in the cruelest way.

His stomach churned at the thought of walking through the front door. Would Anna look weaker? Would Paul falter? And Grandma…if she were still here, she'd know what to say. Without her, they all felt unmoored.

As he passed the familiar road sign welcoming him back to town, CreeksVille's lights flickered in the distance. The streetlamps cast golden pools across the damp pavement. The town hadn't changed, but everything in Sam had.

Anna's diagnosis had struck like a freight train, dredging up memories of their mother's illness. He could still see Anna then—a girl forced to grow up too fast, shielding him from the harshest truths, carrying a burden no child should. He remembered her tucking him in after their father failed to show up for their mother's funeral.

Determined to support her, Sam resigned from the law office and moved back home. Losing Anna was unimaginable, but what she needed most was unwavering hope—his belief that she was strong enough to overcome this.

With every passing mile, Sam felt a renewed sense of purpose. He wasn't just returning to a house—he was returning to his family.

He vowed to create a circle of strength around Anna, alongside Paul, Lizzy, Bob, and everyone who loved her.

By the time Sam pulled into the driveway, darkness had settled fully. The house was warm, and light spilled from the windows onto the front porch like a comforting beacon.

Through the glass, he saw Paul rocking Emma in his arms, her tiny form curled against his chest. The sight sent an unexpected pang through Sam's heart—a reminder that life hadn't stopped moving, even while his world had ground to a halt.

Paul spotted him through the window, carefully laid Emma down, and stepped outside. The cold air hit them both, invigorating and sharp, woodsmoke drifting from somewhere in the distance.

Without a word, Paul pulled Sam into a tight hug. "Glad you're home," Paul said, words rough with emotion. Sam swallowed hard, nodding. "Me too."

Inside, the warmth of the house enveloped him. The fire crackled in the hearth, filling the air with the scent of burning oak. The aroma of baked lasagna lingered, mingling with the faintest trace of lavender from Anna's favorite candles.

"Starving," Sam admitted when Paul asked about food.

"Lasagna's in the oven," Paul said with a grin.

After a shower, Sam sat down beside him in the kitchen.

Their talk was light, but the silence beneath it carried the weight of what lay ahead. Forks clicked softly against their plates, the sound almost hushed.

Sam knew he was no longer the little boy who had once idolized Paul. He was a man now—ready to stand shoulder to shoulder with him for Anna and Emma.

Chapter 44

A circle of courage

The house was unusually quiet, the kind of stillness that only came with late evenings when the world had settled into a lull. The clock on the wall ticked steadily, marking time in a way that felt both grounding and unbearably heavy.

Lizzy sat curled up on the couch, her hands wrapped around a cooling mug of tea. The porch sat in restless silence, every passing gust a reminder that fall was deepening, that time was moving on without her consent.

Her heart was heavy with disbelief. The vibrant, seemingly healthy friend she had always known was now facing breast cancer. Lizzy replayed the signs she had brushed off—Anna's fatigue, her weight loss—thinking them just the struggles of new motherhood.

Guilt gnawed at her. Should she have seen it sooner? Could she have done more?

Bob, ever the constant presence, wrapped his arms around her.

"Lizzy," he said, "you couldn't have known. Anna is strong— she's faced so many challenges before, and I believe she'll overcome this too." His grip on her shoulder was firm, despite the fear in his eyes.

"She will beat this cancer. However, we must be strong for her. Paul, Emma, Sam—they need us now more than ever.

And the café staff need your strength too.

We have to create a hopeful environment around Anna."

Tears streaked Lizzy's cheeks. Bob's words sparked a flicker of resolve. "You're right," she whispered. "I won't let her down."

News of Anna's diagnosis spread quickly through the café. The clamor of conversation dulled, and the usual cheer grew heavy.

Many had watched Anna grow up, and the thought of her facing such a battle was devastating. But soon, grief turned to determination.

"She's beaten odds before," one staff member said quietly. "She'll beat this too."

They began planning small acts of kindness—dropping off meals, covering shifts. The café turned into a hub of quiet hope, an unspoken promise to stand by Anna.

Despite the challenges, a sense of unity grew. Sam's return, Paul's presence, Lizzy and Bob's resolve, and the café's loyalty wove together into a foundation Anna could lean on.

One crisp morning, Sam stepped onto the porch where she sat sipping tea, her gaze on the garden they once tended together. He sat beside her, and the pause between them held only birdsong and the whisper of leaves.

"Remember when we tried planting tomatoes?" he asked, a smile tugging at his lips.

Anna laughed, eyes bright with memory. "It turned into a jungle of weeds."

"Better than the time we tried baking. That cake could've been used as a brick."

"Hey, at least we tried," Anna teased, a smile tugging at her lips.

Their laughter faded, leaving everything unspoken behind. Sam took a breath, his resolve hardening.

"Anna, no matter what happens, we'll face it together. You're not fighting this alone. I promise."

Tears welled in her eyes, but they were not of despair. "I know," she said steadily. "And that gives me strength."

The morning sun spilled golden light across the porch, catching in her hair. The fight ahead would be long, but they were ready—armed with laughter, love, and an unshakable belief in brighter days. They had weathered storms before: a mother gone too soon, a grandmother whose wisdom still lingered, and a father who had never truly stayed. Together, they would weather this one too. And as Anna sat bathed in sunlight, surrounded by love, fear receded just enough to let readiness take root

Chapter 45

Spirit of colors

Anna's life had become a whirlwind of appointments and trips to New York. But today was different—today was her first chemotherapy session at CreeksVille Baptist Hospital.

Determined not to let fear take control, she slipped a notebook into her bag, planning to sketch out new café menu ideas while the drip ran.

The corridor smelled sharply of antiseptic, and her footsteps echoed on the polished floor. She braced herself for what she imagined: a bleak room, disinfectant in the air, patients staring numbly at the walls.

Instead, when the nurse opened the door, a burst of laughter greeted her.

The chemo unit buzzed with conversation, machines beeping in rhythm with the chatter. Pastel walls glowed beneath wide windows, spilling sunlight across the floor. Even the air carried a faint trace of lavender, as if calm had been stitched into the room itself.

Anna hesitated, surprised by the gentleness of it all. Paul squeezed her hand.

The nurse smiled as she settled the IV line. "See? Not so bad."

Across the room, a group of patients waved them over. Their IV poles stood like flags, but their smiles were alive with mischief.

"Are you new?" an elderly man called.

"Yes," Paul said carefully.

"What are you in for?" a woman in neon-pink boots asked, grinning.

"I'm just here with my wife."

"Chemotherapy," Anna added quietly.

The group burst into laughter, bright against the buzz of machines.

"What, you thought we were here for a bingo night?" one teased.

"We do play," Purple deadpanned. "Winner gets the good blanket."

Laughter rolled. Anna's own laugh slipped out, unguarded, and the knot in her chest eased, as though fear had been holding its breath too.

"So, you're here to support her, then?" another woman asked.

"Yes," Paul said firmly.

"Perfect. Make yourself useful." A woman with knitting needles didn't look up. "Coke from the vending machine, please."

"And Skittles for me!" added Pink Boots, wiggling her foot like a signal flag.

Paul chuckled. "Yes, ma'am."

By the time he returned, Anna was laughing with the group. Her earlier fear forgotten.

The sight swelled his chest with gratitude.

Thank you, God.

As the weeks passed, Anna grew more confident. She added long walks to her routine, tried yoga with Lizzy, and allowed herself guilt-free naps with Emma curled against her.

But the surprise was this: she began to look forward to her chemo sessions.

The once-daunting unit had become a circle of friendship.

Each woman went by a color—playful aliases that kept the focus on living.

"Colors make it easier," Purple explained one afternoon, guiding Anna's first clumsy knitting stitches. "If someone recovers or passes, their color is passed on. It helps us look forward, not back."

Pink, with her neon boots and endless one-liners, turned IV drips into punchlines.

Purple, calm, always knew when to lean in with advice. Yellow, with her flirty laugh and habit of calling everyone *darling,* kept the room sunlit even on the hardest days.

And when the previous Magenta rang the bell and left, the name passed to Anna.

It fit. Bold. Spirited. Resilient.

Together, they swapped recipes, parenting hacks, and stories of love. Illness rarely entered the conversation; laughter did instead.

In this circle of warriors, Anna found unexpected strength.

Paul marveled at her change. She still carried fatigue, still fought nausea, but her laughter—gentler now, yet true—had returned.

One evening, Anna opened her café notebook and wrote her new name across the top: *Magenta*. She paused, smiling.

Life's fiercest storms, she realized, sometimes delivered hidden gifts.

And this one had given her friendship as vivid and enduring as color itself.

Chapter 46

Life whispers again

The bakery was always special, but during the holidays, it took on a storybook quality. Garlands looped across frosted windows, the air thick with cinnamon and warm pastries, an irresistible invitation against the drifting night.

Now working full-time beside Lizzy during the holiday rush, Sam fell into the rhythm of the bakery. Customer chatter, peals of laughter, and the ring of the cash register filled the space—ordinary noises that, if only briefly, shielded him from the ache of Anna's illness.

Sometimes, when he caught the sweet smell of gingerbread or saw a child press a mittened hand to the glass, Sam felt a pang—remembering how Anna used to stand in this very spot, laughing as she dusted croissants with sugar.

Each morning, the display cases gleamed with seasonal delights—peppermint macarons, gingerbread cookies laced with delicate icing, and warm apple turnovers drizzled with caramel—each treat a testament to her creativity and passion.

Customers wrapped in thick scarves and wool coats streamed in, shaking off the cold as they ordered steaming coffee and rich hot chocolate piled high with whipped cream.

And for a moment, with the ovens warming the air and the snow falling softly outside, Sam could almost believe life was as bright and simple as the season made it seem.

"Hey," Lizzy said, nudging him lightly as she passed. "You're staring at those cookies like they've personally offended you."

Sam blinked, pulled from his thoughts, and managed a faint smile. "Just thinking," he said, reaching for a tray of turnovers.

Lizzy studied him for a beat longer, her expression softening. "She'd be proud, you know—seeing you here, keeping this place running."

Sam swallowed hard but nodded, the lump in his throat making it impossible to speak. Lizzy didn't press, just patted his shoulder before turning back to the counter.

The moment passed, and soon the bell over the door jingled again, ushering in more customers and pulling Sam back into the present.

Holiday music played from the old speakers in the corner—Bing Crosby crooning about a white Christmas.

Lizzy, moving quickly behind the counter, nudged Sam playfully.

"Hey, you're getting pretty good at those candy cane croissants," she teased, nodding toward the tray he had just pulled from the oven.

Sam smirked, dusting his hands off on his apron.

"I learn from the best," he said, handing a croissant to a little girl bundled in a puffy red coat. She grinned up at him before taking a big bite, her eyes lighting up as the flaky pastry melted in her mouth.

Despite the festive energy, Sam carried Anna's battle with him. The bakery made life feel almost normal. Almost.

The holidays were different this year. But amid the chaos of flour-dusted countertops and peppermint-scented air, Sam found comfort in the small joys—the laughter of customers, the twinkling lights, and the knowledge that, for now, he was exactly where he needed to be.

One night, the bakery finally settled into a peaceful hush. The once-bustling space was now dimly lit under the overhead lamps, shadows stretching across the empty tables.

Melissa lingered behind, methodically wiping down the counters. The rhythmic swish of the cloth against the stainless steel was the only sound filling the quiet kitchen.

The once-full display cases were now nearly empty, with a few scattered crumbs as the only remnants of the day's rush.

Sam had been quiet all evening, moving through the motions with a faraway look in his eyes. As he stacked the last trays in the drying rack, the words slipped out before he could stop them.

"You ever have one of those nights where you're just... tired?" His voice was low, hesitant, as though saying it aloud made the feeling too real.

Melissa set down the damp cloth and glanced over. "Every night in December," she teased lightly, but when his usual smirk didn't come, her expression softened, her gaze turning warm.

The town had gone still. Snowflakes drifted lazily through the air, catching in the glow of the streetlights, the quiet beauty of the late-night hour wrapping the bakery in its own hush.

"You like living here, don't you?" he asked, leaning against the counter.

Melissa gave him a curious glance.

"I do. I always have."

Sam hesitated before asking, "You never thought about leaving? Going somewhere bigger?"

Melissa dried her hands on a towel before turning to him.

"I used to. When I was younger, I thought I'd go to the city to find a job in some fancy bakery. But... I don't know. This place is home."

Sam studied her, something unreadable in his expression.

"I don't know if I could stay here forever," he admitted.

"You don't have to," Melissa said gently. "Just because you leave doesn't mean you have to stay gone."

Sam didn't respond right away. He just nodded, but Melissa saw it—the way his jaw tightened, the way his fingers tapped against the countertop.

A part of him longed to chase opportunities beyond CreeksVille, but another part of him wondered if leaving meant losing something he didn't want to live without.

Melissa, now the head of the kitchen, couldn't shake the feeling that something was troubling Sam. His usual vibrant energy seemed dimmed, replaced by a quietness.

Over the years, she had watched Sam grow from a determined teenager into someone she deeply admired. But lately, his quietness worried her—and it had stirred something deeper within her. She no longer saw him as just a friend.

Melissa approached Sam with two bowls of steaming minestrone,

"Lunch by the fire?" she offered with a smile.

Sam paused, then nodded, a faint warmth in his eyes. They settled near the crackling fire, the aroma of soup wrapping around them like a comforting embrace.

He was about to take his first spoonful when Melissa's hand came to rest gently over his. "How are you holding up, Sam?" she asked, her voice quiet but steady.

Sam nodded, then hesitated, the spoon lowering back to the bowl. "Good," he said, making a half-hearted attempt to lift the spoon again.

Melissa studied him for a moment, her thumb brushing lightly across his knuckles. "You look like a volcano about to erupt," she said gently, a touch of teasing in her voice meant only to ease the weight between them. Her fingers tightened around his. "I'm here if you ever need to talk."

Sam let out a breath that was almost a laugh. "Will you let go of my hand if I promise?"

Melissa smiled softly but didn't let go right away.

Their laughter softened the heaviness between them. In that quiet moment, something shifted for Sam—Melissa wasn't just his "buddy" anymore. And that realization scared him.

One frosty December evening, while Anna and Paul were visiting a specialist in New York, Sam stayed behind to care for Emma. Melissa arrived with warm food as the snow fell heavily, braving the worsening storm.

Hearing her car in the driveway, Sam rushed to open the door. Melissa bundled up against the biting cold, stepped inside, carrying bags of food.

"Are the roads okay?" Sam asked, his brow furrowing with concern.

"Barely made it. The storm hit just before I got here," Melissa replied, shaking the snow off her coat.

"Stay warm by the fire," Sam said, draping a woolen throw over her shoulders. "I'll plate the food."

After dinner, they sat by the fire, jazz curling through the quiet. Beyond the windows, snow swept in wild, silvery sheets, but the turbulence inside was far harder to contain.

Melissa, sensing the moment, finally spoke up.

"Sam," she began, her fingers twisting together, "I feel like there's something we need to talk about. We've been dancing around it for too long.

Sam turned to her, his expression guarded but curious.

"I've been worried about you," Melissa admitted. "And... I care about you, Sam. More than just as a friend."

Her words hung in the air, and Sam sat unmoving. The blizzard swept across the glass, his own unease rising just as fierce.

"Melissa," he said, eyes dropping. "I'm scared of losing what we have. You're my best friend, and...I don't know how to handle this. My life is in chaos right now—with Anna, my career, and everything else. You deserve better than someone still trying to figure it out."

Melissa met his gaze, her eyes filled with understanding.

"Sam," she said gently, "you'll never lose me. I can't pretend I don't feel something more. I love you. We'll figure it out—there's no rush."

Sam felt a wave of relief and emotion wash over him. He pulled Melissa into a tight embrace, anchoring himself in her warmth.

He exhaled slowly. "You mean so much to me, Melissa."

Melissa smiled, her hand still resting on his. "I know. And I'll be here, no matter how long it takes."

For a long moment, he just looked at her, his heartbeat hammering against his ribs. He had spent years keeping his emotions locked away—first for Anna, then for his career, then because he didn't know how to stop running.

But Melissa wasn't asking him to have it all figured out. She was just asking him to give it a try.

He swallowed hard and reached for her hand. His fingers trembled, but Melissa didn't pull away. Instead, she gave his hand a gentle squeeze.

He exhaled and pressed his forehead to hers. The walls he'd built around his heart finally gave way.

The tension melted, replaced by something quiet and certain. The storm outside raged, snow sweeping in wild, silvery sheets and rattling the windows, but inside, a different calm took hold.

Firelight painted their faces in gold, as though the world had paused just for them.

As the storm howled, they stayed wrapped in each other's warmth, knowing the road ahead would be uncertain and filled with challenges. But in that moment, nestled by the fire, they found solace in the promise of something beautiful—something worth fighting for.

Chapter 47

Go on and on

Anna worked in a controlled frenzy. She had double-checked the event order that morning—a large wedding cake for Pine Valley Hotel—but now, staring at the confirmation email, she realized there was a second cake order for another event—one she had completely overlooked.

Her stomach plunged. Two cakes. Same deadline. Not enough hands.

Lizzy peered over her shoulder and let out a low whistle. "Wow. This is bad."

Anna shot her a glare. "Not helpful."

"Hey, I'm just saying—unless you have a secret twin, we will need a miracle."

She ran a hand over her forehead, already feeling the sweat building. "I'll call Melissa. If she can handle decorating one while I bake the other, we might make it work."

Minutes later, Melissa arrived, rolling up her sleeves without hesitation.

"Tell me what needs to be done," she said, a grounding presence amidst the chaos.

As Anna scrambled to prepare the second cake, she kept glancing at Melissa, watching her work with an efficiency that rivaled her own. Every piped swirl of frosting, every carefully placed decoration—it was seamless.

Now, Anna saw it clearly. Melissa wasn't just helping—she was leading.

For the first time, Anna saw her bakery's future without her—and it didn't terrify her. It steadied her.

Ever since scaling back after starting chemo, Anna had wondered if stepping away from the bakery meant losing a part of herself. But standing there, watching Melissa step up, she felt something she hadn't expected—relief.

The bakery was in good hands.

Lizzy popped in just as Anna was wiping her flour-dusted hands on her apron. "Come on, superstar," Lizzy said, nudging her. "Melissa's got this, and I've got Emma. You, on the other hand, have an important date with a recliner and an IV drip."

Anna forced a smile. "I hate that chair."

"Yeah, well, I bet it hates you, too. But you're going to beat this, and I'll be right here spoiling your daughter until you do."

As Anna washed her hands and removed her apron, a new kind of relief began to settle in. It wasn't just about handing over the bakery—it was about trusting someone else to take care of something she had built.

The thought of taking a step back wasn't as terrifying as it had been a few weeks ago. If anything, she felt lighter.

She glanced at Melissa, who was finishing the last cupcake.

"You're staring at me like a proud mom," Melissa teased, piping the last swirl of frosting onto a cupcake.

"Maybe I am," Anna said softly, watching her work.

But the truth was, she had finally come to believe that the bakery would be okay without her.

Flexing her fingers, a familiar motion stirred a memory she hadn't touched in years.

She had been five or six, standing on a kitchen chair and running her tiny fingers through a mound of flour. "It's so soft!" Her face lit up in surprise.

Her mother had laughed, wiping her own hands on a towel. "That's because you haven't learned the messy part yet."

She had watched her mother measure out flour with practiced hands. "Baking is like magic," her mother had told her, tapping a bit of flour onto Anna's nose. "You mix a few things together, and suddenly, you have something new. Something warm. Something good."

Anna giggled, reaching into the dough to grab a handful. "I wanna do magic too."

Her mother had only laughed, gently prying the sticky mess from her fingers.

"You will, baby. One day, you'll do more magic than you know."

That memory hit her at random moments—when she was kneading dough in the bakery, when she tucked Emma into bed, and when she sat beside Paul in the hospital, his fingers curled around hers.

And sometimes, when she was alone, she repeated the words to herself:

You will do more magic than you know.

She stepped into the cold, the bakery lights still shining behind her. Through the window, Melissa set out a tray of her own cookies—a simple mark of trust taking hold.

A few weeks ago, that thought would have stung. Now, it felt like a relief.

She exhaled, watching her breath curl into the cold night.

Today wasn't about the bakery. It wasn't even about letting go. Today was about fighting for herself.

Today, Anna was ready to embrace her journey, filled with hope, resilience, and the belief that magic could still happen, even in the most unexpected of places.

That night, Anna sat in the living room, staring at the flickering fireplace. The house was quiet—Emma was asleep, and Paul had just put away the last of the dishes.

She didn't hear him approach her until she felt his warm hands on her shoulders. "What's on your mind?" Paul asked.

Anna swallowed, still staring at the flames. "I don't know if I can do this.

It's just...I already feel like I've lost so much. My strength, my hair...parts of who I used to be. And now..."

Paul took her hand, threading his fingers through hers. "It's a part of you, Anna. But it's not you."

Anna let out a shaky breath. "What if I don't feel like myself after?"

Paul turned to her, his gaze unwavering. "If you lose pieces of yourself, Anna, I'll hold them until you're ready to take them back."

Tears welled in her eyes, but she no longer felt alone in her fear.

By the next morning, Anna had made up her mind. She gathered Paul, Sam, and Lizzy in the kitchen, their eyes filled with quiet expectation.

"I'm doing the surgery," she announced.

Paul exhaled, relief breaking through his expression. Sam nodded firmly. Lizzy, ever dramatic, clutched her chest as if she had been waiting for an Oscar-worthy announcement. "Finally," she huffed. "I was about to stage an intervention."

Anna chuckled despite herself, grateful beyond words for their unwavering love. "I believe it," she said, meeting Lizzy's grin with one of her own.

Paul stepped beside her and reached for her hand. "We've got you."

Anna squeezed back, her fingers strong.

This wasn't only a fight for survival. It was a choice for life. And she was finally ready to claim it.

Chapter 48

Juice girls meet again

The surgery was scheduled for the following week.
Anna wasn't ready.

But then again, she hadn't been ready for any of it.
Still, she kept going—because deep down, she knew she wasn't fighting for herself alone.
She was fighting for Paul, for Sam, for Emma.
And she wasn't doing it alone.

After the surgery, she still had to go through chemotherapy.
At the chemo unit, Anna found comfort in the familiar faces of her treatment group—the nods, the gentle smiles, the unspoken understanding.
"Glad to see you again, Anna," one of them quipped with a wry smile. "But sad you're still here. Never mind, good luck this time!"
Their humor and camaraderie were the only bright spots in the grueling sessions.

By the third session, Anna barely recognized herself in the mirror. The weight loss, the pale skin, the way her hands trembled whenever she tried to button her coat—it was overwhelming.
She had expected the exhaustion, but she hadn't anticipated feeling like a stranger in her own body.
Paul was there, as always. He carried her bags, helped her into the recliner, and made small talk with the other patients—acting as if everything was fine.
But Anna could see it, the way his hands clenched whenever the IV needle slipped into her vein.
"You're still bad at pretending," she murmured, leaning back into the chair as the first drops of the chemo cocktail dripped into her bloodstream.

Paul exhaled sharply, rubbing the back of his neck.

"And you're still annoyingly perceptive." She smiled faintly, closing her eyes.

"At least one of us is."

She listened to the distant chatter of other patients trying to pretend that this wasn't the worst place in the world to be.

Then, a familiar call she hadn't heard in weeks pulled her from her thoughts.

"Purple's gone," said a woman in the chair beside her.

Anna turned her head slowly to see Helen, one of the chemo group regulars, twisting a tissue between her fingers.

"Gone?" Anna echoed, though she knew exactly what Helen meant.

Helen nodded.

"Last week. Didn't even make it to his final cycle."

Anna felt a lump rise in her throat. She had never learned his real name—just like that, another chair was empty.

Paul reached for her hand and squeezed.

Anna swallowed hard, forcing herself to breathe through the ache in her chest.

Not now. Not here.

"You okay?" Paul asked.

Staring blankly at the wall across from her, the sterile whiteness of the room felt suffocating, a reminder of everything she was battling.

The empty chair where Purple used to sit loomed large in her mind, a stark reminder that the fight against cancer was not just a personal struggle—it was a relentless war that many did not survive.

Anna's voice broke as she spoke. "I don't think I can do this anymore."

Paul's head snapped toward her.

Sam, who had been scrolling absently on his phone, froze.

"Anna—" Paul started.

"No, Paul. I can't.

I can't keep doing this."

Her fingers curled into the blanket.

"I look in the mirror, and I don't even know who I am anymore. I can't taste food. I can't sleep without feeling like my body is turning against me."

Her eyes brimmed with tears. "And now people are disappearing. And what if, one day, it's me?"

The words burst out before she could stop them.

Sam made a choked sound, his breath catching.

Paul flinched.

She had never said it out loud before.

She had never let herself.

Tears slid down her face. Paul reached for her, but she shook her head.

Her chest rose and fell in shallow, uneven gasps. "I don't want to die, Paul."

It was barely a whisper.

Sam sucked in a sharp breath and pushed himself up from the chair so fast it scraped against the linoleum.

"Don't say that," he snapped. "Just—don't."

Anna turned her head to look at him, startled.

Sam's fists clenched, his knuckles bone-white. His chest rose unevenly, his body trembling as if he might shatter.

He looked furious—and terrified.

"You're not dying," he ground out.

"You're Anna. You beat everything. You don't get to—" He turned away, rubbing a hand over his face.

Paul stared at the floor, his hands clasped together tightly.

For a long moment, no one spoke.

Anna had never seen Sam like this.

She had been the strong one his entire life. The big sister. The one who took care of him when their mother got sick, the one who made him feel safe.

And now, he looked at her like he didn't know how to keep standing.

Her heart twisted.

"Sam," her voice was weak.

He shook his head. "No. I just—I can't—" He ran a shaking hand through his hair. "I can't lose you, too."

That broke her.

A sob escaped before she could stop it.

Paul reached for her again, and this time, she let him pull her close. Her shoulders shook as everything she'd held back finally broke free.

Paul wrapped his arms around her tightly.

His palm was warm—steady and real—and for a heartbeat, that simple touch steadied her more than any medicine could. The chemo pump clicked softly beside them, its quiet rhythm reminding her that life, however fragile, still went on.

Across from them, Sam dropped into the chair, burying his face in his hands. His whole body shuddered as he fought to hold himself together.

For the first time, no one tried to be strong.

No one tried to say, *"It's going to be okay."*

Because right now, it didn't feel okay.

Slowly, Sam reached out and wrapped an arm around Paul. The embrace was awkward, uncertain—but real.

Paul froze, then exhaled and leaned in. Anna watched her brother and husband cling to each other, their silence saying everything words could not.

In that fragile quiet, she felt something shift—not strength, not courage, but a delicate grace that came from simply being seen.

The fight wasn't over. But for now, she allowed herself to break—and to be held.

Chapter 49

I see a shadow

In the hardest seasons of life, love revealed its truest form—not through words, but through the quiet endurance of those who refused to walk away. This was where loyalty was tested, where devotion meant showing up again and again, even when hope felt thin.

By the fourth cycle, Anna had grown frail—a shadow of her former self. The relentless side effects came in waves—nausea crashing like a turbulent sea, exhaustion pressing down until even sleep felt heavy.

"Her hair, once thick and strong, now fell away in clumps—each strand a small memory left behind on the pillow."

Paul pretended not to notice, but she could see the sorrow in his eyes every time he found strands scattered like fallen leaves.

The bakery, once a sanctuary of warmth and sweetness, became a place she could no longer bear. The smell of cookies now turned her stomach.

Some mornings, the weight of the world bore down on her, making it a struggle to rise from her bed.

She hated feeling like a burden.

Hated seeing Paul's exhaustion.

Hated the way Sam pretended he wasn't scared, and how Lizzy blinked back tears when she thought Anna wouldn't notice.

But most of all, she despised the pity in their eyes—more bitter than the smell of medicine.

One afternoon, Lizzy burst into Anna's room carrying a basket of wigs—curly, straight, blonde, pink. "You're getting a makeover," she announced. "It's non-negotiable."

Anna raised an eyebrow but couldn't help smiling. Lizzy plopped a big blonde wig onto her head, teasing it high with her fingers. "Well, hello, Dolly Parton," she said, grinning.

Anna caught her reflection in the mirror and let out a shaky laugh. "All I'm missing is a rhinestone guitar," she whispered.

"You've already got the sparkle," Lizzy replied softly. For a moment, laughter replaced the steady hum of machines. The room brightened—not from the lights, but from the love that shimmered quietly between them. Sometimes, hope came dressed in sequins and laughter.

The absence of Purple and Yellow, two members of her chemo group, cast a shadow over the room. Anna couldn't help but wonder if they had recovered—or if they hadn't.

The chemo unit was where hope clung to the flicker of monitors and the steady whisper of IV pumps. In the waiting room, life still stirred—soft words between loved ones, a laugh breaking through, a cry swallowed back. And always, the stale bite of lukewarm coffee lingered.

Paul spent hours there—sometimes sharing quiet smiles with other caregivers, sometimes just holding Anna's hand as she dozed. It was there he met Jane, an older woman whose husband's cancer had relapsed. Despite her struggles, she always asked how he was holding up, her warmth a stark contrast to the coldness around them.

Once, when Paul confessed the helplessness that dragged him down like a tide, Jane stirred her tea and said softly, "Caregivers suffer as much as patients—maybe even more. But we keep going, because they need us to believe. Life doesn't stop for cancer. There are still bills, meals, and visits. We learn to carry it all."

Inspired, one evening, Paul designed a small poster for the chemo unit: "If you are on the Juice, call us for a free hot meal."

He left the café's number below. When Anna saw it, her eyes filled with pride, a flicker of light breaking through the dark.

"Anna often wondered how love could still bloom in places where pain lived. But somehow, it always did."

Soon after, nurses pinned it at reception. Patients began to call, hesitant at first, until they realized the offer was genuine. For them, the café became a beacon of kindness, a reminder they weren't alone.

Having put his law school plans on hold, Sam took over the evening chores without hesitation. When Paul was at the hospital, Sam bathed Emma and read her bedtime stories.

On other nights, he sat quietly by Anna's side, making sure she was never alone. He shoveled the driveway before the snow settled, brewed Anna's favorite peppermint tea, and ensured Paul got a few hours of rest between caregiving and running the hotel.

Their support system wasn't built on grand gestures—it rested on the quiet, unwavering presence of those who loved fiercely. Cancer had changed everything, but it had not broken them. Together, they built a world where hope, laughter, and love thrived in the smallest, most meaningful way — like light finding its way through stormy clouds.

Chapter 50

In the arms of hope

As Christmas approached, CreeksVille transformed into a winter wonderland. The festive decorations sparkled, creating an ambiance of joy amidst the heaviness they all felt.

Lizzy sat beside Anna on the couch, her hands wrapped tightly around a cup of tea that had long gone cold, the warmth of the mug a faint reminder of comfort. The Christmas lights twinkled around them, their reflection shimmering in Lizzy's unshed tears, creating a bittersweet atmosphere that hung between them.

"You don't have to be strong all the time, you know," Anna said, reaching over to place her hand over Lizzy's, their connection grounding them amidst the storm.

Lizzy let out a shaky breath, her grip tightening around the cup. "I don't know how to do this, Anna. I don't know how to watch you stop fighting."

Anna swallowed hard, nodding. "I know."

"I'm scared," Lizzy admitted, her eyes shining, the weight of her emotions thick in the air. "I know you're trying to prepare us to make it easier. But it's not easy, Anna. It won't ever be easy."

Anna exhaled slowly, leaning her head against the back of the couch.
"I'm scared, too."

Lizzy turned her head sharply, startled by Anna's admission. Anna rarely let her fears show, keeping them tucked away like secrets beneath layers of love and resilience.

"I don't want to leave Emma. Or you. Or Paul. But I don't want to spend what time I have left being poked and prodded, clinging to a miracle that may never come," Anna continued, her eyes steady though sorrow burned behind them, her heart's warmth a small light in the dark.

Lizzy wiped at her eyes, nodding. "I just… I don't know how to imagine life without you in it. You've been my anchor, Anna. Without you, I don't know where to put my feet."

Anna smiled softly, her mind slipping backward, past the fear and the hospital visits, to a younger version of herself walking into the bakery for the first time.

Mrs. Lewis had sent her down to "help at the bakery for the summer," and Anna remembered standing just inside the door, the bell still jingling above her head, the smell of warm bread and powdered sugar wrapping around her like a blanket.

Lizzy was behind the counter that day, her hair tied back in a messy bun, flour streaking her cheek, smiling as if she had been waiting for Anna all morning. "There you are," Lizzy had said, wiping her hands on her apron. "Mrs. Sophia's granddaughter finally shows up—I was beginning to think you'd changed your mind."

Anna had laughed nervously, but Lizzy had disappeared into the back and returned with a crisp white apron. "First things first," Lizzy announced. She tied the apron around Anna's waist with a theatrical flourish, then reached for a paper cap from the shelf and set it gently on her head.

"There," Lizzy declared proudly, stepping back to admire her handiwork. "Officially a member of the CreeksVille family. No turning back now."

Anna had giggled, feeling oddly proud despite the flour dust clinging to her hair. By the end of that first day, they were sitting on overturned flour buckets in the kitchen, sipping coffee and talking like they'd known each other forever.

From that moment on, Lizzy was like the sister Anna never had—and Anna became the same for Lizzy. Together, they made the bakery a second home. Bob, with his terrible jokes, soon joined in, doting on Sam as if he were his own son.

Somewhere in the distance, the bakery bell jingled in her memory, reminding her that family wasn't just who you were born to—it was who stayed, even in the hardest seasons.

Over the years, the three of them became a team, wrapping Sam in the kind of love that made him grow up knowing he had a village behind him.

A wistful smile played on Anna's lips, a bittersweet light in her eyes. "You don't have to. Because I'll always be there—in Emma's laughter, in the smell of bread from the café oven, in every crooked scarf I ever knitted for you."

Lizzy let out a small, tearful chuckle, the sound a thread of joy amidst their sorrow. "God, those scarves were ugly."

Anna laughed, squeezing Lizzy's hand, their bond stronger than any fear. "They were made with love, though."

Lizzy's laughter faded as she looked at her best friend, her heart breaking as the harshness of reality sank in.

They sat together, their shared reality hanging between them like a heavy fog, until the faint voices of carolers drifted through the frosted windows—a quiet reminder that the world was still turning, and for now, they could simply stay.

Chapter 51

The last tree standing

One crisp December afternoon, the air was sharp with the scent of pine and frost. Bundled in scarves and heavy coats, the family piled into the truck, fabric crinkling with every movement.

Christmas classics crackled from the radio. Lizzy sang along, wildly off-key yet brimming with cheer.

"I swear, Lizzy, you could make Santa rethink Christmas," Sam teased.

"Oh, hush," she shot back, nudging him. "I'm just adding to the spirit."

Paul chuckled from the driver's seat as the truck wound toward the CreeksVille Christmas Tree Farm.

The farm, powdered with snow, looked like a Christmas card—fairy lights strung along fences, a red barn with a giant wreath, the mingled scents of evergreens, cider, and roasted chestnuts.

"Baby tree! I want a baby tree!" Emma squealed, clapping her mittened hands.

Anna smiled indulgently, nodding. They returned home with two trees, decorating them over cocoa and fruitcake. Emma giggled as she draped tinsel around her baby tree.

Paul and Sam hoisted Anna onto Paul's shoulders so she could place the angel on top. Emma, perched on Sam's shoulders, set a golden star just beneath it.

"Santa's coming!" Emma cried, pressing her tiny hands against the frosted window.

Paul adjusted a ribbon on a gift. "Santa's going to have a lot of cookies tonight."

From the doorway, Sam smiled at the scene—until the faint crunch of footsteps on snow reached their ears.

Then came the singing.

Carolers stood in the glow of the streetlamps, their song weaving Silent Night into the cold air. Snow drifted through the light, catching on scarves and mittens.

Among them was Melissa. On the line "sleep in heavenly peace," her gaze slipped from the hymnbook and found Sam. It was brief—almost secret—but it held.

Her singing didn't falter; if anything, it warmed. Sam felt the room fall away, the other sounds fading around her clear tone.

When the final note faded and the door closed, the warmth inside seemed suddenly too still. Sam's chest was tight, as if the echo of her look—and her song—had settled there and refused to leave.

That night, CreeksVille seemed to glow a little brighter, as if the town itself were keeping watch over them all.

Anna nudged him. "What's going on with you and Melissa?"

Blushing, Sam confessed, "It's complicated. Our lives are so different. She loves this town. I'm heading back to New York to practice law. I can't see her leaving CreeksVille."

Anna thought for a moment, her brow furrowing slightly.

"She doesn't have to make the move—you do."

Paul chimed in, leaning forward with interest.

"I moved here for your sister, and I don't regret a minute of it. Are you in love with Melissa?"

Sam hesitated, running a hand through his hair.

"I love her. That's not the problem."

Paul leaned closer, sensing the tension.

"Then what is?"

Sam sighed, uncertainty written across his face.

"Melissa belongs here. My life's in New York. I don't know how to choose one without losing the other."

Anna squeezed his hand gently.

"Love doesn't survive on its own. It needs sacrifice and effort. If she's the one, you can practice law here in CreeksVille."

Sam stared into the fire, lost in thought.

Outside, the carolers' voices drifted away, and the snow fell in whispers, cloaking the town in serene silence.

The baby Christmas tree, twinkling in the corner of the room, cast shadows across the walls.

And somewhere in Sam's heart, the first shape of a decision stirred—quiet but resolute, like the first light of dawn.

Chapter 52

The light beneath the tree

On Christmas Day, Lizzy arrived with Bob, their arms full of gifts and wine.

Emma squealed as Bob lifted her high, his hearty laugh filling the house.

Over lunch, the talk drifted to Sam and Melissa.

"Stop discussing my love life!" Sam groaned, though he was smiling. Laughter bubbled around the table; the house wrapped in warmth.

Afterward, Anna—frail but radiant—declared they were going to the Christmas market. That afternoon, she passed out scarves she had knitted in the chemo ward, each stitch a labor of love.

The market bustled with carols, roasted chestnuts, and children's laughter. Paul pushed Anna's wheelchair carefully along the cobbled streets while Emma darted beside them, touching everything—ornaments, wooden reindeer, baskets of peppermint sticks.

"Now this," Bob declared, rubbing his hands together, "this is the real reason for Christmas."

"Family and togetherness?" Lizzy teased.

"That," he grinned, "and an excuse to drink mulled wine at noon."

Anna chuckled as the two bickered, treasuring the easy banter. A gust of wind tossed snow over their coats. Emma squealed, tongue out.

"Mama, look! Snowflakes taste like Christmas!"

Anna brushed a curl from her daughter's forehead. "That's because Christmas is made of magic, sweetheart."

Paul squeezed her hand. "And so are you."

Later, the stalls of funnel cakes, sausages, and pretzels tempted them again.

"Didn't you just eat an hour ago?" Lizzy teased Bob.

"That was lunch," he replied solemnly. "This is market food. Entirely different category."

Emma tugged Sam's sleeve. "Uncle Sam, chocolate pretzels!"

Sam smirked. "Didn't you just have dessert?"

"That was lunch dessert. This is a carnival dessert."

Anna laughed, content to watch them argue over festival food.

Paul bent to her. "Hot cocoa? Extra whipped cream?"

"Always," she said, smiling.

That night, with Emma asleep, Anna and Paul curled together on the couch. A single candle flickered.

Paul memorized everything—the way Anna traced the rim of her mug, the way she melted into his side.

"Best Christmas ever," she whispered, warmth flickering through her like candlelight.

He kissed her hair, holding her close. "Yeah. It really was."

Her breathing slowed as she drifted into sleep. Paul stayed still, listening to the hush outside—the wind, the faint carols fading in the night.

He held her as if he could stop time, realizing that no Christmas would ever feel this perfect again.

After the laughter, carols, and warmth of family, the house settled into a peaceful night.

Fresh snow blanketed the streets, lamplight stretching long across untouched drifts. The town seemed to have curled up for the night.

Upstairs, Sam sat in his room, the tick of the clock filling the stillness. In his lap rested Melissa's gift—a notebook wrapped in deep red fabric embroidered with delicate gold thread. He traced the cover with his fingers before untying the ribbon.

May you fill your life with moments to cherish. –Melissa

It wasn't just a notebook; it was a canvas, a future waiting to be shaped.

Anna's voice echoed in his mind: *"You could practice law right here in CreeksVille."*

What if Melissa were the one? What if staying in New York meant losing her? His corporate attorney career wasn't as flexible as Paul's patent practice, but as he held the notebook, questions that once felt heavy now seemed small.

When he thought of Melissa—her laughter, her eyes, the comfort of her presence—he felt an undeniable sense of belonging.

Taking a deep breath, Sam opened the notebook and picked up a pen.

Meanwhile, Melissa's Christmas table overflowed with food, laughter, and chatter—siblings, parents, grandparents, all talking over one another in a cheerful din. And yet her thoughts drifted.

She looked again at the photo Lizzy had sent: Sam in his sweater, smiling easily. The words slipped out before she could stop them.

"God, I love you."

She pressed the phone to her chest, whispering a prayer for a Christmas miracle.

Just then, her phone buzzed. Her breath caught. A message from Sam:

A snapshot of *The Nutcracker* poster with a note— "Can this be our first date?"

Her heart soared. "Thank you, Jesus!" she exclaimed, startling her family.

"Have you won the lottery, dear?" her grandmother asked, amused.

Melissa hugged her tightly. "Something like that," she laughed, cheeks flushed.

Chapter 53

The Christmas gift

That Saturday evening, the house glowed softly, the Christmas tree lights casting golden patterns across the living room.

"Okay, be honest," Sam said, stepping out of his room and doing a slow turn. He wore a crisp button-down shirt, dark slacks, and a jacket that looked suspiciously new.

Anna looked up from the couch, a mischievous spark in her tired eyes. "Well, well. Someone's taking this seriously."

Paul set down his book, nodding in approval. "Melissa's going to swoon."

Sam rolled his eyes, but a faint blush crept up his neck. "Just making sure I don't look like a dork."

Anna's smile softened. "You look perfect. And Sam…" She reached out, squeezing his hand. "I'm glad you're doing this."

He nodded, throat tight, then grabbed his coat. "Wish me luck."

Paul grinned. "Go make it count."

That night, they went to The Nutcracker—Melissa's favorite. The theater glittered with lights, the winter air crisp and magical. Afterward, Sam led her to dinner along the river promenade.

The restaurant felt intimate, a fire crackling in the hearth. Melissa, dressed in black with a wool jacket, embodied her quiet, effortless elegance.

Their laughter came easily, but Sam's decision thrummed inside him, bright with excitement. Finally, he set down his glass.

Sam watched the firelight play across her face and felt something in his chest settle. The answer felt simple.

"I've been thinking about moving back to CreeksVille."

Melissa froze, tears springing to her eyes. "You mean it?"

He nodded. "Yes. I want to be here—with my family, with you. I've been thinking about this for a while, and it feels right."

His gaze didn't waver. "I love you, Melissa."

Tears spilled as she laughed through them. "I'm sorry—I'm just so happy."

Sam reached across, taking her hand. "I am, too."

Later, outside her house, the car idled in the driveway. The porch light caught her face, and he couldn't look away.

"I've wanted to do this for so long," Melissa whispered.

"Me too," Sam admitted.

Their breath clouded in the cold, and the world seemed to still with them.

Melissa's mittened hands twisted together, her smile tremulous but sure.

Sam reached up, brushing a stray strand of hair from her face.

"You're beautiful," he said softly.

And then the space between them closed.

Their lips met in a tender, long-awaited kiss. The world fell away, leaving only their embrace and the gentle fall of snow.

When they pulled apart, Sam grinned. "Can I come in?"

Melissa laughed. "I live with my parents, remember?"

"And I live with my sister."

They both burst out laughing, the absurdity only sweetening the moment.

As she disappeared inside, Sam drove off into the snowy night, grinning to himself, a warmth in his chest he couldn't suppress.

This Christmas had given him more than cheer—it had given him a future.

From the window, Melissa watched his taillights fade into the snow, her heart so full it ached—as if Christmas itself had answered her prayer.

Chapter 54

Will upon the moon

The past year had been among the most grueling of Anna's life. Most days, she barely had the energy to see Emma. The time she had longed to spend with her daughter, Paul, and Sam slipped away, replaced by hospital rooms, harsh fluorescent lights, and the constant ache of exhaustion.

At first, she had fought fiercely, defying every wave of sickness with clenched fists and stubborn resolve. Lately, though, she found herself sinking into the quiet acceptance of a body no longer winning the battle.

One evening, after a brutal round of chemotherapy, Anna sat in the dim light of the living room, her breathing shallow, despair pressing down on her.

Then, as if sensing the darkness closing in, Emma burst into the room, Mary trailing behind. Her small hands clutched a handful of wildflowers from the garden, their stems bent, petals barely holding on.

"Look, Mommy! They're for you!"

Anna's fingers trembled as she reached for them. The colors seemed almost too bright, too alive against the fatigue dragging her down. But Emma's joy was relentless, her eyes wide with innocent delight.

"Aren't they pretty?"

Anna swallowed past the lump in her throat. The flowers weren't perfect—wilted in places, petals missing—but they carried love. Chosen just for her.

"They're beautiful." She clutched them to her chest as if they were a treasure.

In that moment, Anna resolved to find meaning in the days she had left.

She began painting again, though her hands were weaker now. Some days, she managed only a few strokes before exhaustion overtook her. Each painting felt more fleeting, as if she were trying to hold time before it slipped away.

One afternoon, she sat by the window, her brush moving sluggishly across the canvas. The wind howled, rattling the glass, but inside Anna felt an unexpected calm.

She painted a sunset—an explosion of gold and violet—a farewell to the sky she had always loved.

Small, joyful fragments became her lifelines: Emma's brightness filling the house, Paul's constant presence, Sam's unwavering loyalty, Lizzy's tireless optimism.

These moments felt sharper now, as if her mind were recording them carefully, afraid to forget.

Lying on the couch one afternoon, she closed her eyes and listened. From the next room came Emma's quick footsteps, followed by Sam's exaggerated gasp as she tackled him.

"You got me!" he laughed.

Emma's giggles rang out, bright and carefree. Anna held onto the sound, letting it wrap around her like a familiar song. Please *don't stop playing,* she thought, *even when I'm gone.*

The toll was undeniable. The double mastectomy, radiation, and chemotherapy had left her frail, a shadow of the woman she once was. She reached up, tracing the smooth skin of her chest where scars had replaced what once had been.

The woman in the mirror was both herself and a stranger— strong, yet fading.

Then Paul entered, his eyes filled not with pity but with love— steady and whole. "You are more than what's been taken from you," he said, gathering her into his arms.

She closed her eyes, letting his warmth anchor her. For a moment, she imagined staying—a future not slipping through her hands.

But deep down, she knew.

Yet it was love that kept her going. She would not leave Emma without knowing—without feeling—how much she was cherished.

Many nights, as Anna tucked Emma into bed, she whispered stories of her own childhood—tales of adventure, of wonder, of the woman she had been before the sickness took hold.

"Did Grandma tell you bedtime stories, too?" Emma asked sleepily one night.

Anna swallowed the grief tightening in her throat.

"She did," she said, "And when I was little, I thought she'd always be there."

Emma yawned, curling into her pillow.

"You'll always be here, too."

Anna brushed back her curls and smiled gently. "Yes, baby. Always."

And in that moment, she wished more than anything it could be true.

As time passed, so did Anna's strength. Each brushstroke slowed, each moment of love grew more precious.

She discovered that even the smallest fragments—Emma's tiny arms wrapped around her, Paul's steady hand in hers, the golden sun dipping below the horizon—held enough beauty to fill a lifetime.

And maybe, just maybe, love itself was enough.

Chapter 55

I surrender all

The wind howled through the trees, shaking the last stubborn leaves from their branches. A brittle frost coated the world, the morning air sharp enough to steal one's breath.

Gray clouds hung heavy and unmoving, casting a muted light over everything below.

Inside, the windows were misted, the fire crackling softly—its warmth no match for the heaviness in the room.

Anna wanted one quiet evening alone with Paul.

When she asked him, Paul gave a dramatic bow.

"The honor is mine," he said, bringing a smile to her face.

Excited but apprehensive, Anna called Lizzy, who whisked her off on a shopping adventure.

Though her frail frame made finding the right dress a challenge, the outing turned into a joyful occasion, filled with loud laughter that drew amused glances from other shoppers.

Anna ultimately chose a floral wrap dress and a navy blue cocktail gown, her spirits buoyed by Lizzy's infectious energy.

That evening, Paul recreated their first date on the hotel terrace. Fairy lights sparkled above, music played in the background, and a breathtaking mountain view stretched before them.

Paul lifted her gently, and together, they swayed to *Unchained Melody*. In his arms, all that remained was the timeless connection between them—untouched by illness, untouched by time.

After their dance, Anna leaned against Paul on the sofa as they gazed at the stars.

"You look beautiful," Paul said.

Anna laughed. "You wouldn't believe the struggle to find a dress that fit. Every woman dreams of shopping in the teen section, and today, I finally did!"

Paul chuckled; his eyes filled with love.

Anna's expression turned serious. "Paul, do you love me?"

"Any doubt?" he teased, but her grave tone made him pause.

Tears welled in her eyes. "I want to stop the treatment," she whispered, her body trembling.

"I can't do this anymore.

I don't want to live as a shadow of myself.

I need to leave with some dignity."

Her voice broke as she clutched his hand. "Sweetheart… I need your permission to let me go."

Paul's heart clenched. For a long moment, he just looked at her—at the pain etched into her face, the strength beneath it.

When he finally moved closer, Anna pressed her cheek against his chest. His heartbeat was wild, pounding hard and uneven, as if his body refused to accept what she was asking.

He wanted to beg her to keep fighting, to stay one more day, one more hour—but the plea died in his throat.

In that moment, a memory flickered—their wedding day, Anna's eyes shining as he slid the ring onto her finger.

"In sickness and in health," he had promised, his voice steady then, never imagining how fiercely those words would one day be tested.

Loving her meant keeping that vow now—even when it meant letting her go.

He closed his eyes, one hand trembling as it found the back of her head. Then, with a deep, steadying breath, he forced the words out.

"Anna, I want nothing more than to see you free from this suffering. If this is truly what you want…"

His voice caught before he finished softly, "I will stand by you."

Anna sobbed, the tears falling freely now, soaking his shirt as she clung to him.

"I hope you can forgive me," she whispered against the sound of his heart, which was finally slowing—beating not with panic, but with the quiet, unbearable weight of love.

"There's nothing to forgive." Paul's voice was steady. "I love you, Anna. Whatever you choose, I will be your greatest strength."

They sat together, the weight of their decision settling around them. Beneath the quiet stars, Anna found comfort in Paul's unwavering presence, their love a beacon in the night.

Anna felt a profound sense of peace as the fire crackled, and the night deepened. The weight she had carried for so long seemed to lift, replaced by a quiet acceptance.

Her body was frail, but her heart swelled with love for the family she had built, for the memories they had made together.

She thought of Emma, whose laughter filled their home with light. Anna prayed her daughter would always know how deeply she was cherished—that this love would guide her, even when Anna was no longer there.

Her thoughts turned to Paul, her rock through every storm. His strength had carried her when her own had failed, his love an anchor she could cling to when the world felt too heavy.

And then there was Sam, her beloved brother. She marveled at the man he had become—kind, steadfast, resilient—and hoped he would carry forward the lessons of love and perseverance they had shared.

The flames in the hearth had burned low, yet their glow lingered—a soft, steady light holding back the darkness.

With gratitude in her heart and the warmth of love surrounding her, Anna let her eyes drift closed—no longer afraid of what came next.

Outside, the wind still howled, but inside, the last embers glowed—small, steadfast, refusing to go out too soon.

Chapter 56

Hope changes shape

The room was hushed. The air vent's steady breath was the only sound. Pale light washed over the walls, quiet and still.

Anna sat upright—composed but pale—her hands folded loosely in her lap. Beside her, Paul sat rigid, his fingers clenched together. Across from them, Dr. Barry glanced down at his notes, the rustle of paper the only movement.

In the corner, Sam stared at a smudge on the wall, shoulders drawn tight. Anna drew a slow breath, then spoke with quiet finality. "I've decided not to continue with chemotherapy."

Her words landed in the room like sudden stillness—too quiet, too heavy to ignore.

Paul tensed, his fingers tightening. "Anna… are you sure?"

She turned to him, her tired eyes filled with quiet certainty. "Yes, Paul. I am."

Dr. Barry met her gaze with understanding. "It's a difficult decision," he acknowledged. "We can discuss symptom management and palliative care. There are ways to keep you comfortable."

Sam shifted in his chair. "But Anna… you could try a different approach. Another specialist. Another trial—"

She shook her head. "I'm done, Sam. I've thought about this for a long time. It's my decision."

Sam wanted to argue, but every plea caught in his throat. She looked too tired to fight for anyone else's comfort.

Paul exhaled, his heartbeat drumming. He wanted to plead, to bargain. But something in her posture—so calm, so resolute—silenced him.

Dr. Barry nodded. "I respect your decision. You've been incredibly strong through this."

Anna offered a faint smile. "I just don't want to spend the time I have left in a hospital."

Later that day, the scent of lamb and bread filled the family room.

Paul, quiet. Lizzy, watchful.

A fork scraped against a plate, then nothing.

Anna's eyes swept the table. Each face. Each memory.

She cleared her throat.

The room stilled.

"I have something important to tell you all."

Paul stiffened beside her. Melissa put down her fork. "Anna, what is it?"

"Anna exhaled, looking down for a moment before meeting their eyes. 'I've made a decision.' Her gaze drifted across the table."

Silence stretched. Even the fire seemed to hold its breath.

"No more hospitals."

The words landed like stones.

Paul's father set his glass down with a dull clink. "Anna... you mean permanently?"

She nodded. "Yes. I don't want to spend my days in a hospital anymore."

Melissa swallowed, pushing her chair back slightly. "But... isn't there still hope?"

Anna gave her a tired, gentle smile. "Hope isn't only about fighting. Sometimes, it's about choosing how you want to live."

Lizzy looked down at her hands. "I don't know what to say."

Bob cleared his throat, his eyes rough with unshed tears. "You've fought so damn hard, Anna. I just... I wish it weren't like this."

Paul hadn't spoken the entire time. Anna turned to him, reaching for his hand. "Paul?"

His jaw tightened as he stared at the table, then he finally looked at her. His eyes softened, and he gave her a small, steady smile—a wordless promise that he would be by her side. Her fingers tightened around his. "Thank you."

Anna sat on the sofa, leaning against Paul for support. Her eyelids drooped, exhaustion settling into her bones.

Paul's mother rose. "I'll check on Emma."

Melissa stood abruptly. "I—I'll do the dishes."

Paul's father and Bob remained still.

Lizzy finally spoke, barely above a whisper. "I don't know how to do this, Anna."

Anna smiled. "You don't have to. Just be here."

Lizzy nodded, her throat tight.

Paul adjusted the pillows beneath Anna's head, tucking a blanket around her. He leaned in and kissed her forehead.

"I love you," he whispered.

Anna murmured, her lips curving into a faint, drowsy smile.

He gripped the porch railing until his knuckles whitened, fighting the scream lodged in his throat. The night air bit his face, but it was nothing compared to the hollow ache in his chest. He stared up at the starless sky, thoughts spiraling.

A hand touched his shoulder. He turned to see his father. Without a word, Paul stepped forward and embraced him. His father held him as silent tears soaked through his coat.

In the kitchen, Melissa scrubbed wine glasses with too much force, tears slipping down her cheeks.

Sam entered, his face pale. "I'm scared, Melissa," he said. "I don't know if I can do this." The words lingered, raw and unguarded.

Melissa turned, fierce despite the tears. She cupped his face. "We will do whatever it takes to make her comfortable. We'll be there for her—together. Okay?"

Sam nodded, holding onto her like a lifeline.

In the living room, Lizzy sat curled in an armchair, watching Anna sleep. A single candle flickered nearby, its lavender scent mingling with the faint aroma of burning wood.

She clasped her hands in silence, offering a quiet prayer—not for miracles, but for peace.

Paul returned and sat beside Anna. She stirred, her hand reaching for his.

He took it, kissing it gently.

"I'll be with you every step of the way, Anna. Always."

Her eyes lifted to his, heavy with exhaustion, before she drifted into sleep.

Paul leaned back, watching her, heart aching. He understood now—

Hope hadn't left them. It had only changed shape.

Chapter 57

Edge of a storm

Sam slipped into the room, eager to see his sister. The laptop cast a pale glow over Anna's face as she worked. At last, she closed it with a sigh and looked up, a tired smile tugging at her lips.

"Come sit with me," she invited, her expression easing as the tension left her face.

After stopping chemotherapy, Anna seemed to have a little more energy. Sam perched on the edge of the bed, his eyes searching her face—not just for exhaustion, but for something deeper.

"I need to talk to you about something," Anna said, her tone shifting.

Sam raised an eyebrow. "That sounds serious."

Anna took a breath, meeting his gaze. "I want to meet our dad."

The words hung between them. Sam stilled, silence filling the room for a moment.

He blinked, startled. "Now? After all these years?"

She nodded. There was no hesitation, no second-guessing—just quiet resolve.

"That can be arranged," Sam said after a pause. "How about this weekend?" she asked, trying to soften the gravity of the conversation.

Sam studied her face for a moment before nodding. "Okay. This weekend."

A quiet understanding passed between them. Gently, he tucked her under the warm covers, an old habit from when they were kids, when she used to do the same for him. Leaning in, he brushed a light kiss against her forehead.

He looked at her with teary eyes. "You're my hero, sis."

Anna's lips curved slightly as she tightened her grip on his hand. "And you're my champ, little brother." Her eyelids fluttered, sleep tugging at her, her words barely holding. "You're the best."

Sam sat there for another moment, watching her drift off before finally slipping out of the room.

In the kitchen, Paul was deep in conversation with Emma, who was perched in her highchair, shaking her head furiously at her least favorite vegetable—carrots.

"No carrots, Daddy!" Emma declared, her tiny arms crossing in defiance.

"Come on, Em," Paul coaxed, holding up the spoonful of mashed carrots. "One bite. Just one."

Emma's lips twisted in a stubborn pout. Just as Paul leaned in with the spoon, she turned her head sharply—sending the orange purée flying straight at his face. The bright orange splattered across his cheek like war paint, and Emma burst into giggles.

Sam barely contained his laughter as he walked in, tossing Paul a napkin. "Wow. She's got great aim."

Paul groaned, wiping the purée from his cheek. "Yeah, tell me about it."

"Let me try," Sam said, grabbing a fresh spoon. He crouched in front of Emma, leaning in conspiratorially.

"Emma, if you eat your carrots, you'll grow strong like Spider-Man." Emma's skeptical eyes locked onto him. "Spider-Man?"

"Yup. And Spider-Man loves carrots," Sam nodded, dead serious.

Emma considered this. Then, after a long, dramatic pause, she opened her mouth and accepted the bite.

Paul stared in disbelief. "You've gotta be kidding me."

Sam smirked, raising a triumphant hand. "Victory."

Paul shook his head, laughing as he gave Sam a high-five. "I'm calling you for every meal from now on."

As the laughter faded, Sam's smile lingered for a moment before slipping away. The lightness in the room felt suddenly unsteady. "Can we talk for a second?"

Paul picked up Emma from the highchair, setting her down with her toys before turning back. "What's up?"

Sam hesitated, then asked, "Did you know Anna wants to meet our dad?"

Paul exhaled, nodding. "Yeah. We talked about it this morning." Sam folded his arms. "Do you think it's a good idea?"

Paul ran a hand through his hair, his expression thoughtful. "I don't know. But if she wants to do it, I won't stand in her way."

Sam let that sit for a moment, then nodded. "Yeah. Me neither."

Later that evening, Sam sat on the couch, phone in hand. His thumb hovered over the call button before finally pressing it.

After a few rings, a familiar voice answered. "Hello?"

Sam took a breath. "Hey, Dad. It's Sam."

A brief pause. Then: "Yeah."

"Listen, Anna wants to meet you."

Another pause.

"Anna?" Jake's tone was quiet, almost disbelieving.

"Yeah," Sam confirmed. "She'd like to see you."

Jake exhaled sharply. "I—are you sure?"

"She is."

Jake was silent for a beat before he spoke, his voice rough. "Yes," he said, then again, steadier this time, "Yes. Of course. When?"

"This Saturday," Sam replied, his own voice quieter now.

When the call ended, Sam sat there for a long moment, the phone still in his hand. Knowing his father, he wasn't sure this was the right decision—whether Jake would show up, or if his presence would bring more pain than peace.

And yet, beneath the doubt, something unexpected stirred in his chest. Not dread. Not fear. Maybe… anticipation.

He realized he wanted something he hadn't admitted in years—for Jake to finally show up, not just on Saturday, but in their lives. For Anna to have that moment, that closure, before it was too late.

But the thought cut deep, like standing at the edge of a storm—one that might clear the air or leave wreckage behind.

Chapter 58

It's everybody else

Jake hadn't expected to hear from Sam, and the call left him surprised and anxious. The idea of meeting Anna after so many years felt surreal, stirring a mix of emotions he couldn't quite place.

For years, he had convinced himself that leaving his family had been the right choice—not just for himself but for them as well.

His world was painted in shades of solitude and regret, the call from Sam a jarring reminder of a past he had tried to leave behind.

Jake leaned back in his chair, the wood groaning beneath him. Silence pressed against his ears. The walls held no warmth—only peeling paint and years of solitude.

Dust clung to the furniture, gathering in corners where time had stopped. A flickering bulb cast uneven shadows, making the space feel smaller, almost suffocating.

Saturday loomed. And though he'd never say it out loud, the thought of facing Anna unsettled something sharp and sour in his chest.

Not guilt. Not love.

Just the quiet, choking fear of being seen—for exactly who he was.

He sat with a beer in hand, pondering the surreal notion of seeing Anna again.

His mind drifted back to the past—meeting Sarah, the bright spark she brought into his life, the whirlwind of their youthful romance.

Excitement faded into loss, a sense of displacement that only grew. When Anna was born, joy was brief, replaced by the growing divide between him and Sarah, her ambition pulling her away.

They met as teenagers, working at his parents' Farmhouse Ham Store. Jake struggled with school and eventually dropped out.

The store offered him reliable work and a sense of stability, even if it wasn't glamorous. Sarah, full of energy and ambition, brought a spark into his otherwise monotonous days.

They married young, and for a time, Jake believed life would always stay simple and happy.

But after Anna was born, everything changed. Sarah became more determined to build a better life for their daughter.

She talked about moving to the suburbs, getting a bigger house, and giving Anna opportunities they never had.

Jake couldn't understand why she wasn't content with their downtown apartment and quiet, predictable life. He liked the simplicity and comfort of it.

As Anna grew older, Jake felt distant from her. She seemed fiercely loyal to her mom, Sophia, and her grandmother.

When Anna scraped her knee or needed advice, she went to Sarah or Sophia—not him.

He told himself it was natural for girls to cling to their mothers. But sometimes, he caught the way Anna looked at him—like she was bracing for disappointment. He hated that look. It made him feel like a stranger in his own home.

When Sarah started nursing school on a scholarship, Jake supported her, even helping Anna with Sophia's assistance. But he resented the changes it brought.

He felt like an outsider in his own home, constantly judged for not meeting Sarah's expectations. By the time their son, Sam, was born, the cracks in their marriage had widened.

Sarah's criticism wore on him, each word chipping away at his patience. She accused him of being lazy, of watching too much TV, of not pulling his weight.

Jake couldn't understand why she was so hard on him. He wasn't abusive—what more did she want? To him, Sarah's drive for success felt like an attack on his way of life.

Sophia only made things worse. Jake always felt like Sophia was whispering in Sarah's ear, turning her against him. He hated how she looked down on him, always siding with Sarah.

He convinced himself that Anna saw him the way Sarah and Sophia did—unworthy, a failure.

The more isolated he felt, the more he withdrew—spending nights on the couch, flipping through channels, wondering where it had all gone wrong.

One day, Jake decided he'd had enough. He walked away from it all.

He told himself it was for the best—for everyone. He deserved to be free from the constant criticism.

Over the years, Jake clung to the belief that he had been the victim. He told himself that Sarah had driven him away, that he had no choice but to leave.

It was a convenient belief, easier than facing the truth: that he had failed as a husband and father.

As he took another sip of beer, Jake wondered what Anna wanted from him now. Surely, she had a good life without him.

Maybe she wanted to tell him how wrong her mom was to drive him away. But another part of him felt uneasy. What if Anna wanted answers he couldn't give? What if she saw through his excuses and confronted him with the pain he had caused?

Anna had always chosen her mother and grandmother over him. She'd never looked at him the way a daughter should.

"I'm not the villain," he whispered, the lie tasting bitter even as he said it.

Jake leaned back in his chair, the wood groaning under his weight. The day was coming, unavoidable. And with it, the reckoning he'd spent years outrunning.

Chapter 59

A mirage

Sam hung up the phone with his father, his thoughts circling how Anna might react to seeing Jake after twenty-five years.

For three years, Sam had tried to mend the distance with his father, but each attempt left him drained.

Jake, with his six-foot frame and broad shoulders, bore the harshness of fifty-six years. He looked older than his years—his weathered face and guarded stance shaped by decades of bitterness and disappointment.

Jake's dismissive remarks about Anna's illness cut deep. "Her mother had cancer too—it must be in the genes."

Even when he feigned concern, his detachment showed through. He spoke of Emma and Paul with the same coldness, reducing Paul to nothing more than "Anna's husband," as if the man himself didn't matter.

Sam realized early on that Jake had no desire to revisit the past. He often waved off deeper discussions with phrases like, *"What's bygone is bygone."* This dismissive attitude made Sam wary of the upcoming meeting, sensing that Jake's presence might bring more trouble than peace.

For Anna, the decision to meet Jake stemmed not from a longing for reconciliation but from a desire for closure. For years, she had harbored resentment toward the man who abandoned her, her brother, and their mother without explanation.

The absence of a father during pivotal moments, especially when their mom was sick and after their mother's death, only intensified Anna's anger.

Now, facing her own mortality, Anna felt the weight of bitterness pressing down on her heart. She hoped the meeting would bring clarity—was he truly the villain she believed him to be, or merely a flawed man who made terrible choices?

In this tangled web of fathers and daughters, Anna sought to untangle her feelings and find peace. With each passing day, the need for resolution grew stronger, propelling her toward a confrontation she had long avoided.

On Saturday, Sam collected Jake and brought him to Anna's home. At the door, Paul greeted him with a steady handshake and courteous introduction, relieved him of his coat, and ushered him inside.

"Anna is in the family room with Emma," Paul said, gesturing toward the cozy space.

Jake followed them in. Anna sat on the sofa, and her daughter Emma was asleep beside her. To Jake's surprise, Anna looked up and said, "Hello, Dad," her gaze steady, her manner calm and polite.

"Hello, Anna. How are you feeling?" Jake asked, hoping to bridge the gap between them.

"I'm okay," she replied, maintaining a distant tone.

Paul gently scooped up Emma, murmuring that he would put her to bed, leaving Anna, Sam, and Jake alone for the first time in twenty-five years.

Sam leaned down to kiss Anna's forehead before sitting by her feet. Jake settled into the chair by the fire, feeling the warmth of the flames contrast with the chill in the air. After a moment, Paul returned, offering Jake a drink.

"Whiskey?" Paul asked.

"Yes, please. On the rocks," Jake replied.

Sam stood up. "I'll grab a beer," he said, leaving Anna and Jake momentarily alone.

An awkward pause stretched between them until Anna broke it with a simple question. "Where are you staying?"

"I live on Maple Street," Jake replied. "Near the retirement home where I work as a cook. Only fifteen minutes from the bakery."

He had lived so close all these years, yet never reached out—and that, more than anything, made him unworthy.

"Oh," Anna said, nodding. "What do you cook?"

Jake shared a few details about his work, but their conversation felt thin, as if they were acquaintances rather than father and daughter. The distance lingered, casting a shadow over every attempt to connect.

The night before, Anna had envisioned this moment—hoping for vulnerability, an apology, or even a simple acknowledgment of the pain he had caused her.

But as she sat across from him, she felt no anger or sympathy— only a profound sense of detachment. Her gaze fixed past him, as though he were just another visitor passing through her house.

Jake had taught her nothing but absence—and now even his shadow no longer had weight. She had built a life without him, and it was enough.

When Sam returned with a bowl of peanuts and Paul handed Jake his whiskey, the atmosphere shifted. Paul began peeling an apple and slicing it into small pieces, which Anna accepted with a faint smile, grateful for the distraction.

Jake spoke at last, low and serious. "I've been waiting for this moment for many years," he said, his gaze fixed on Anna.

She and Sam exchanged wary glances, the tension in the room palpable.

Jake continued, "I tried to find you once. I stopped by the old house, but the couple renting it said you were married and had moved on. I even went to the retirement home where your grandmother was staying. I told her I wanted to see you and Sam."

Jake hesitated, then added, "She threatened to sue me for back child support if I ever came back to town."

Sam's crooked smile appeared. "Grandma Sophia? Barely five feet tall? She punched you?"

Jake hesitated, then muttered, "She punched me."

Sam blinked. "She what?"

Jake nodded defensively. "She told me to lean in, and I thought she would say something important. Then—bam—she hit me right in the nose!"

Jake touched the bridge of his nose unconsciously, as if the sting still lingered.

Anna blinked, stunned by the image. She hadn't expected this— any of it. A part of her wanted to remain cold and distant.

Her gaze flicked to Sam, whose mouth twitched, fighting a grin. Something unspoken passed between them, a flicker of shared memory and years of hurt—and then the absurdity of it all chipped at her resolve.

Her lips twitched despite herself. She grabbed the nearest pillow and pressed it to her face, a quiet laugh escaping before she could stop it.

When she lowered the pillow, her expression had softened just slightly. "Atta girl, Grandma," she murmured, her voice low, almost reluctant.

Suppressing his amusement, Paul turned to Anna. "Are you ready to call it a night?" he asked lightly.

Anna stood, leaning on Paul for support, while Sam helped her up. She offered a distant thank-you to Jake for visiting.

Jake's mouth curled into a bitter half-smile, satisfaction flickering in his eyes as if Sophia's punch proved his point—that everyone had always been against him.

As she turned away, she caught the bitter curve of his mouth—and felt the last flicker of pity she might have had for him vanish.

As she headed to her bedroom, Paul exchanged a mischievous glance with Sam, the corners of his mouth twitching in a barely contained grin. The room felt lighter, the earlier tension fading into shared laughter.

Once inside, the couple burst out laughing, imagining their grandmother punching Jake.

A knock on the door interrupted their laughter. Sam entered, his face lit with barely contained humor. The three of them laughed until tears streamed down their faces.

"I shouldn't be laughing…but God, it feels good," declared Anna. Paul murmured, "We should have framed that moment for eternity."

Chapter 60

A magical beginning

The cabin by the creek was alive with warmth. Sam moved through the room carrying wine and hors d'oeuvres, his smile stretched a little too wide, his hands just a bit too fidgety.

Anna raised an eyebrow. "Sam? You're up to something."

He paused, grinning. "Can't a man host dinner without being interrogated?"

But as the room quieted, he cleared his throat. "Alright, everyone. I do have something to share—especially with you, Lizzy."

A flicker of surprise passed through Lizzy's eyes. The others leaned in.

"You might want to start hiring soon," Sam said. "Because come spring…I'm leaving the café."

Anna's face tightened. "Why?"

Sam stepped onto a chair, his words ringing out. "Because I've accepted a job as a corporate attorney at a local firm!"

The room exploded—clapping, cheers, a mixture of pride and disbelief.

Anna clasped his hand, eyes gleaming. "You did it."

Lizzy pulled him into a hug. "You'd better come back for coffee and my sarcasm."

After the laughter settled and dinner plates were cleared, Sam rose again and clinked his glass. "One more thing."

He led everyone out to the balcony. The winter air kissed their cheeks, but what stole their breath was the sight before them: hundreds of candles glowing in glass jars, red roses trailing the railing, the creek shimmering in moonlight.

For a moment, no one spoke. The only sound was the fire crackling at the balcony's edge.

Then Sam turned to Melissa and took her hand. His voice was steady, carrying through the hush. "Melissa Angelina Davis," he said, dropping to one knee, "will you marry me?"

The world seemed to hold its breath. Melissa's eyes brimmed, her lips parted. Snow drifted slowly around them, like confetti from the heavens.

"Yes," she whispered, then stronger, through tears: "Of course, yes."

Cheers erupted. Laughter spilled into the night as Sam slid the ring onto her finger. She buried her face in his shoulder, laughing and crying all at once.

Paul grabbed him in a hug. "You romantic fool."

Sam laughed. "I learn from the pros."

As hot chocolate and champagne flowed, stories spilled and laughter soared. Melissa danced with her niece near the fire. Anna leaned into Paul, her hand resting over his.

Jake stood apart for a moment, watching it all. Smiling. But not fully part of it. In his coat pocket, a letter weighed heavier than it had all week. He had carried it for days, waiting for the right moment to hand it to Sam—or maybe to Anna. But as the fire crackled and the laughter swirled around him, he hesitated. Not tonight.

Anna glanced his way. Their eyes met—no anger, no warmth. Just something...human. A fragile truce in the flicker of candlelight.

And in that hush before midnight, with snow settling gently around them and love stitched across every corner of the cabin, it didn't matter who had come late to the story. What mattered was that, somehow, they were here now—together, trying.

Chapter 61

The bishop is moving

The morning after the engagement celebration unfolded like a tapestry of light and warmth. Sunlight spilled through the cabin windows, casting shadows across the wooden floors.

In the kitchen, Anna was already moving about with quiet energy, the scent of pancakes and bacon drifting through the air, her heart still buoyed by the joy of the night before.

One by one, the others stirred from sleep, drawn by the comforting aromas. Sam appeared last, still riding high on the excitement of his proposal, a sleepy grin stretching across his face. His excitement lingered in every gesture, every breath.

"Morning, everyone!" he called out, a grin spreading across his face. "I can't believe how magical last night was!"

"Good morning, Mr. Fiancé!" Anna teased, flipping a pancake. "How does it feel to be engaged?"

"It feels amazing," Sam said, glancing at Melissa, still curled under the sheets, joy written plainly across her face. "I can't wait to start planning our future together."

As the others gathered around the table, laughter and lighthearted banter filled the room. The atmosphere was thick with love and excitement, and everyone reveled in the shared joy of the new couple.

"I hope you know you're stuck with us now," Paul joked, nudging Sam. "You can't just escape to your fancy attorney job without us!"

"Yeah, we'll be expecting regular updates on your life as a corporate attorney," Melissa added with a wink. "And don't forget to bring us all those attorney perks!"

The group chuckled, and Sam raised his glass of orange juice. "To new beginnings and lifelong friendships!" he declared, his eyes sparkling with gratitude for the family he had chosen and the one he was about to build.

After breakfast, the group decided to spend the day outdoors, embracing the winter wonderland that surrounded them. They were bundled up in warm coats, scarves, and gloves, ready to create memories that would last a lifetime.

As they stepped into the snow, it crunched delightfully beneath their boots. With every step, laughter echoed through the trees as they engaged in friendly snowball fights and built snowmen adorned with hats and scarves.

The crisp air invigorated their spirits. Sam ran through the snow, his laughter mingling with Melissa's as she pelted him with a perfectly aimed snowball. He caught her in his arms, twirling her around as their friends cheered.

His happiness was radiant and unfiltered. He had everything he had ever wanted—Melissa, his new job, and a loving family. Life had never felt this full. And yet beneath it all, a quiet ache for Anna lingered.

But at a distance, away from the warmth and joy, Jake stood watching. His hands were stuffed deep into his coat pockets, his breath curling in the cold air. He saw the way they all moved together—Sam so naturally a part of them, so deeply entrenched in their love and belonging.

And Jake hated it.

He hated how Sam looked at Paul like a brother and how Anna regarded him with pride. He despised how Melissa leaned into him, anchoring him further into this group that had no room for an outsider like Jake.

He clenched his jaw, frustration tightening in his chest. Sam was his son. Jake had lost everything once—his family, his place in their lives—but he wouldn't lose Sam. Not completely. Not to them.

This wasn't where Sam belonged. Their laughter, their history, had pulled him in, reshaping him into one of them. Jake had to remind him of the truth—of who he was, of who his father was.

Taking a deep breath, Jake forced a casual smile and stepped forward, joining the snowball fight. His laughter mingled with the others, but unlike Sam's, it wasn't effortless. It was calculated.

As the sun began to set, painting the sky in hues of pink and orange, the group gathered around a fire pit they had set up. They roasted marshmallows, made s'mores, and shared stories, their hearts warm despite the chill in the air.

"Remember, this is just the beginning," Sam said, looking around at his friends. "We're all in this together, no matter where life takes us."

They toasted to love, friendship, and new beginnings. Melissa leaned into Sam, her heart overflowing with happiness.

Jake stood at the edge, glass in hand, the fire catching only half his face. He raised it with the others, but his thoughts were far away.

Sam was already moving forward too fast, too completely.

Jake tightened his grip on his drink. He wasn't going to let this happen.

Sam was his son. And he wasn't going to lose him to them. He belonged to him, not to this family of borrowed ties.

Anna glanced toward Jake, her expression clouding with sadness for a fraction of a second before shifting into something unreadable.

She had never trusted easily, and old wounds didn't heal overnight. Though Jake had made an effort to join their laughter today, the quiet way he withdrew now made her uneasy.

Paul noticed it, too. He was good at reading people, at sensing the subtle tension that lingered beneath surface pleasantries. While everyone else reveled in the moment, Jake's smile didn't quite reach his eyes. It was as if he were toasting to something else entirely.

Paul's hand instinctively found Anna's, giving it a gentle squeeze. She met his gaze, and though neither of them spoke, the same thought flickered between them.

Jake wasn't laughing with them. He was circling. Watching. Waiting.

He wasn't here to reconnect; he was here to reclaim—Sam, and the life he believed was still his.

Chapter 62

The last spring

As winter gave way to spring, CreeksVille blossomed with color. Tulips flared red, yellow, and purple across the thawing earth; streams rushed free, and the air carried renewal.

During this season of change, Jake began showing up more often—first at the doorway, then at meals, and finally at family gatherings where his presence almost felt routine.

Anna neither encouraged nor resisted. Anger had long since burned out, leaving only indifference. Jake mistook her quiet for progress.

Emma called him "Grandpa Jake" with innocent delight. Paul's polite nods carried no more than courtesy, though Jake took them for respect. He told himself that time was stitching him back into their lives.

With each visit, bitterness gnawed deeper. He saw Paul everywhere—comforting Anna, guiding Sam, steady at Emma's side. Where Paul fit naturally, Jake felt only the hollow of absence.

One Sunday, Jake saw him on the porch, coffee in hand, Emma playing close by.

"I just wanted to thank you for taking care of my family while I was away," Jake said, his tone measured. Paul didn't answer. He set down his cup and turned toward Emma. "Need some water, sweetheart?"

From the doorway, Sam's words cut in. He stood there, arms crossed.

"You sound as if you went off to war," he said evenly. "But you weren't away, Jake. You left."

Jake's face barely shifted, though something flickered in his eyes. He sighed, weary with practiced regret. "If your mom and grandma hadn't made life difficult, I would've stayed. I can't change the past."

He sighed, the sound heavy, almost convincing—as though he'd told this story so many times he now believed it.

Sam's reply was simple. "No, you can't."

Jake forced a chuckle. "Paul's a good man. But a father's role can't really be replaced."

Paul turned. "No. It can't." The words hung in the air, quiet but absolute.

From inside, Anna watched through the window. For years, she had wondered what it would mean to have her father back. Now she saw the truth—there was no missing piece.

Only Jake, rewriting the past to suit himself. Closure was not coming. She had already moved on.

With a quiet sigh, Anna turned away, picking up Emma's coloring book from the table.

Sam kicked at a loose stone on the path, his jaw tight, eyes clouded with the anger he rarely let spill. Anna studied him for a moment, recognizing the same storm she had carried at his age—the same ache for a father who had never stayed. She reached out, resting her hand over his.

"Sam," she said gently.

"You can yearn for the love of your blood relatives, but you can't let that yearning close your heart. Sometimes the deepest, truest love comes from unexpected places—from those who choose to stay when others walk away."

He glanced at her then, and though the frustration hadn't entirely left his face, she saw the words settle, anchoring him in a way that silence never could.

Later, Paul wheeled Anna along the creek path while Sam pushed Emma's stroller. Lizzy and her husband joined, their laughter easing the heaviness of the day.

Anna lifted her phone, capturing the sunrise light, Emma's carefree giggles, Paul's easy smile, and Sam's unwavering calm.

Her cancer had reached stage four, but she had no regrets about leaving treatment behind. She had chosen clarity. Every photo, every glance, every laugh mattered more than the time she had left. Emma's laughter, Paul's devotion, Sam's gentle courage—these were the things that mattered.

The creek rushed alongside them, its song steady and sure, carrying the day forward.

Chapter 63

Broken promise

The lamp threw dim shadows across the walls. Beyond the window, CreeksVille lay in hushed silence. Lavender lingered in the air, the ghost of the tea Anna once loved.

Sam sat beside her bed, his fingers lightly brushing against hers. The warmth that had once filled her hands had faded, but she was still there—his Anna.

She looked beautiful with her pixie cut. He had always thought so, though he never told her enough. Many nights as a child, he had woken to find her sitting beside his bed, watching over him. She thought he was asleep, but he had always known.

He remembered the whispers in the dark, the quiet promises she made when she thought he couldn't hear.

"I love you, Sam. No one will ever take you away from me. I promise."

Now, here he was—watching over her.

Anna stirred, her eyes fluttering open, a small smile playing on her lips as she saw him.

"Hey, kid." Her voice was weaker than he liked.

Sam let out a breathy laugh, though his throat felt tight. "I haven't been a kid in a long time, you know."

Her eyes twinkled, just like they always had when she teased him. "You'll always be my kid, Sam."

He swallowed hard, gripping her hand a little tighter. He had so much to say and so little time.

"I was thinking about when we were little," he said. "When Mom passed, it was just us. I remember how you held my hand at the funeral and wouldn't let go, even when I told you I was too old for that."

Anna chuckled. "You were so little."

"You were eighteen. And you were already acting like a mom." His smile wavered as he looked down at their intertwined hands. She had been his sister, his protector, his everything.

"I don't think I ever told you," he continued, his eyes shining with emotion.

"But I knew then, even as a kid, that I wasn't alone. That I would never be alone as long as I had you."

Sam kissed her hand, holding it to his lips. His eyes were red, the kind that come from too many sleepless nights. "You promised you would never leave me."

Anna's eyes glistened, a single tear slipping down her cheek.

"You were just a kid yourself," he said, shaking his head. "And you had to grow up overnight. You gave up so much for me, Anna. And I don't think I ever really told you how much I—"

His throat caught. He closed his eyes, drew a deep breath, and looked at her again. "How much I love you for it. How much I appreciate you."

Anna's hand squeezed his—weakly. "Oh, Sam."

He leaned closer, his hand tightening gently around hers. "You raised me. The man I am today—who I became—that's because of you."

His lips trembled as he added, "And Paul."

She let out a small, tired laugh. "Paul would love to hear that."

He smiled through his tears. "He's not here right now, so don't tell him. He'll get a big head about it."

Anna let out a slow, quiet breath. "You were always mine to take care of, Sam. But somewhere along the way…you started caring for me, too."

"I'd do it forever if I could."

She gave a faint smile, her voice barely above a breath. "I know."

"I'm so proud of you."

His throat clenched. "I know."

She smiled at that, a sleepy kind of warmth in her expression.

"You were always enough, Sam. You always will be."

He pressed his lips together, fighting back a sob as he leaned forward, resting his forehead against her hand.

"I don't know how to let go of you."

Anna's fingers brushed against his hair.

"You don't have to. I'm always with you."

Sam sucked in a sharp breath and tilted his head toward the ceiling.

"Dear God, you must love my family a lot—first my mom, then my grandma… and now my sister."

Tears poured down his cheeks, his chest tightening with grief, with love, with everything he couldn't put into words.

Anna exhaled—a slow, peaceful breath, as though she had been waiting for his words. Her fingers relaxed in his grip, a trace of tension leaving her face as the burden of pain eased away.

Sam swallowed hard, lifting her frail hand to his lips one last time.

"I'll be okay," he said, though the words tasted like a lie. "Because you made me strong."

He let out a shaky breath, his voice breaking.

"I promise, Anna. I promise I'll keep going. For you. For Paul. For us."

Long after, she slipped into sleep. And long after that, the stars flickered in the night sky, watching over him—just like she always had.

The house was silent.

Paul stood in the doorway, watching Sam, still seated beside the bed, Anna's hand cradled in his. The faint lamplight bathed them both in a golden hush, as if time itself had slowed.

Paul stepped inside quietly, laying a hand on Sam's shoulder. Sam didn't look up, only shifted slightly to let Paul sit on the other side of the bed.

"She's resting," Sam said softly, his voice hoarse.

Paul nodded, reaching for Anna's other hand. He traced the faint blue veins across her skin, his chest aching. "You've been with her all night."

"I didn't want her to be alone."

"You did right," Paul said, his voice steady but thick.

A quiet moment passed, the three of them bound together by the stillness.

Down the hall came the sound of Emma's light footsteps, Lizzy's soft whisper coaxing her back to bed. The ordinary sounds of life felt almost unbearable in their calm

Paul brushed a strand of hair from Anna's forehead. "You fought so hard," he murmured. "But you don't have to anymore."

Sam's eyes glistened. "She told me I was always enough," he said, his voice breaking. "I didn't know how much I needed to hear that until now."

Paul's throat worked as he swallowed. "You were enough. For her. For me. For all of us."

Sam's lips trembled. "I don't want her to go."

Paul didn't answer right away. Instead, he leaned forward, pressing a long kiss to Anna's temple, then whispered so softly Sam barely heard: "If she does, she'll go knowing she was loved."

The fire in the hearth had burned low, glowing embers casting faint light across the room, as if waiting for what would come next.

Paul reached for Sam's hand across Anna's sleeping form. Sam gripped it tightly, grounding himself in the connection.

"We'll be here," Paul said. "Together. However long this takes."

Sam nodded, his jaw set, tears streaking silently down his face. The night stretched on—quiet and sacred—as if holding them all in its palms.

Chapter 64

You must bloom like a tulip

The late-afternoon air carried the tender warmth of early spring, brushing Anna with a fleeting touch. Sunlight filtered through budding trees, scattering fractured patches of gold along the gravel path.

The wind carried the scent of earth and blossoms—honeysuckle, damp grass, cherry—sweet, but already fading.

Paul's footsteps crunched rhythmically on the gravel as he slowly pushed the wheelchair forward. The creek beside them murmured, its clear water glistening under the sun, reflecting the pale blue sky.

A pair of birds flitted from branch to branch, their chirps carrying through the quiet, a reminder that life still sang on.

Anna closed her eyes briefly, tilting her head into the breeze. The wind brushed her skin, whispering of life and memories, of all the seasons she had once run through.

It played with the loose strands of her hair, lifting them gently as if nature itself refused to let her go.

Paul glanced down at her, his chest tightening. She looked so much lighter than before, as if she were slowly fading into the very air around them. Yet in her eyes, there was peace—a quiet acceptance he wasn't ready to acknowledge.

The breeze carried the distant laughter of children playing in the meadow beyond the creek, their voices rising and falling like a melody neither could join, but both could still hear. Life continued, spilling over with warmth and vibrancy. And yet, in this small, quiet moment, time felt suspended—just for them.

As they neared the old oak tree by the lake's edge, Paul slowed the wheelchair, allowing Anna to take in the view. She inhaled deeply, her chest rising with effort as if trying to hold onto the air, the scent of spring, the feeling of the sun on her skin—everything.

And Paul, watching her, wished he could bottle this moment, freeze it in time, and keep it forever. Because deep down, he knew—this was one of their last walks together.

A warm breeze rustled the leaves, and Anna leaned her cheek against Paul's hand.

"I love you," she whispered.

Paul wrapped his arms around her from behind, pressing a tender kiss to her forehead.

"I love you beyond love," he murmured.

As they neared the house, Anna's voice grew feeble.

"Can we stop by the garden?"

The tulips, vibrant and full of life, caught her eye. Each bloom reminded her of joyful afternoons spent nurturing the garden, of laughter spilling into the air as they planted tulip bulbs in the shape of a heart.

Turning to Paul, her gaze grew serious.

"You, too, must bloom like these tulips."

Paul chuckled, teasing her for being philosophical. But the sincerity in her eyes stopped him. She cupped his face, her hands firm yet gentle.

"Emma needs a blooming dad, not a mourning husband," she said.

Paul felt a lump rise in his throat. He looked away, swallowing hard, but Anna leaned in, her kiss filled with love and understanding.

That evening, twilight cast its golden hues across the sky as Paul wheeled Anna back to her room. The gentle creak of the wheelchair echoed a poignant reminder of the fragility of the moment.

The house was steeped in a sacred stillness. A golden lamp glow pooled in the corners, shadows flickering with each shift of the nearby candle flame. The air carried lavender and chamomile—familiar, soothing, and edged with finality.

The wind barely stirred the trees, their branches standing still against the deep indigo sky.

Inside, the hospice room was simple and unobtrusive. The bed by the window gave Anna a view of the fading sunset, its blankets neatly layered for comfort.

The nurse moved in quiet rhythm, adjusting pillows with gentle precision. Paul didn't take his usual chair. Instead, he slid onto the bed beside Anna, gathering her into his arms. Their bodies fit together as if they had always belonged this way.

She felt so small now, so light, her warmth fragile but still present. He rested his chin gently atop her head, his fingers tracing over hers in slow, lingering circles.

The house, though full of love, felt unnaturally still. It was a different kind of quiet—laden with unspoken words, final moments, and an understanding too deep for language. Even the clock on the wall seemed hesitant to tick, its hands sliding almost soundlessly toward the inevitable.

"Would you like some pain medication?" the nurse asked.

With a smile and a gentle shake of her head, Anna replied, "No, thank you. Maybe later."

Paul settled beside her, resting his chin atop her head, his fingers brushing lightly against hers. The quiet rhythm of her breathing matched the thrum of his heartbeat.

"Do you remember our honeymoon in France?" Anna asked, her voice barely above a breath.

Paul nodded, his throat tightening. "Of course I do."

A wistful smile touched her lips. "That little village with the cobblestone streets, the flower market, and the enchanting library—it felt like we'd stepped into a storybook," she murmured.

Paul closed his eyes. "It was the happiest time of my life."

Anna's breathing grew shallower, and her gaze drifted as if she were seeing something beyond the room, beyond the moment.

In her mind's eye, a memory—or perhaps a vision—began to unfold.

She saw a red train pulling into the station of a quiet French village, its wheels clattering gently over the tracks.

A low, melodic horn echoed through the valley, announcing its arrival, blending with the rustling of spring leaves in the breeze. The golden afternoon light stretched across cobblestone streets, casting long, dappled shadows.

A gentle wind carried the faint perfume of wildflowers and blooming wisteria, their delicate petals swaying from stone archways. Clusters of daffodils and violets peeked through the cracks between weathered stones, their colors vibrant against the sunlit haze.

The distant chime of the village clock tower merged with the train's final, rhythmic hiss as it came to a stop. An old man played a slow, wistful melody on his violin near a quiet fountain, the notes floating through the still air like a gentle farewell.

Anna watched as the doors opened, revealing her mother standing inside the train, radiant with joy. Nearby, her grandmother waved enthusiastically, waiting beneath the shade of an ancient oak, her presence as warm as the sunlit air.

A deep peace settled over Anna as she stepped forward, her hands reaching for theirs. But before she crossed the threshold, she paused.

Turning back, she saw Paul.

His eyes were full of love, and she knew—he would carry her with him always.

She took one step back, pressing a gentle kiss to his lips. The warmth of his skin, his familiar scent, and the love in his touch were all she had ever known. All she had ever needed.

"Thank you," she whispered, her breath no louder than a breeze. Yet it carried every memory, every moment, every ounce of love she had ever known.

Paul pressed a kiss to the top of her head, his tears spilling. "Thank you, Anna," he said, his shoulders shaking. "For everything."

With a final smile, she turned, stepping onto the train.

The doors closed behind her. The train gave a gentle lurch, then slowly began to move. Paul watched as it pulled away, disappearing into the golden light, carrying his love beyond his reach.

Moments later, her body stilled in his arms, her breath fading away.

Paul froze. His heart pounded in his chest as he gently shook her.

"Anna, sweetheart, darling, are you okay?" His voice trembled with desperation.

The nurse entered the room, her expression shifting as she realized what had happened. She approached quietly, placing a gentle hand on Paul's shoulder.

The world around him seemed to collapse. He stared at Anna's serene face, free from pain, and his heart shattered. She looked so peaceful, almost as if she were merely asleep. But the stillness in the room was deafening—a silence that spoke of an irrevocable loss.

Paul lay still, holding Anna close. Her absence pressed against him like a physical weight. Memories of their love, their laughter, and the life they had built together flooded his mind, each one bittersweet in its vividness.

He rested his chin atop her head, tracing her fingers in slow, lingering circles.

He bowed his head. "I'll take care of Emma," he whispered. "And I'll keep blooming—just like you said."

Chapter 65

An eternal moment

Sam, Melissa, and Lizzy sat on the porch of the café, sipping tea as the sky darkened with heavy clouds. The world outside carried on as if nothing had changed, but Sam's chest felt tight, as though he were bracing for something unseen.

Then his phone rang.

He stared at the screen—Paul's father, Thomas.

Sam swallowed hard before answering.

"Thomas?"

There was a pause, a slow inhale. Then Thomas spoke, calm but heavy: "Sam, you need to come home."

Sam sat up straighter, his stomach twisting.

"Is it Anna?"

For a heartbeat, no one spoke.

"Yes."

Melissa's hand covered her mouth, her eyes filling with tears before Sam could even look at her.

The drive back was suffocating. It felt like an eternity.

By the time they pulled up to the house, the sight of the ambulance parked outside and the somber faces of waiting relatives confirmed their worst fears. Sam barely registered Lizzy's hand, squeezing his before he stumbled out of the car, running inside.

The room was too quiet. Paul stood motionless, his gaze fixed on Anna's still form.

Sam felt the world tilt. His legs gave out beneath him, and he sank to the floor. Thomas knelt beside him, wrapping him in a quiet embrace.

Melissa, pale and tearful, looked up. "Where's Emma?" The question barely escaped her lips. "She's with your mom," Mary replied, her voice thick with sorrow.

The Riley home felt suffocating in the hours that followed.

She lingered in every corner—the scent of her perfume clinging to the blankets, her favorite sweater draped over the armchair as if she might walk in at any moment and slip it on.

Sam's shoulders sagged, his eyes red and swollen. Paul moved through the house like a ghost, carrying out necessary tasks on autopilot, but his presence was just an echo of the man he had been.

In the corner, Emma played quietly, her small giggles breaking through the silence like wind chimes against a storm.

Paul caught glimpses of her, a stark contrast to the grief that engulfed him. She sat cross-legged on the floor, her doll cradled in her arms, blissfully unaware of the storm brewing in the hearts around her.

The sight of her innocence was both a refuge and a dagger to Paul's soul—a reminder of everything that had been lost.

That night, Paul lingered at the threshold of Emma's room, watching her tiny chest rise and fall in gentle rhythm.

She had drifted off mid-sentence, her fingers still curled around the stuffed bear Anna had gifted her, its fur slightly worn from countless hugs.

Paul's heart twisted. How long before she started asking where her mother had gone?

How long before she realized that the warm embrace she craved would no longer be there?

Careful not to wake her, he tucked the blanket around her, smoothing a strand of hair from her forehead.

In the dim light of the kitchen, Paul poured himself a drink. Then his gaze landed on Anna's favorite mug sitting by the sink.

Her sweater still hung over a chair, its sleeves folded neatly as if waiting for her return.

His eyes flicked to the calendar on the fridge, marked with her neat handwriting—birthdays, anniversaries, little notes that once filled their days with meaning.

Now, they were just reminders of what would never be.

His breath came short, tight bursts. The world had moved on without her.

With a quiet thud, the glass slipped from his grip, shattering against the floor.

The sound echoed through the hollow house, and Paul gave in to the grief he'd been holding back for days.

Gripping the counter, he bowed his head, his body trembling as grief surged through him like a tidal wave.

Tears blurred his vision, hot and relentless.

Lizzy sat alone on her kitchen floor, the shadows stretching long across the room. The refrigerator hummed, a stark contrast to the heavy silence that enveloped her.

She clutched an empty ice cream carton. It had been their ritual—midnight ice cream on hard days, laughter woven into every spoonful. But now, the only sound was her ragged breathing, the quiet that came when absence felt too loud.

"Help me, God. Please help me," she breathed, her voice breaking in the stillness.

Bob stood in the doorway, grief settling heavy in his chest. He had loved her like family, but it was Lizzy who had lost a part of herself.

He crossed the room in silence and sank beside her, gathering her trembling shoulders into his arms.

"You've got to pull yourself together, honey," he murmured, gentle but firm. "Anna wouldn't want this."

Lizzy didn't answer; she just leaned into him, her body sagging beneath the weight of loss.

Her gaze drifted to the table, where two small wooden boxes sat side by side. Their names were engraved on them—one for her, one for Bob—an unspoken promise left behind.

Bob reached for hers and pressed it into her hands.

"I Will Always Be There," she read aloud. The words shimmered in the dim light, carrying Anna's presence into the space between them.

Later, at the kitchen table, Lizzy cradled a steaming cup of tea, the warmth seeping into her fingers as she traced the edges of the box.

She hesitated before opening it.

Inside, nestled among delicate keepsakes, was a letter. Her heart clenched at the sight of Anna's familiar handwriting—so effortlessly alive on the page.

Taking a deep breath, she unfolded it, her hands trembling.

"Dear Lizzy," it began, the playful tone igniting a flicker of warmth within her.

"If you're reading this, it means I've succeeded in surprising you from beyond! I can almost hear you gasping and muttering, 'That cheeky woman!'"

A chuckle escaped Lizzy's lips before she could stop it. The sound was foreign but welcome.

"You're probably saying, 'I'm juggling a million things as it is!'" Lizzy wiped at her tears, half laughing.

Anna always knew exactly what she would say and what she would need to hear.

The words wrapped around her like a hug, filling the emptiness in the room.

Anna had written about their memories, their inside jokes, their shared dreams. She had written about life, about moving forward, about love that never ends.

Tears streamed down Lizzy's cheeks, but they were no longer just of sorrow.

They were of understanding, of gratitude, of resolve.

Anna had left her with something more than grief.

She had left her a promise.

Lizzy pressed the letter to her heart, inhaling deeply.

"I've got this, Anna. I promise," she said to herself, conviction glinting in her eyes.

Somewhere beyond the veil of loss, she could almost hear Anna's laugh—knowing, full of life.

The hearse pulled away slowly, its taillights glowing red against the gray morning, flickering embers vanishing into the fog.

Chapter 66

A full bloom

The day of Anna's wake dawned bright and serene, a July morning washed in light. The tulips, her favorite flowers, stood in full bloom—a fitting tribute to a life that had brought so much color and warmth to those around her.

So many came to pay their respects that the funeral had to be postponed until the following day. The funeral home overflowed with friends and family, each carrying cherished memories of Anna.

Paul moved with quiet determination, ensuring every detail was as she would have wanted. Sam, though grief-stricken, worked tirelessly to honor his sister's memory, his presence a pillar amid the storm of loss.

Anna's daughter, Emma, too young to understand, wandered through the crowd, her small hands reaching for familiar faces.

Her presence was a poignant reminder of Anna's legacy—a flicker of innocence and resilience amidst the grief, as if Anna's spirit lived on through her.

The ambiance of Anna's funeral hung heavy in the air, a palpable mix of sorrow and remembrance that settled over the Riley home.

The morning blazed with light, indifferent to the sorrow that lingered within, where every room seemed to breathe loss. Friends and family gathered, their faces a tapestry of tears and quiet reflection as they navigated the emotional labyrinth of grief.

A murmur filled the living room, punctuated by the occasional sob. Flowers adorned every surface, their vibrant colors bittersweet—a tribute to the life Anna had led.

The scent of lilies and tulips mingled with the faintest hint of incense, a calming presence that seemed to hush the pain, if only for a moment.

In the corner, a table held framed photographs of Anna—capturing moments of laughter, quiet joy, and love that now felt almost out of reach.

Her smile radiated warmth from every image, a stark reminder of the light she had brought into their lives. Guests paused by the table, their fingers tracing the frames, sharing whispers of memories that echoed like distant songs.

A hush fell over the crowd when it was time for the eulogies.

Sam stood first. His hands trembled as he gripped the podium.

"She was my sister, my mother, and my father all in one," he said, tears brimming in his eyes. "Without her, I wouldn't be here. She gave me everything—her love, her life, her dreams. And now, I'll carry her dreams forward."

He paused, his breath ragged, before stepping back into Paul's embrace. Paul stood with his gaze fixed on the casket, his hands clasped tightly behind him, holding himself together by sheer will.

Next came Lizzy. Her voice wavered as she recounted their decades of friendship, then brightened with a laugh.

"I'll never forget the day Anna turned on the mixer without adding water—flour exploded across the bakery, dusting every poor customer at the counter.

And then there was the time she poured coffee into the dough instead of water. I won't say who handed her the cup, but that's how her famous coffee cookies were born. Trust Anna to turn a blunder into a signature treat."

Lizzy paused, eyes glistening yet playful. She looked up and gave a small salute, sending a ripple of laughter and tears through the room. "And of course, the night we bought cookies from Mrs. Jones and accidentally got high—we spent hours convinced we were characters from Harry Potter."

A tearful smile broke across her face as the memory carried both laughter and a pang of ache.

Laughter rippled again—a brief reprieve from sorrow. It was the kind of memory Anna would have wanted them to hold onto, a reminder that she had lived, loved, and laughed fully.

Melissa rose slowly from her seat, her hands trembling as she clasped them together. The hush in the room deepened as she drew in a shaky breath.

And then, she began to sing.

Her voice was soft at first, uncertain in the silence, but as the words carried into the air, they gathered strength. The melody wrapped around the mourners like a thread of light, soft and unbroken.

"I Will Always Love You" swelled and softened, each note a testament to love and loss, stirring emotions long held in silence. Tears blurred faces, a shared release weaving them together in grief.

Sam closed his eyes. He had heard that song once before—his mother had sung it to them on the hardest nights, when grief pressed too close. Hearing it now, in Melissa's voice, felt like something inside him breaking open.

His throat tightened, but when Melissa's voice faltered, he found himself standing. His voice joined hers, rough at first, then steadier, rising with hers until the two of them wove together—a duet of love and loss, brother and friend bound by the same promise to Anna.

The room shifted. People leaned forward. A few clasped hands. Tear-streaked faces.

And then Lizzy rose. Without a word, she gathered Emma into her arms. The little girl stirred, resting her head on Lizzy's shoulder, her tiny hand clutching at Lizzy's sleeve. Carrying her, Lizzy stepped closer, and when the chorus swelled, she added her own voice.

Three voices now—Melissa's steady, Sam's breaking but resolute, Lizzy's strong and sure. Together, they filled the room, lifting the song into something larger than grief, larger than any one person.

Emma stirred again, her eyes half-open, and in that instant it was as though Anna herself had joined them—woven into every note, every breath.

By the time the final words fell into silence, the room was trembling with the weight of it. No applause. No movement. Just a sacred stillness, as though everyone present understood they had just witnessed something eternal.

After the service, guests moved to the café—Anna's cherished second home.

The familiar aroma of coffee mingled with the scent of freshly baked pastries, creating a comforting atmosphere amidst the heartache.

For a while, no one spoke, only sitting together in quiet reflection. Then, slowly, laughter began to weave through the crowd.

They shared stories, speaking her name, recounting the quirks, the kindness, and the mischief that made Anna who she was.

They honored her not just in their sorrow but in the joy of remembrance.

In that space, grief began to loosen its grip, softening as Anna's spirit echoed in their words, in their laughter, in the love they still carried for her.

Friends and family leaned on one another, the warmth of connection a balm for their aching hearts. They vowed to keep Anna alive in the way she would have wanted—by living, by loving, by remembering.

And as the sun dipped below the horizon, casting golden light over the town she had called home, they knew—Anna would remain with them, in every tulip that bloomed, every burst of laughter, every act of love freely given.

Chapter 67

Carrying the beat

The entrance to the café bloomed with life—a sea of vibrant flowers, flickering candlelight, and heartfelt notes pinned delicately to the walls.

Inside, the aroma of fresh pastries mingled with the voices sharing stories punctuated now and then by ripples of bittersweet laughter. It felt as if the walls held Anna's presence, echoing her warmth and joy.

"Anna used to love these cookies," someone said, pointing to a tray of chocolate chip treats on the counter.

"Remember how she'd always mess up the timer?" another chimed, prompting warm chuckles.

As their sadness began to ebb, it was replaced by a quiet joy as they recalled Anna's quirky humor and her relentless determination to brighten everyone's day. Her spirit lingered in every corner of the café, in the recipes she perfected and the smiles she inspired.

With the café bustling with familiar faces, Melissa stepped into her new role, ensuring the place continued to thrive.

She kept the menu simple—offering coffee, soups, and pastries—while managing daily operations. Yet every action felt like a tribute to Anna, a way to preserve her legacy.

The walls—once merely a backdrop—transformed into a tapestry of love and remembrance. Colorful photographs of Anna laughing and living life to the fullest adorned the space alongside handwritten notes from patrons.

Each new message felt like another thread weaving into the rich fabric of the community she had built.

As Melissa tied her apron that morning, a wooden box on the counter caught her eye. Paul had left it there earlier, and her heart skipped a beat upon recognizing Anna's handwriting on a sealed envelope.

Her hands trembled as she unfolded the letter, her fingers tracing the familiar curves of Anna's script.

Dear Melissa,

If you're reading this, then I suppose it's official—you're not just part of the family; you're stuck with me forever. And since being your sister-in-law comes with certain privileges, I'm pulling rank and handing over something very close to my heart.

I'm giving you my share of the café. If anyone can keep its magic alive, it's you. You've always had a way of bringing people together, of making a place feel like home. I know you'll do the same for this place.

But there's more. I've always dreamed of extending the café's warmth to those who need it most. Remember the meal program Paul started for chemotherapy patients? It was one of the best things to ever come out of this place, and now it's yours to carry forward. Promise me you'll keep it going—rally the community, sprinkle your magic, and make it extraordinary.

Thank you for being you—for your kindness, your strength, and your huge, generous heart. I'll miss you more than words can say.

With all my love, Anna

Melissa folded the letter slowly, her fingers lingering on its edges, trying to hold onto Anna's presence just a moment longer. She tucked it gently into her apron pocket, whispering, "I miss you too, Anna."

Taking a deep breath, she entered the kitchen, enveloped by the comforting aroma of freshly baked pastries. She reached for a towel and pulled open the oven door, a wave of warmth washing over her as golden croissants crackled in the heat.

The scent wrapped around her like an embrace, stirring memories—Anna teaching her to make the perfect croissant, their laughter over flour-dusted countertops, and Sam sneaking in for warm pastries.

Tears filled Melissa's eyes as she remembered how Anna had welcomed her into the family long before she became her sister-in-law.

As the day unfolded, Melissa held Anna's words close to her heart, guiding her ahead. The café had evolved into more than a business; it was a mosaic woven with love, laughter, and compassion.

With each customer who walked in, Melissa felt the legacy of her promise to Anna—to keep the café alive and nurture it as a sanctuary for the community, just as Anna had always envisioned.

She could almost hear Anna's laughter mingling with the clinking of cups and the chatter of patrons, creating a sweet symphony of memories that would never fade.

Today, as she prepared meals for chemotherapy patients, Melissa felt Anna's guiding hand in every stir of the pot and every slice of bread. After all, love was the secret ingredient that made every dish extraordinary.

And as laughter rose and the scent of fresh bread drifted through the café, Melissa knew this wasn't just a café. It was Anna's heartbeat—carried forward, still alive, still shaping the world she left behind.

Chapter 68

Bad blood

Jake stood beside Sam and Lizzy during the wake, anger simmering beneath his self-pity. Anna's death wasn't about the daughter he had lost—it was about him. She had died without giving him the chance to reclaim his place, and now he had no way to rewrite the years he had thrown away.

To Jake, Anna's death felt like an injustice, and he laid the blame squarely on Paul.

"If only my daughter had continued her treatment, she'd still be alive today," he lamented to anyone who would listen, his voice tinged with self-pity and bitterness.

At just thirty-eight, Anna's life had been cut far too short. Jake carried a profound sense of failure, buried beneath misplaced resentment toward Paul.

He despised Paul's place in Sam's life—every bond between them deepened his own sense of failure.

The truth was, Jake felt small—just as he always had in the presence of his late wife, Sarah, his brothers, and even his parents. He projected these feelings onto Paul, whom he perceived as smug and superior, though the reality stemmed from Jake's own guilt for abandoning his family.

Jake couldn't fathom that someone like Paul might genuinely care for another man's child without ulterior motives. Instead, he harbored fantasies of reclaiming his place in the family despite having forfeited it years ago.

Jake had carefully planned his move to CreeksVille. With his mother's passing a year earlier and no ties left in the neighboring county, he saw Sam's letter as an invitation to rebuild. But his motivations weren't pure.

He viewed his family—especially Sam—not as people to reconnect with, but as a lifeline. Jake envisioned a future where Sam would support him financially in his old age.

He hoped Anna's passing would strengthen his bond with his son, believing that shared grief could help him manipulate Sam's decisions.

By positioning himself as a guide, Jake intended to quietly claim control over the family's assets, particularly Anna's share of the café and the house.

The day before the wake, Jake joined Sam for a drive under the pretense of running errands. Once the road stretched quiet before them, Jake cleared his throat.

"It's hard to believe she's gone," he began, malice threading through his voice. "If only Paul had convinced her to keep fighting. A husband should do that—protect his wife."

Sam's knuckles whitened against the steering wheel. "Dad, it was Anna's choice. Paul stood by her, like any good husband would."

Jake let out a derisive laugh. Paul stood by her? No—he stood by and let her die. Sam jerked the wheel into the supermarket parking lot and slammed the car to a stop. His chest rose and fell with restrained fury. "What exactly are you trying to say?"

Jake leaned closer, speaking low as if they were conspirators. "I'm saying you need to be smart now. Anna's share of the café—why should Paul get it? He'll remarry, move on, and you'll be left with nothing.

You've worked harder for that café than anyone. And the house? That should be ours, yours, and mine. Family blood, Sam. Not an outsider."

Sam's jaw clenched. "Paul is my family."

Jake sneered. "He's not blood. Remember that. When the grief fades, he'll forget you. But me? I'll always be your father. We could set things right—together. Anna's gone, but you and I…we can make sure what's left doesn't slip through our fingers."

The words hit Sam like poison. He slammed the gearshift into park and turned on his father, eyes blazing. "Stop. Just stop. You left us. Paul picked up the pieces you threw away. He gave me a home when you didn't care if I had one. Don't you dare call yourself the one who stayed."

Jake opened his mouth, but Sam cut him off, his anger breaking through. "Anna's memory isn't yours to twist into some scheme. If you can't see that, then maybe you've already lost me too."

Silence filled the car, thick and final. Sam stepped out, slamming the door behind him, leaving Jake in the echo of his own bitterness.

But Jake wasn't finished. His bitterness spilled into the days that followed. He spread rumors about Paul, portraying him as manipulative and accusing him of distancing Anna from her family and discouraging her treatment.

He leaned back, rubbing his jaw, his voice low and brooding.

"I had the papers ready. If I'd just had the chance to talk to her alone… she would've signed them."

Sam's chest tightened. The certainty in his father's voice made his stomach turn—as if Anna's silence had been consent, as if her choice not to sign meant nothing.

"Paul is the reason I've had a stable life. Anna is the reason I didn't end up in foster care. He gave me a home, a family, and a sense of purpose. You left. And now you think you can walk back in and tear all of that apart?"

Jake's face hardened, but he had no response. Sam's words cut through the excuses and self-pity, laying bare the truth Jake refused to acknowledge.

As Sam closed the door behind him, he felt a mixture of relief and sadness. Confronting Jake had been necessary, but it wasn't easy. For too long, Sam had carried the burden of his father's shortcomings, allowing Jake's toxicity to weigh on his peace of mind.

Standing in the quiet of the night, Sam took a deep breath, letting the cool air fill his lungs. He thought of Anna—her strength, her unwavering love for their family—and Paul, whose quiet support had been a foundation in his life.

That night, Sam made a pivotal decision: he would no longer carry the Buchman name. He would be a Riley. And in that choice, it felt as if Anna's hand rested on his shoulder, steady and sure, as though she were telling him he had done the right thing.

Sam stared up at the night sky for a long moment, then turned back toward the house, his steps lighter, his resolve clear.

Inside, Jake slumped back on the couch, the room spinning around him. His jaw worked as if chewing on the silence Sam had left behind.

What an idiot, he thought bitterly, reaching for the bottle on the table.

Chapter 69

I belong here

The evening after the wake, Sam received a call from the bar; he rushed over to find his father, Jake, slumped over the counter, drowning his grief in alcohol. With the bartender's help, Sam managed to get Jake into the car and drove him home.

The acrid smell of whiskey filled the car, making the tense ride feel suffocating.

Sam helped his father into the living room at home, carefully lowering him onto the couch. Slurred but insistent, Jake muttered, "We could move to New York, you know? Start fresh. This town just brings grief."

Sam brushed off the comment, turning to leave, but Jake pressed on, his tone laced with condescension. "That Melissa girl? She'll only hold you back. In New York, you could have someone better."

The words hit Sam like a blow. He froze mid-step, frustration and anger bubbling to the surface. Closing his eyes, he clenched his fists to hold himself together. Without a word, he turned back, walked to the table, and carelessly dropped a set of keys onto its surface.

"You're welcome to stay in Mom's house for as long as you want," Sam said coldly, his face devoid of emotion.

Jake perked up at the offer, suddenly more energized. "Good," he replied, sitting up straighter. "Now, about the bakery. You should go after Anna's share. It's your right, son."

Sam stepped closer, his anger now dangerously close to the surface. Jake looked so small in that moment—diminished by years of bitterness, selfishness, and regret.

Sam's low but firm voice cut through the tension like a blade. "Let me make something clear," he said deliberately.

"I'm not a Buchman anymore; I'm a Riley. I carry the name of the man who raised me. My mom didn't want to die as your wife, and I don't want to live as your son."

The slam echoed through the house, leaving a ringing silence in its wake. Sam stood there for a long moment, staring at the man who had once been his father.

There was nothing left to salvage—not anger, not pity, not even hope—only the clean, cold resolve to cut the last thread tying him to this house.

The night air felt sharp, bracing, almost clean. Sam stood on the porch for a long moment, staring up at the stars, letting the anger bleed out of him until all that was left was resolve.

The next morning, Sam stood at the courthouse. This wasn't just paperwork; it was a declaration of independence, a step toward reclaiming his identity.

Jake's name had always felt like a heavy, cold shadow—a reminder of abandonment, the void his father left, and the burden Anna had shouldered.

He saw Paul at his graduation, standing in the back row of the bleachers. While most parents clapped politely, Paul had been on his feet, whistling and cheering like Sam had just won a championship.

His cheeks had burned as he fought a grin—but it felt good, someone finally proud enough to make noise about him.

And then there was that night on the couch, a movie flickering across the screen. The story had caught them both off guard, raw and close to the bone, and Sam had felt the sting of tears he couldn't stop.

He'd braced himself for teasing, but when he glanced sideways, Paul's eyes were wet too. No jokes, no shame—just the two of them, letting it spill, side by side.

His hand hovered for a moment, the pen heavy between his fingers. This was more than ink on paper—it was a clean break, a new beginning, a promise to himself that the past would no longer own him.

Sam bent over the paper and wrote the name that finally felt like his own—Samuel Riley.

The words felt foreign yet empowering, like a suit tailored perfectly for him, carrying the legacy of love and resilience instead of pain.

That night, Paul approached Sam with a wooden box, its surface smooth and polished, carrying the wear of love. "This is from Anna," Paul said, handing it to him.

As the sun dipped below the horizon, casting a warm, golden light over the backyard, Sam sat alone, the box resting on his lap. The laughter of children playing nearby filled the air—a poignant reminder of the joy Anna had always sought to cultivate.

Sam opened the box to find a collection of letters written in Anna's neat, familiar handwriting. His hands trembled as he picked up the first envelope.

Inside were words of love, wisdom, and encouragement, each sentence a thread in the tapestry of Anna's spirit.

She wrote about her hopes for him, her belief in his potential, and the strength she saw in him. She reminded him of their humble beginnings and the sacrifices they had made together.

One letter, in particular, caught his eye.

Anna wrote:

"Sam, I know you will go on to do incredible things. You've always had that fire within you—the one that refuses to give up, no matter how hard life gets.

I want you to chase your dreams as an attorney, find love with Melissa, and build a life you can be proud of. That's all I ever wanted for you—to see you happy, loved, and thriving. So, make my dreams come true, little brother."

Sam read the letter aloud to Melissa that evening. Each word seemed to carry Anna's spirit, weaving a bridge between the past and the future. The letters spoke of resilience, of facing challenges with courage, and of holding onto family.

Sam stood beneath the stars, a new resolve settling in his chest. He looked skyward and murmured, "I'll make you proud, Anna. I promise."

The stars shimmered, as if listening.

Melissa joined him, slipping her hand into his. Together, they stood beneath the vast sky, their grief easing, lightened by love.

Neither her illness nor her passing defined Anna's legacy. It was a living, breathing force—a testament to her strength, love, and the indomitable spirit she had passed on to those she left behind.

As Sam and Melissa walked back into the house, they carried the lessons Anna had imparted and the light she had left behind. At that moment, Sam knew he truly belonged—not just as a Riley, but as a part of the beautiful, unbreakable tapestry of family and love that Anna had so carefully woven.

Chapter 70

My lamp in the storm

The next day, as the procession to Anna's final resting place began, Paul, Sam, Bob, and the others carried the coffin together. Each step was heavy, pressed down by loss, yet lifted by the strength of love.

It was a farewell to Anna and a celebration—a tribute to a woman whose life had left an indelible mark on everyone she touched.

After the funeral, Paul's home overflowed with friends and family, their murmurs and shared grief filling the spaces between them.

Lizzy and the café staff prepared a comforting feast, ensuring no one was left hungry—for food, warmth, or solace

Conversations ebbed and flowed, punctuated by quiet moments of shared grief and bursts of laughter as memories of Anna eased the heavy atmosphere.

Tucking Emma into bed, Paul stepped onto the porch, seeking solace under the quiet night sky. Memories of his arrival in CreeksVille with Anna flooded his mind—a journey that had brought hope, love, and a sense of belonging.

A gentle tap on his shoulder pulled him from his reverie. Sam stood there, offering him a drink.

They sat together watching the stars emerge one by one. The stillness between them spoke volumes, each man finding comfort in the other's presence.

Jake joined them, breaking the quiet. Draping an arm over Sam's shoulder, he said, "Let's put this grief behind us, son. Maybe a fresh start in New York?"

Sam stiffened and shrugged Jake off, stepping away.

"Jake, I told you last night—we're done."

His words were tinged with restrained emotion. They hung in the air, heavy with finality.

Sam took a deep breath, his hands tightening around the folded paper. He had rehearsed this moment in his head a thousand times, yet now that it was here, his throat nearly failed him.

"Paul," he said, handing over the document. Paul took it, unfolding the crisp paper with careful fingers.

Silence stretched between them as Paul read, his eyes scanning the name at the bottom—**Samuel Riley.**

When he looked up, his eyes shimmered. Sam swallowed hard.

"I wanted this for a long time. To be a part of this family, truly."

Paul pulled him into a firm embrace, his voice thick with emotion.

At that moment, Lizzy peeked out from the doorway, holding a food tray.

Wiping his eyes, Sam chuckled.

"Can we eat now?"

Paul laughed, realizing their bond ran deeper than ever. At that moment, family was redefined—not by blood but by love and loyalty.

Later that night, after the last guest had left and Emma was fast asleep in her bed, Paul sat on the porch steps, elbows resting on his knees, staring into the dark expanse of the night. The cold had settled deep into his skin, but he barely felt it.

Sam had just gone to bed. The word "Sam Riley" still echoed in Paul's mind.

Paul exhaled, his breath curling in the night air. He hadn't expected that. Not ever.

He had spent months afraid of losing Sam to his manipulative father, scared that one day Jake would say the right thing, spin the right lie, and take him away. The thought of it had tightened Paul's chest more times than he could count.

But tonight, Sam had made his choice. And it wasn't Jake. It was Anna. It was them.

Paul swallowed hard. The house behind him was quiet, save for the creak of old wood settling. The funeral, the endless condolences, the blur of the day—it was all over now. And yet, his heart still felt unbearably heavy.

He looked up at the sky, at the thick clouds that refused to part.

"You hear that, Anna?" he murmured, his breath rough with exhaustion and grief. "Sam's a Riley now."

Saying it out loud made his throat tighten. He rubbed a hand over his face.

"You'd be proud of him."

He paused, his chest rising and falling with a deep breath.

"You'd be proud of all of us, I think."

Paul didn't know if he believed in anything beyond this life. But if Anna were anywhere—if she could hear him—he wanted her to know.

He wanted her to know that her name lived on. That Sam had chosen to carry it. They were still here, trying to hold on and be enough for Emma.

He looked into the night sky. "I hope you're watching," he said quietly. "I hope you know we're doing our best. Even when it hurts like hell."

The wind picked up, rustling the trees in the distance.

It wasn't an answer—but somehow, it felt like one.

Paul lingered a moment longer before rising and heading inside.

The grief would always remain, but so would the light—steady, flickering, alive—like Anna.

Five years later

Years after that winter of loss, on a crisp December evening, the Riley home was filled with warmth once again.

The first Christmas without Anna had felt unbearable. The second softened, the third became ritual. By the fifth, grief had settled into something gentler—a presence rather than a wound.

Raising Emma alone had been a journey filled with heartache and joy for Paul. He kept Anna's memory alive through bedtime stories, baking sessions, and small traditions that ensured Emma would always know the mother who had loved her fiercely.

Lizzy, Bob, and Melissa had been his steadfast support, while Sam, despite his demanding legal career, remained deeply involved in their lives.

But today, joy had returned to the Riley home. Paul stood before the mirror, adjusting Sam's tie with a proud grin. "You look dashing in that tuxedo," he declared.

Sam chuckled. "Paul, you're getting sentimental."

"Just let me have my moment," Paul said with mock indignation, straightening Sam's lapel one last time.

"Dad! We're going to be late!" Emma called from downstairs, her excitement filling the house.

Grandma Mary descended the staircase with Emma, who twirled in her pink flower girl dress.

"They're waiting for me at the church!" Emma exclaimed, her radiant smile lighting up the room.

Emma and Lizzy rushed into the bride's dressing room at the church. Melissa stood before a full-length mirror, her wedding gown cascading gracefully to the floor.

Sunlight streamed through the window, illuminating the veil draped over her shoulders and the bouquet of red roses in her hands. Her mother, sister, and cousins fussed over her final touches, their chatter filling the room with warmth.

When the organ began to play, the church doors opened. Emma led the procession, scattering petals along the aisle, her joy infectious. Behind her, Melissa's older sister, Dr. Melody Davis, walked as the maid of honor, flanked by Lizzy and Melissa's sister-in-law as bridesmaids.

As the bridal march began, Melissa entered, escorted by her parents. Sam stood at the altar, his breath catching as he saw her. She looked ethereal, the embodiment of every dream he had ever dared to have.

The ceremony was brief but heartfelt. When the pastor pronounced them husband and wife, the couple walked back down the aisle, their smiles shining as brightly as the sunlight streaming through the stained glass.

Jake, now looking old and tired, sat quietly among the other guests, his gaze fixed on Sam, Paul, and Emma at the altar. Their easy camaraderie twisted like a thorn in his chest.

He should have been standing there as the groom's father, sharing in the moment's pride. Instead, he sat on the sidelines, a guest in a family that had moved on without him.

He offered a thin smile and muttered an excuse before slipping out unnoticed. The celebration belonged to others now, and the night carried on without him.

The reception at Pine Valley was a joyous affair. Sam and Melissa's first dance was a tender moment that brought tears to everyone's eyes.

Melissa and her father swayed in a heartfelt dance, the moment steeped in love and nostalgia. The music broke the hush of the room, and the sight of them together sent a ripple of emotion through everyone watching.

Paul hesitated when it was time for the best man and maid of honor's dance, but Melody, Melissa's sister, twirled confidently onto the floor, teasing,

"We're a family of fine dancers. Just follow my lead."

Paul laughed nervously but soon found himself swept up in the rhythm. As the music ended, applause erupted, and he escorted Melody back to the table.

"I've heard much about you and your work from Melissa," Paul said. "It's a pleasure to finally meet you, Dr. Davis."

"Please, call me Mel. My close friends and family call me that."

Paul blushed slightly but nodded. "Mel, it is," he said.

They found themselves on the dance floor again as the night continued. Their conversation flowed effortlessly, and a surprising connection formed between them. Later, they stepped onto the balcony to enjoy the crisp night air.

"How long are you in CreeksVille?" Paul asked.

"Just tonight," Mel replied. "I'm in the middle of a tour in Nepal with Doctors Without Borders. I've got another year left."

Paul hesitated before asking, "And after that?"

Mel's expression changed. "I'm planning to return to CreeksVille to work with my parents," she said, her voice tinged with nostalgia.

She shared memories of Anna, whom she had known since childhood. "Anna was a pure soul," she said sincerely.

Paul nodded, emotion flickering across his face. "She was," he agreed quietly.

As they moved to go inside, Mel's stiletto caught in the lace of her gown. Struggling to free herself, she laughed, "I'm a disaster tonight."

Paul knelt to untangle the fabric. As he did, Mel hesitated and asked softly, "Can I call you?"

Paul looked up, his expression thoughtful but warm. "Yes," he replied.

The evening ended with laughter and promises. Beneath the twinkling stars, there was a sense of hope—a feeling that even amidst loss, life had a way of unfolding beautifully.

As Sam and Melissa drove away that night, a trail of sparkling lights twinkled in their rearview mirror, marking the start of a new chapter.

The celebration had been everything they had hoped for—a night filled with love, laughter, and the quiet presence of those who had shaped their lives, even those who were no longer there—but whose love still lingered in every laugh and every light.

Chapter 71

Return to joy

Winter returned to CreeksVille—but this time, it carried laughter instead of tears.

The Riley home brimmed with warmth and the sound of life—proof that even after the longest winter, the heart remembers how to bloom.

Outside, snow sifted down over CreeksVille, stilling the world beneath a soft white hush.

Sam arrived with his family, laughter trailing behind them.

The door swung open to Emma—ten, her mother's mirror—her grin lighting the doorway.

Before anyone could step inside, two-year-old Anna Riley—named after her late aunt—her curls bouncing with excitement, dashed past her cousin and leaped into Paul's arms.

"Uncle Paul!" she squealed, her giggles filling the crisp air.

Paul laughed, lifting the little girl high into the air.

"Well, hello there, my little Anna!" he said, brimming with joy.

Lizzy and Bob rushed forward, scooping the energetic toddler into warm hugs.

Behind them, Sam and Melissa entered, their faces flushed from the cold. Dr. Melody followed closely, gently closing the door to keep the winter chill at bay.

The living room welcomed them with warmth, the scent of freshly baked cookies, cinnamon, and Christmas cake weaving through the air.

Emma carried the tray of cocoa, steam rising from the mugs, topped with whipped cream and sprinkles—a tradition her mother had treasured. She passed them around, her hands careful, her proud smile giving her away.

The evening unfolded in a delightful swirl of laughter and shared stories. Children eagerly unwrapped presents, their joyful gasps filling the room as colorful wrapping paper scattered to the floor.

Little Anna clutched a new stuffed rabbit to her chest, her wide eyes brimming with wonder.

Later that evening, as the family gathered around the piano, Bob's fingers danced over the keys, leading a heartfelt rendition of *"Silent Night."* Their voices intertwined in a symphony of love and remembrance. Above the piano, a portrait of Anna gazed down at them, her warm smile a reminder of her enduring presence.

For Paul, this moment was transformative. Surrounded by laughter and love, he marveled at the strength of the bonds they had built—bonds forged through resilience and shared memories.

Outside, the snow-covered town provided a serene backdrop to the warmth within, embodying the true spirit of Christmas: togetherness.

Years later, on a crisp December evening, the Riley family gathered once more in their cozy living room. The fire crackled in the hearth, flames dancing across the walls. Laughter rose like music, filling the room with a sense of belonging and gratitude for their journey.

Paul sat comfortably by the fire, his arm protectively draped around Emma's son, Eric, who dozed peacefully on his lap, wrapped in the knitted shawl that once belonged to his great-grandma, Sarah.

The soft texture of the shawl enveloped him like a warm embrace, a tangible connection to the love of generations past.

Nearby, Emma leaned against her husband, their fingers intertwined, the warmth of their connection palpable. Lizzy and Bob exchanged knowing glances, their laughter like the tinkling of bells, brightening the atmosphere as they shared a joke that only they could understand.

The sweet, spicy aroma of cinnamon-spiced cookies and rich Christmas cake wafted through the air, mingling with the lively conversation.

Sam watched his three grown children, poised at the threshold of their own adventures, anticipation lighting their faces.

In them, he saw echoes of those who came before—his grandmother Sophia's wisdom, her gentle voice a comforting whisper in his mind; his mother Sarah's kindness, radiating from his children like a warm hug; and his sister Anna's unbreakable love, a bond that transcended time.

Though his children had never met these remarkable women, the thread of family wove them together, an invisible tapestry both strong and delicate.

Lizzy's heart swelled as she watched Eric, a love she once feared she'd never feel. Life had surprised her with miracles, the greatest of them being Emma—a daughter not by blood but by love.

Emma had grown into a woman of quiet strength and purpose, carrying her family's compassion into the world through her *Meals for Chemotherapy Patients* program—one that now touches lives far beyond CreeksVille.

Bob reached over and ruffled Eric's curls, his eyes crinkling with pride.

"I think he's got your stubborn streak, Emma," he chuckled.

Emma grinned.

She glanced at Lizzy, who met her gaze with an understanding that only a daughter could share. No words were needed—just the quiet knowledge that this bond, this family, was the greatest gift they had ever received.

Just then, Dr. Melody walked in, her warm presence adding another layer of comfort to the evening. With a gentle smile, she carried a tray lined with steaming mugs of apple cider, their golden liquid swirling with fragrant spices.

"Here we go," she said, her eyes soft with affection. "A little warmth for this beautiful night."

She handed the first mug to Lizzy, then Bob, her eyes twinkling with knowing affection as she made her way around the room.

When she reached Sam, she lingered for a moment, squeezing his hand as she passed him a mug.

Sam looked up at her with gratitude, his fingers wrapping around the warmth of the cider.

"You always know what's needed," he murmured.

Dr. Melody chuckled.

"It's a gift, Sam."

Lizzy raised her mug. "To Judge Samuel Riley—the man who brings order to the courtroom and chaos to Christmas dinner."

The room erupted in laughter, and Sam grinned, the moment settling over him like a blessing.

The laughter lingered, softening into a contented quiet as they reached for their mugs.

As everyone took their first sips, the rich blend of cinnamon, cloves, and apples seemed to melt away the cold of the winter night. The warmth seeped through them—not just from the drink but from the love that filled the room, the bond that time and distance could never fray.

Sam reached for Melissa's hand, squeezing gently, feeling the warmth of her palm against his. No matter where life took them, this love—this family—would always be their anchor, a steadfast presence in the ever-changing tides of life.

Together, they stepped into the future, their lives intertwined in a tapestry rich with the vibrant colors of love, resilience, and joy.

Each thread carried a story—loss, healing, laughter, tears—braided into a bond.

Outside, the snow shimmered faintly beneath the porch light, and beyond it, the garden slept beneath winter's hush.

There, nestled in the frozen soil, the first shoots of Sarah's tulips waited for spring—a promise that love, like life, always finds a way to bloom again.

Lives don't hold because the fabric never frays.
They hold because, when it does, we learn to weave.

Dear Reader,

Thank you for taking the time to spend with *Threads That Weave Us*. I hope the characters stayed with you and that their journey meant something to you, however big or small.

If you enjoyed the book, I'd be deeply grateful if you took a moment to leave a review on Amazon or Goodreads. Reviews not only help other readers find the story, but they also truly mean the world to authors like me.

You can also follow me for updates on upcoming titles, behind-the-scenes glimpses, and more:

Facebook: **Facebook:** facebook.com/ManjulaPothuriAuthor

Website: www.manjulapothuri.com

Thank you again for reading. Your support makes stories like this possible.

With gratitude,

Manjula Pothuri

Author's Note

This book was written in a season when loss seemed to arrive all at once. In the months after my father's passing, my mother's absence left an ache that felt just as sharp.

Writing became my lifeline, the way I honored what was taken and what still remained. These pages are stitched together with pain, yes, but also with a fierce love that refuses to be forgotten.

If you've ever had to say goodbye too soon, carry burdens you didn't choose, or fight to hold on to hope when everything changes— this story is for you.

Even when the storm feels endless, I promise—light finds its way back.

Manjula Pothuri

About the Author

Manjula Pothuri writes emotionally rich, character-driven stories about love, loss, and rediscovery. With roots in India and a life spent across continents, she draws inspiration from the cultures, people, and landscapes that shape her journeys.

Her debut novel, *Secrets That Hold Us,* became a #1 bestseller on Amazon's free charts, touching thousands of readers with its heartfelt exploration of memory, healing, and second chances.

Her second novel, *Threads That Weave Us,* continues that tradition—an intimate, uplifting family saga that explores the power of resilience and the bonds that hold us together.

Manjula writes from the heart, supported by the unwavering love of her husband, daughters, and close friends—whose faith in her words has made these stories possible.

Also By Manjula Pothuri

Secrets That Hold Us: A heartfelt novel about memory, healing, and second chances.
Available on Amazon – search by title or author.

Upcoming Titles by Manjula Pothuri

Between Us and Ourselves: Four women, four journeys. A story of truth, friendship, and the power of second chances.
The Soul That Called: A moving exploration of love, identity, and the ties that connect strangers into family.
Crow Sings A Sonata: A deeply felt novel about grief, forgiveness, and the truths we dare to speak.

Visit www.manjulapothuri.com to explore blurbs of upcoming titles and stay in the loop.